NEVER KNEW ANOTHER

NEVER KNEW ANOTHER

ANOTHER

BOOK ONE OF THE DOGSLAND TRILOGY

J.M. MCDERMOTT

NIGHT SHADE BOOKS
SAN FRANCISCO

First Edition

ISBN 978-1-59780-215-4

Printed in Canada

Night Shade Books
Please visit us on the web at
http://www.nightshadebooks.com

To the people who watched over me when I wrote
this book, and who watch over me still

Mother, Father, Brother, Sister

This one goes out to all of you.

CHAPTER I

My husband and I placed the head from the body we had found upon a rock face at the top of a hill, where the sun and moon would always fall upon it. He had worn the uniform of a king's man in life, but he had demon in his bloodline, and he had stained the earth where he had fallen. My husband and I prayed there, with the head on the stone, to the goddess Erin, and raised our eyes to the sky, to her. We fasted and fasted all day. We drank only water when the moon slipped from behind the clouds. We prayed and we prayed. In morning twilight, Erin granted me the vision. I cried out in pain. *Where is my body?* screamed the skull. *Where is Rachel?*

He and Rachel were lovers as true as any in the city. She left him. He died chasing her.

I asked my husband if he would die for me. He said no.

Jona would have said the same until the moment he realized what he had done.

His mind was mine now. I could sift through his memories, if I knew what to seek; I could reach into the lives of the people around him, as they were known to him. His human mother's hand on his face, his days and sleepless nights, and his great love all floated over the surface of my world. His human mother's hand on his face, his days and sleepless nights, and his great love all floated on the surface of the world. I looked into my forested hills, and saw where he had walked among them—how he had seen my home and longed for his.

My husband touched my hand. Even when we were human, we spoke to each other as wolves. *Anything?*

His mother was human. His father is already dead. There is another demon's child. Maybe two.

To his city, then, to walk behind his life, and search for memories. The seed of Elishta must be burned away to ash, no matter who they are or who they were. Those born to such blood pollute life where they walk.

What was his name?

Jona. There are two others—Rachel Nolander, and... The second's name is on the tip of my tongue.

They might lead to others. Give it time. His name will come. All things will come.

My husband and I had found the corpse near a bluff. We smelled it before we saw it. Something had burned a hole in the sunflower smell. When we found the corpse, it was face down, half-buried in mud and stiff and cold.

Everything living had died where the tainted blood pooled. Tiny red mushrooms—all deadly—sprouted like warts. This noxious corpse wore the uniform of a king's man.

My husband had frowned. *I was lucky, the last time. There was only the one. He had no brothers or sisters. These two others may lead to more as we find them.*

My beloved had found one long ago, when he was a young man, and I was not yet born. After he killed it, the poison of the man's blood left him sick for months. It burned off all his hair. I look at him and cannot imagine him without his long, silver hair all down his back.

He had told me stories from that demon's memories, of a life spent in hiding in back alleys and hillsides. The demon only went into cities to steal pigeon cages, and baby pigeons. He had loved to watch his pet birds fly. When he was found, all his pigeons had to be killed and burned. No one could allow hawks and cats to catch them and spread the stain from the demon's sweaty palms stroking their backs.

Demon children were not common anymore. The Nameless of Elishta had been driven deep underground, where they could not make children with human mothers. We found this one a grown man, dead on the ground, like an artifact from ancient times. We had pulled his head loose from his body, with thick leather between our hands and it. We had to be careful not to get any blood on our skin. We had placed it on a stone in full light of sun and moon, and Erin blessed me with the demon child's mind.

My husband and I pulled the wolfskins over our backs upon our return to the place where the body had been found. We pressed our noses into the earth along the perimeter of the bluff, searching for signs that would spark my awareness—another body, a lost tool or precious thing, a smell of someone, any sign that called to Jona's memories. Rachel's smell was all, to him. Her trail led north and north. We found nothing else here. He was not of the woods, like us.

Ants have no souls to lose. We gave the tainted skull back to the body while we cleaned away the bones. We planted two red queens in the his gaping mouth, and blessed them both to quicken their hungry daughters. When only bones remained, we planted tough dandelions to eat the worst of the stain from the earth. We'd harvest the first generation of dandelions before they spread their white seeds. Then, we will plant sunflowers. This first generation of sunflowers will be short and covered in thorns, but those sunflowers' children will be better. In a few generations, the flowers won't need to be burned.

Someday sunflowers will once again bloom here. They will be as tall as men, and smell sweet.

***

We led our pack of wolf brethren north along the road to track the raiders to the edge of our territory, following the trail of Rachel. We stopped at the boundary of the blasted field. The red valley was the edge of our territory. A war had ended here. Deadly magic stopped both armies and the man who cast the spell, Lord Sabachthani, declared it a victory for his city over theirs. The spell had stopped all life where it spilled over the ground. Blasted sand, a faded red color like old blood, poisoned the ground at the boundary of the kingdoms here. My husband and I stopped at the valley's red boundary line. We served a kingdom of men, here. We could not run past the valley with the wolves. The pack would continue on without us, hunting north. My husband and I were Walkers, not true wolves. We had to stay behind, to sift through Jona's memories for signs of the stains of this kingdom. We howled our sorrow at our running brethren, and the dust cloud they kicked up with their paws, until we saw them at the far side, pressing on into the hills beyond. We could not mourn their passage. We had our work, for Blessed Erin. My husband and I planted new weeds at the edges of the sand. We cut down the ones that had died before they could flourish. We spread grass seeds in the red mud where runoff from the hills pooled into a puddle in the dead sands. This old wound would have to wait. We had to hunt the demon children, and the new stains made across the land, uncontained by hills and time.

There was a watch tower from the city near this place. The king's men there were polite, and little else. They said that some small skirmish had happened before we found the body. People had died. The ones that had been found near the watch tower were sent home to their families to be buried, and no one got sick from their bodies. That's all they knew. Young men, all of them, and bored. They wanted us to leave so they could play cards, again, pick fights with each other, and roll dice. We were not of their world, nor they of ours. They asked us what we wanted. We asked for supplies. They gave them. As we left, I turned back and saw them slouching and rubbing their necks. Jona's mind knew none of these boys, and none of them knew Jona. In the city, this would change. King's men knew each other.

The ants had been given enough time to finish their work by then. My husband and I returned to the ant-stripped bones to collect the clean skull. I lifted it gently with strips of burlap wrapped around my hands. We placed the skull inside a wicker box.

I stripped the rest of the uniform from the demon bones to give to the city proof of his heritage, if it came to that. The uniform was nearly destroyed, but enough strips of cloth and leather remained where the demon child's acid blood hadn't completely destroyed it that it was recognizable. I wrapped my hands in stiff soldier's leather to do it. I knew I was being stained, but I felt nothing. It could have been any bones. I held his skull up, turned it in my hands. If I hadn't known he was a demon's child, and smelled the stain, I'd have thought it the skull of a normal man. He was hardly deformed at all. He must have been a few generations removed from the father of the stain. His memories lingered, still, where the soul had sunk into the demon-stain in the bones. I needed to keep his skull close to me to reach his mind's remains.

We placed the uniform in the box as well.

My husband put that box inside of a bag. He put this bag inside of a larger box of solid oak. He put this box on strips of heavy burlap spread between two branches. We would drag the box back towards the city.

As we traveled, we wrapped our hands in oiled burlap as if we had been burned. We rinsed with holy oil every day until the taint faded.

The city sits on a bay beside a long peninsula that noblemen had cut loose with a canal to make their island against the rest of the city. Who could blame them? The mainland side stinks of shit, smoke, and fish. It is on our land, but we never go there without a reason. The Church of Imam is stronger than ours there, and they do not want us running wolves through the streets. In this task, they will welcome us with open arms: we purify the demon stain and root out anyone left who carried it. If they had found the body, they'd have done it gladly, but we were better at it. We could pull the wolfskin over our backs and hunt.

My husband and I did not want to leave the woods, but our duty was our duty. We left the wisdom of the wolf packs of the region to keep the woods a while without us, Blessed Erin's loyal Walkers.

***

My mother, a mountain Walker, told me about cities long before I ever visited one. She said that Blessed Erin grants all creatures and all plants three tasks: *Eat*, *Sleep*, and *Love*. But, she cursed mankind with intelligence, and from that moment no man ate easily, slept easily, or loved with the practical candor of a fish. Most had already forgotten the curse, so wrapped up in what they believed really mattered, somewhere in their city that really mattered to them. To them, the curse that had pulled them away from the ground had become a blessing. These were the men and women who built cities.

Where does a city begin? Where does it end?

A traveler before I was married and settled down with one kingdom and one pack, I once stood at guarded gates, and saw nothing but grass past the horizon. I pulled the wolfskin from my back to make myself a young woman. I stood up. I leaned against the guard, and asked him where the city was, this place that I could neither see nor smell beyond the horizon whose boundary we had found along the road. The guard gently eased me away from his arms. He told me that their city began an inch from where I had stood.

I have traveled to cities where I spent all my time outside the gates, wandering from playhouse to tavern to home to park. All that time, everyone I met called themselves a citizen though none had seen inside the walls of their own nation.

Once, I passed through a city with seventeen walls, each more difficult to pass through than the last, with codes of dress and bribery required to move from one layer to the next, from the gates to the temple at the center.

I do not know what makes a city what it is, exactly. I will never truly know. I know that people clump together and call themselves home and part of a city.

I was born in a cave beyond the mountains. The first time my feet touched the ground, the pine nettles stung me. The rocks made me shiver when my skin pressed into them. The water was brisk and filthy. The air was clean as snow. I learned that every tree fights for sunlight in the canopy, but this happens so slowly that the combat looks like peace.

This is what I thought of cities: Each person is a tree, crawling on top of another to reach the sunlight. Random chance planted seeds in patches of light, and these seeds grew to become larger trees. They were all like a strange forest.

My husband and I arrived in a city that I shall call not *Woodsland*, but, rather, *Dogsland*. That is the name for human places in the language of the wolf packs.

***

We journeyed south from the hills and through swamps for three days until we reached the main road. We moved slowly, the skull in its heavy box dragging behind us in a travois. We followed the men's path to the city, walking the grass beside the road, where old wheel ruts wouldn't pull the ends of the sticks apart.

We saw the walls before we reached them. They were taller than hills. Outside these walls, small buildings pressed against the merging trails. Someday, a new wall will be built around the new buildings, and this new wall will be bigger and more magnificent than the last.

The forest continued on beyond the human settlements. Trees are patient. They cede all ground to their usurpers, knowing they will always return to claim the ground again, eventually.

We call the city by the name our wolf pack gave to it. They say it is a dogs' land. The dogs run the streets, tear into the trash heaps, and chase the cats away from the balconies. The dogs piss their boundaries into the mud. That is *Dogsland*, they say, and you smell the dogs everywhere. Why the dogs would want a place crowded with those bellicose monkeys is unknown to the wolves, but it is the dog shit and piss that walls the place off to the wolves. And good riddance to bad wolf land. The farmland isn't as bad, but it is better deep in the hills, where the retiring soldiers receive parcels of land and try to carve farms into the hills. They stay long enough to lose their sheep to wolves, and watch their crops wither. When spring comes, they sell the land back to the king, and fade from our lands. I assume they go back to the city. They leave behind huts that keep the rain off wolf backs in the night. What dogs stay behind fade into the woods when the packs come, run wild and die alone. They belong in the cities, among men, and not in the forested hills.

My husband and I live where the forested hills and distant emissaries of the city press into each other, at the boundary of things, serving both man and beast. Some farmers live on, and fight on, growing wheat. They are the flock we serve the most, among the men. The city church is no place for wolves, and no place for Walkers.

Leaving the forests, I wondered how long it would be until we could turn home again. The stain had to be broken. The ground had to be healed. How long would it take? We knew many things because we were Walkers. We smelled a man's life in his skin, and sometimes his death. We felt the flow of life around us, like Sentas' dreamcasting with koans, but we did not see in metaphors as in a dream. We saw with holy eyes, smelled the secrets of the land. We knew so many things simply being raised to be the servants of Erin. We could merge into the mind of a dead man. We could wear the wolfskin over our backs and run with wolves. In all these things we knew, and all our blessings, we did not know how long it would take to clean this stain and hunt the demon children survivors, and all who aid them.

***

At the magnificent gates of Dogsland, guards inspected all the cargo and caravans and wagons—even ours. They had such serious faces. They poked the cattle, and pinched the wheat. They stuck their blades into boxes to find smugglers' secrets. They were on alert. Something must have happened if they investigated even our little box so thoroughly.

We were so small with only us two and our boxes within boxes wrapped in leather and burlap, dragged behind us on sticks. We told the guard that it was best not to dig too deep into the box, for it contained a demon's skull. He did not listen. We let the guard open the first box. He dipped his blade into the second. He bumped against the bone. His ears turned white, and his jaw tightened. He had felt a skull against his blade before. He needed no more proof.

We told him, for the second time, that it was a demon's skull. We touched a leaf to the edge of his steel where it had banged against the bone. The leaf wilted there. We told the guard to sheathe his blade, and purify the whole thing at Erin's temple before he accidentally nicked anyone. He nodded, his skin white.

"Where did it come from?" he asked.

"Near the red valley. He was wearing a uniform like yours," I said. "A corporal of the king's men, dead in the woods."

"Oh," said the guard, "Oh. I bet he was the traitor."

"Who, specifically," I said, "and where do we locate his friends and family?"

I knew the dead man's name, but I wanted to hear him say it.

He might say another name for the demon child than the one I knew, and lead me deeper into the truth of this lost life. Even good memories fade into untruth, and I had to sort them all out. This was Jona's home, all the days of his life. Everywhere I looked, I felt his history in a blurred flurry of déjà vu upon déjà vu.

The guard looked at his boots. "Are you going to kill his family?"

I shrugged. "If they are of demon blood, we will have them burned at the stake by the king's men with the blessing of the Church of Imam," I said. "Unless we find them in the woods. In the woods, they are ours to kill."

He was trying not to look me in the face. He was so young. I bent a little downward to catch his gaze. "Other then that, I do not know what we will do to his friends and family, but we will obey the laws of the city in all things," I said. "We will hand any sinners over to you and yours."

The guard nodded at us. He opened his mouth to say something, but changed his mind. Then he coughed. "I knew that fellow when he was alive," he said. "Didn't know him real good, but I knew him. Nobody knew he was of demon. Jona was his name."

"He may have been a good person, somewhere inside of the twisted stain of Elishta, but with demon children, the evil rises in their blood and they fall a little more every day, until they become…" I trailed off, inviting the soldier to speak into my silence. I waited and waited.

He spoke at last. "…Traitors. Yeah, I get it. Corporal Jona Lord Joni's his name," said the guard, "and his Ma lives in the city, but I don't know where. Sergeant Nicola Calipari is the one that killed him, I hear. Sergeant's… Well, I don't know where he is, but you can find him if you need to if you ask around. Everybody knows Calipari. That's all I know."

"Thank you," I said. "How well did you know Jona?"

He squinted down at the box between the two branches. He

frowned. "Passing good, I guess," he said, "Walked the rounds a few times before he got transferred to Calipari's unit and I got over here. We did a bit of this or that. He never turned on me. Seemed good as anybody."

"He probably was for a time. If they die before the blood influences them too much, part of them may escape damnation in Elishta, with their wicked fathers."

He snorted. "You really believe that shit?"

"I believe what I believe," I replied. "What is your name? I may want to find you again, ask you more questions."

"I'm Christoff," he said, "Corporal Christoff. No last name. Never knew my folks. Named myself when I became a man."

"A pleasure." I bowed to him. "My name cannot be pronounced without a wolf's tongue, Christoff, so forgive me if I withhold it. Where do you worship?"

"Nowhere."

"Well, did you ever worship anywhere?"

"My orphanage was a temple's place. Not Erin, though," he said, "Imam."

"And you do not return?"

"No. You're free to go anywhere you want. Look, I don't have time to talk about this shit."

"I only ask because you're going to have to clean your blade at a temple. Imam is a bit more expensive then Erin, and it's not your fault that you were doing your job." I held a bag of coins out to him.

He opened his hand, uncomfortably. This would look like a bribe, in broad daylight. I placed the bag of coins into his palm, and I closed his fingers over it, holding them closed.

"If the temple must destroy your sword," I said, "tell them that Erin's Walkers sent you to get the blade cleaned. They will give you another."

The coins were too much for just a cleaned blade. The extra weight would pay for the funeral that I smelled in his skin. I pulled him closer. "It wouldn't hurt to light a candle for Jona,"

I whispered. "We are, all of us, feeling for the worlds that move between the cracks in our senses. Light a candle for your friend. Good hearts push through many boundaries. Have faith, Christoff. Have faith in something."

Christoff nodded. I hope he prayed before the sickness came. I hope he lit a candle and prayed for someone's soul before the disease came out of his skin and made him beg for his own life in the long night.

We would never meet Christoff again in any of our stories or walks of life. I could smell his death coming soon. Yesterday he had run into something—a wooden crate's nails, or a jagged candlestick. He had cut himself deep with the metal. I smelled the lockjaw that would kill him soon. If I had kissed his cheek, I'd have tasted it there, in his sweat.

I imagine there must be a girl at his funeral to cry and cry, a damp cloth with legs. Her love will spill from the corners of her eyes for weeks. Poor creatures, these young lovers, and a story left untold. I reach into a demon child's memories, while good people live and die so quietly, and no one studies their memories for signs of good things done, and good people. Nothing will remain of Christoff in this life, except perhaps this imagined girl's heart.

Christoff, I felt your whole life like a thundercloud.

These cities, each crack and crevice opened tears my heart away with a sadness of things lost. I saw too much. None of the people here tried to lead an unspectacular life. Christoff, I wish my work could bend to you, and to all your hurting brethren in the misery of Erin's curse of cities. The stink of death was everywhere, here, and my husband and I could do nothing. Purify the ground; pray for these lost loves, lost lives, and lost souls.

Blessed Erin, may our task be quick. Bring my husband and I back to your woods, where death is the same as life. Give us again the place where the only glory is to eat a little longer in the winter.

CHAPTER II

We do not fully understand the fate of the demon-cursed. Corporal Jona, the Lord of Joni, might even still be alive inside his bones, his soul attached for an eternity to the tainted flesh. I toyed with the box, and wondered if Jona's spirit still lingered, watching the world he had left. Could he see the fabrics of life like Senta mystics? Could he see the truths of the world like us? Did his human soul wander the woods, silently weeping her name to the starlight: *Rachel... Rachel...*

Too late for his soul, we must study his life.

***

First, before we stopped at one of the churches of Erin in the city, my husband and I dragged Jona's skull and uniform to the captain of the City Guard. We insisted upon a visit with him, right away. We wanted to make a scene there. If demon's children could live here so long undiscovered, and serve in the king's men, the city guard needed to be reminded of their failure, and the severity of it. We waited in the captain's office while he washed his hands and face to meet with us respectfully. We carefully placed the demon's skull upon blank papers on his desk, so the empty sockets could stare directly at the captain while we spoke.

The captain stopped at the door when he saw the skull. He spat and told us to put it on the ramparts or take it away, but never let the traitor look upon his captain again. We left it there while we spoke with him, to stare at him. It was his responsibility to catch them here, and now the church of Erin was involved because we found the skull. We wanted to make a scene, and shame him.

Names came to me when I saw the captain, and faces. I knew the captain would not know more than he had already told us. He had not been in the Pens with Jona. "Nicola Calipari," I said. "Where is he?"

"That old dog? I don't know," said the captain. "If he's on duty, he could be anywhere. His people will know where he went. Last I heard, he worked the Pens, near the abattoirs, but I know he made inspection rounds. He was on inspection when the corporal showed his true colors. Of course, records don't mean anything for an old-timer like him. His men might be lying to me just to keep him on the books until he gets the farm. Last I knew he was in the Pens. Could be anywhere."

We wanted to shame the captain, for allowing a demon child to work in his command for so long. We tested his blood for demon stain, to shame him. We commanded him to test everyone in his command. Let them bleed and know why they bleed.

We spread a sheet of his finest heartwood paper under his open palm. We nicked him with his own dagger, and let him bleed a few drops onto the page. Then we held the paper over a steel bin, and set the paper on fire. When the fire reached the blood, the red stain held the smoldering line of ash back. He was not a demon's child.

The captain bowed to Erin, and promised to cleanse his blood at a temple of Erin that very night, even if he didn't need it. He kneeled before me and begged for a blessing.

My husband placed the wolfskin paw upon the head of the man and spoke the blessing for the man. It was the first time he had spoken since arriving in the city. I had missed the sound of his human voice. I placed a red flower in the captain's hair—red, the color of blood and hunting.

We told the captain that we would seek his help when we were ready, whenever we were ready. We asked for his patience in this matter. He nodded. He closed his eyes. We left him there, kneeling and praying. The king's men would know we were here. They would let us work in peace, even unto blood and death.

Outside, I took my husband's hand. "Speak to me again. Let me hear your voice. Speak to me that I may remember who you are."

He sniffed the air. *It's hard, here. I remember what it was like for the demon's child from long ago—how he felt here. It still lingers in me, though decades have passed. This place terrified him. And, it saddens me. It isn't our home. We don't belong here.*

"For me?"

"I'll try," he said.

***

We went down near the animal pens where the butchers kept their beasts. The animals arrived on river ships to the edge of the ocean water. They were shoved from dark cages below deck until they came to the city on ships, shoved from one dark cage to another, waiting for the death they can smell all around them, pressed together in the heat and the mud. The Pens district was where the smell was the worst.

This was Jona's home. Every street was his. His ancestral lands sat in the center of it, his house was hidden somewhere inside the new buildings that sprouted up around it, obscuring its place. There were people here he had known for years. I nodded at my husband. *This.*

I know. Can't you smell his stain here?

And, I could, eventually. If I pushed Jona back from my own memories, and tried to ignore the rising waves of his life here, I could feel the taint in the air, like an edge of metal cutting at the stink of animals and death.

When we reached the Pens' guard station, Sergeant Calipari wasn't on duty. The new sergeant grinned and told us to call him 'Pup', not Sergeant, but I knew that before he spoke. Pup had been promoted since all the other guards Jona knew had died except for Calipari. It wasn't the stain. This was a dangerous place, and dangerous work. Pup said that Nic was ill, and on leave for good. He wasn't coming back.

Nicola Calipari had killed the betrayer, Jona. He alone had felt the demon child's tainted blood spilled all over his skin at the moment of Jona's death. The old sergeant would be trapped in poisoned visions of the dark soul he had destroyed when he had stabbed his friend, mistaking these for mere nightmares. He was going to be sick as dying.

I looked around the room. I saw a thousand moments. I saw them merge into one moment. I could still smell Jona, here, under all the smells of scrivener's ink and interrogation room blood. I opened my mouth to speak, but my husband touched my arm. The new sergeant pointed to the edge of the city, past the walls, where Calipari had gone to be close to his beloved. Calipari thought the stain would kill him. He didn't want to die in a cluttered room above cluttered rooms, alone. He wanted to die in Franka's arms. Pup spoke so quietly about Calipari's death.

My husband scoffed. "He won't die. Jona's blood wasn't that strong. He will make everyone around him very sick. Why do men like you ignore the temples when you are in need? You give alms, and pray for help alone, but never let your face be seen by mortals when you seek your interventions."

Pup shrugged. "I wouldn't know about that stuff, sir," he said. "Anything else I can help you with?"

The tavern was far beyond the city walls, to the east. My husband and I left Jona's skull with the church of Erin in the city. We pulled the wolfskin over our back and charged through the streets. We were wild dogs, running, big like wolves. Women screamed and men drew back from us.

My husband had lied to the sergeant. Nicola might die. He might take people with him in death. We had to run.

***

We were back to the wall, and beyond it, but this time at the far eastern edge. The swampy pine forests stretched out across the hills with the black, muddy veins of roads. I smelled the wind against my face. We were home.

Night fell, and we didn't stop. We kept our wolfskins on our backs and loped overland straight through woods.

We smelled the tavern before we saw it. Drunk men had lost their way to the outhouse and had leaned into the trees. I smelled it all over the roots at the ground against my nose. I smelled the cook fire dusting the trees. Lamplight in the dark guided weary travelers to a place of rest.

My husband stopped at the edge of the light. He told me to go forward; he would search the perimeter for any signs of the other two demons.

I looked up at the building. The bottom floor bustled with travelers and local farmers. In the rooms above, travelers slept, and the owner slept, and his staff slept after drinkers abandoned the bottom floor.

I went to the barn first. I smelled someone human there, and heard a child breathing. The horses whinnied nervously at my scent. But I needed to see in the dark a little longer, so I kept wolfskin.

I recognized the boy when I saw him. Franka's son was sleeping on some hay, waiting for men to come with their horses and a few coppers for his trouble. He snored with his mouth slack, and flies buzzing around his teeth.

I pulled my hand and back free from the wolfskin to reach into my pack. Stretching my hand out, I poured holy spring water over his head. It must have been very cold. He woke with a start.

"Drink this water," I growled.

"Wha…?" stammering, he stood up, clumsily backing into the wall.

I remembered myself. He was a child, and me, a wolf in the shadows. I pulled the wolfskin from my back completely. I smiled as warmly as I could, a woman in full, and kind.

"I am Erin's Walker," I said. "Do you know what that is? It is someone who helps people. I'm here to help. You're Franka's son, aren't you? I've seen you before, but you do not remember me seeing you. Drink this."

"I…?" He shook his head, wiping sleep from his brain. I watched his face as his mind struggled to name what he had just seen. A dream, surely. A woman rising up from the body of a wolf, speaking to him.

I handed him the water. "Drink this."

He took the water, sniffed it, smelled the sweet flowers that had blessed the bottle. He drank hesitantly. "It's good," he said, surprised. He took a deeper swallow.

"You're going to have to spend some time in the temple," I said.

"I've never been to temple," he said. He wasn't looking at me. His back was to the wall. "I should get my ma."

"She isn't feeling well, either, is she?"

"Not for weeks. Bellini doesn't want sick people working," he said, "so I have to pick up the slack for ma."

"Good man." I ruffled his wet hair. He pulled away as if I had struck him.

***

Inside the public house, the owner woke at the noise of doors opening. When he saw me and my husband, he was quick to realize we weren't paying customers. He eyed me, waiting for the trouble to start. His name was Bellini.

"People are dying here," I said. "We came to help."

He nodded, sternly, and told Franka's son to lead us upstairs. He'd be up later, behind us. The boy took me upstairs, to the top floor, where the slate roof kept the sun's heat long into the night. The staff slept here, sweltering in beds too hot for paying guests.

Franka's son knew the way without a light. I followed him down a black hallway lined with buckets of rotting vomit. The heat did not improve the odor. No maid would serve this floor, and Franka was too sick to deal with these buckets herself, without encouragement. At least Bellini had the good sense to isolate the sick.

The boy opened a door at the end of the hall. Moonlight spilled over him from the doorway. "They're sleeping," he whispered. I walked in to the room. A woman and a man snored beneath an open window, curling into each other like wild roots despite the heat.

I had seen enough to know how deep the stain would run here. The whole place might need to be burned down. I turned to the boy. "They shouldn't be together at a time like this," I said. "He will only quicken her illness. You need to go downstairs, now, and tell Bellini to get everyone out of the inn. Everyone needs to leave. Go."

The boy did not go far. I don't think he understood what I was asking him to do. I don't have children. I can't make sense of them. Wolf pups would have understood everything, and instinctively known to flee this tainted hallway.

The bodies in the bed moaned. A woman's voice, as thin as dying, rose from the tangled sheets. "Who's there?"

I pushed the boy back from the door, and stepped into the room. I closed the door behind me. "I'm from the Church of Erin. I have come seeking a woman named Franka and a man named Nicola Calipari," I said. "You are sick. I can heal you."

The man awoke, too. "Who sent you?" he demanded. I recognized his voice from Jona's memories, weak as it was. He was so frail. He tried to sit up in the dark, but couldn't muster the strength. Franka pushed him down. Even in low light, I saw the man before me and knew his cheeks and eyes had sunken into his face since the day he drove a blade into Jona's body.

"You need help," I said. "The illness that plagues you is the poison of tainted blood, from Jona." I grabbed clothes from the floor, and threw them at the bed. I could burn their clothes, later. We didn't have the captain's men here to enforce our commands. We'd have to work in stages. "Dress yourselves and come to the yard. Take anything that burns with you. Your bedsheets. Your clothes. Your books and papers. Bring it all." I looked behind me towards the sounds of the first floor. Men were shouting. My husband was shouting. Bellini was not going to clear the building. "Actually," I said, "let's throw it all out the window. We'll burn everything."

I opened the room's only window. I leaned out. I howled to my husband below. *I have them. Burn their things below.*

He howled back to me. *I hear.*

The mattress was the first thing to go through the window. It was little more than a large bag of feathers and hay sewn shut. It wasn't hard to shove it through the gap. Little goose feathers floated down from holes in the seams. Next, I threw all the clothes they weren't wearing, and all the buckets of the hall.

Sergeant Calipari could barely stand. Franka helped him into a chair. He heaved where he sat, but there wasn't much inside of him. It spilled across his chest and stayed there. He didn't have the strength to clear it away. She wasn't as weak as him, yet.

I pushed Franka away from him. I told her to keep cleaning. I cleaned him up while Franka worked, throwing papers and the pillows from the furniture. She must have been embarrassed that anyone found her in such disarray. She must have been embarrassed that she hadn't been able to help the sick as I could. I made Calipari swallow dandelion wine with mint to settle the burning inside of his guts. I didn't have enough with me. It would take weeks to clean away the worst of his demon-fever. He was too sick to speak. We had to turn the tide inside of him, and burn everything he had touched that could not be cleaned.

***

In the yard, the fire attracted a crowd. Everywhere the demon stain had seeped in from Calipari's deep fever of sweat and vomit, the fire caught it like kerosene, and coughed up balls of fire. People came out of their rooms to watch. Spectacle was more effective at clearing the building than our holy command.

My husband had already left, running through the dark to reach the nearest temple. We would need more supplies to fight the demon's death tide rising inside his killer.

The drunks cheered now. Later on, their hangovers would be worse and the occasional bout of coughs would linger long into the night. Some among them might die, if they had been here night after night, drinking in the stain. My husband would try to walk the farms and houses here while I stayed with Calipari. The temple would help. Even Imam's clergy would try to help. Death does not care whose god you serve.

***

I stayed with Calipari, in a cleaner room, on the second floor. After a few days, Franka was healthy enough to work downstairs. I couldn't convince her not to work. We tried to quarantine the place, but Bellini only allowed us to block off the inn rooms. The tavern remained open against our command. We would fix that soon enough.

First, we focused on the man. As the stain faded from him, Sergeant Calipari was able to talk for long periods of time. With Calipari's face and voice to feed Jona's memories, a candle flickered in my mind, burning steady, then growing clear as scenes separated from each other. But Calipari himself was a hollowed out shell of the battering ram with legs that Jona had known. He should have been a tightly wound spring, not this feather on a mattress.

"What are you looking at me for?"

I had been staring. It made him uncomfortable.

I closed my eyes. "Do you feel strong enough to talk a while?"

"Yeah," he said. The weakness of his voice betrayed him. I waited a while more. He said nothing else.

I smiled. "This isn't an interrogation. I'm just picking up the pieces, healing the sick, and making sure there are no more."

He still didn't speak.

"We won't hurt anyone, I promise. We're trying to help."

"Well," he said. With my eyes closed, I imagined his face, his mouth screwed up like he was about to spit out the side where there was a gap in his teeth. "I don't know. It wasn't right, but, I know what happens when demon stains get involved. I don't want to think about what comes next. Never good when we can't handle it ourselves. You aren't even human like us. You're this other thing, a wolf or a priestess or something."

I opened my eyes and reached out to touch his arm. "I'm human, Sergeant. I'm also a wolf. The divine goddess Erin wills me so."

"What do you want to know, anyway?"

"Anything you want to tell me. If you want, you can just tell me about Jona. You don't need to implicate anyone. We won't be arresting anyone. If there's a crime, we'll hand the criminal over to the king's men."

He didn't say anything for a long time. He was right not to believe me. I don't know how familiar he was with church law, but my husband and I could kill anyone who carried the stain, or burn down any building. If he knew the extent of our duties, he wouldn't speak a word. He rested silently, considering. I thought it a sign that he knew more than he was giving me. It could have been fatigue. He fell asleep for a time, as did I in my chair. Franka came up from downstairs with soup, and woke him up with a gentle hand. He ate what he could stomach of it. I didn't touch a drop. I stayed there, quiet and still. Franka did not touch my arm to offer soup.

It took a long time, but Calipari finally spoke. "People get sick," he said.

"They do."

"People die?"

"Sometimes."

"I know some people that died," he said. "Lost plenty good boys. Lost so many. Some of them, I know why. Some of them, I don't. You expect it to happen sometimes, especially you walking about down with the worst of everybody. Still…"

I nodded. He still had trouble looking at me. I had come here to save his life, and he couldn't even make eye contact because he knew what might happen if he spoke. He knew something I could use. "Help me," I said.

"Yeah, I guess I should."

He did.

***

Jona was the Lord of Joni. He still had the family home, but no lands in the city or out of it. All the good furniture and finery were long sold off. The house stayed together because they only used a little bit of it, and watched the roof for signs of rot. His mother sewed dresses for noble families luckier than hers.

Jona's father's fortune had been stripped during the war. Smuggling was illegal, but everyone did it in wartime. Jona's father wasn't smuggling things the king needed, and he had so much land that could be sold off to pay for war. For his crimes, the Joni lands were confiscated, and he was hung next to common thieves, disgraced and poor.

My husband and I would have to dig up the body, later, and burn the ground where we found it. Jona's stain probably came from his father, a demon's child himself.

After the lord's death, the war continued for months, and food was expensive. Jona's mother had nothing but land to sell for it. Trees came down as the ground was sold. Jona watched what was left of his family's estate devoured by the streets and shops and abbatoirs of the city that took his father to take the family's land. He watched from his bedroom window while men with hammers and sweating backs placed stone upon stone. He wore black the day his father died. He kept wearing mourning black long after his father's death, because his mother told him to, because she had to sell land to buy bread for her son, and the king hadn't even left the widow half a coin from the ancestral treasures. Land to sell was the only wealth they had left. Jona wore cheap wool, itchier than hay, and watched the workmen building where once he had swung from the trees, carefree in white silk.

Jona's grandfathers were all dead, and her mother's brothers had died in the war. Without a patriarch, the family fell hard into poverty. Jona's mother found work as a seamstress.

Her son grew up tall, and strong.

Jona entered the city guard. His mother threw him out of the house for swearing an oath to her husband's murderer. He wasn't doing it for the king, but she'd never understand that. The best that she could ever do is see how it could help her son improve their life. After he trained, out in the countryside, he returned to the city. He lived in barracks for a while, scrivening until he was promoted to Corporal to walk the street. He traded coin for cards and dice. His mother came for him in the barracks, and begged for him to come back into her house. She was an old woman alone. She had no one else, and she loved him. With time, she came to see the wisdom of his choice, even if she still hated the king. He could become an officer someday. He'd earn the fleur instead of buying it like the other young nobles. He'd bring honor back to the family name, marry well, and maybe things would be better for the grandchildren.

He loved the work. He was good at it, and it filled his days with something meaningful.

That's what the sergeant knew. That was what the world knew.

I asked Calipari if he knew which parent held the demon taint.

He nodded. "It was the father."

"How do you know?"

"Jona told me before I killed him."

"Have you checked?"

"Of course not," said Calipari. "This is a nasty business. If the king and the captain want her checked, they can send someone else. It was all in the report."

"Was it?"

"Did the captain say anything about checking her?"

"No. He didn't mention a report, either."

"Well, she's pretty old, and there are lots of reports. Too much paper in the guard, you ask me. If I spent more time with a good bat in my hand and less time with the cheap quills they kept sending me, the Pens'd be a different place. Be a better place. I've seen Jona's ma a few times. She won't have any more kids at her age, and I don't want to burn anyone."

He looked over my shoulder. I was sitting by the window, and he was lying in bed. He looked out at the blue sky, and the rolling sea clouds that had survived the journey this far inland.

I waited for him to speak. I folded my hands, and raised my eyebrows. I let my silence draw him out.

"She didn't betray the city," he said.

I leaned in close to him. I spoke close so he would listen. "If she housed a demon as wicked as Jona, she betrayed the whole world of men," I said. "He never slept. He couldn't. The stain inside of him kept him awake all night. While all decent folk were sleeping, he was killing people. He was working for the worst criminal in the city all night long. His mother probably knew when she saw the money coming in. I will test her blood myself. We will not hand her over to the guard lightly, but if she helped a demon child murder innocent people…"

Calipari looked at my hands. They were human. When he spoke, his voice was weary. "That's not my business," he said. "That's Captain's problem now, not mine. Jona saved my life. I killed him for it."

"Why did you do it if you didn't like it?"

He looked me in the face. I recognized this face. Calipari was a hard man, ready to fight when it was needed. He was fighting now. "Jona betrayed the city, and the king's men. Good boys died because of him. It wouldn't be a duty if it was easy. And it's not my duty anymore, so I won't do it. Please, leave his ma alone."

"It's amazing she's still alive," I said. "Every man with two masters must choose his side. He chose a third path. He betrayed all his masters for you and for Rachel."

"How do you know that?" he asked.

"I am Erin's Walker, Sergeant. I see inside the demon child's mind, even in death. I see all that he remembers. I know there is more for you to tell me."

"How can you do that?"

I shook my head. "You did the right thing, Sergeant. Eventually, every demon-stained mortal succumbs to the wickedness in their blood. You might have saved that part of his soul that passed as human. You can save more people from the Nameless deep in Elishta."

He looked back to the window, and the gathering clouds. "No," he said. "Men like him and me don't get saved. I know what I did was right. I hate that I did it. Jona was one of my boys for almost three years."

"Have you killed many people?"

"Of course," he said, "but they were all criminals. Even if they were good sometimes, nobody was any good for long where I was stationed. And I know Jona wasn't all bad. He was human, too, wasn't he? He wasn't just a demon child. He was a man, too."

"Did you burn a girl last winter?"

"Yeah," he said. "We found that one. Bled true. Anchorites

missed her. She was sneaking out at night like a dumb kid. Got in trouble. Didn't even know what she was, inside."

"She bled true," I echoed.

"Burned her alive. She'd done nothing to deserve it." Calipari sighed, and looked down at his hands. "She was a demon's child, too. If there's two… I guess everyone needs to go looking around for more. Two of them, one after another, you'd think the crusades were still on."

"There may be more. My husband and I will try to find them. There were only three that Jona knew about, including himself, and of these three only Jona is dead. The girl was not one of them. Jona ruined the tests with his own blood to condemn that girl," I said. "She died because Jona sent her to burn instead of the true demon child. There are others he sent to you to protect people who did not deserve protection. They weren't burned, of course, but they were hung. You hung them like thieves."

Calipari put his hands to his eyes. "Please, don't tell me this." He coughed, his chest shuddering. He pulled his hands away. His face had hardened into a stone. "How many?"

"Do you really want to know? This wasn't your fault, but his. The deed is done."

His courage broke. "No, I don't want to know." He turned away from me. The window was open. If he could have sat up, he could have seen Franka with her son, riding a horse in the yard while her mother watched over him. The boy wasn't his, but he was the only father that boy would ever know.

"How many was it?" His voice was tight, his eyes turned from me. "Tell me."

"Nineteen, with the girl."

"Elishta but that's a lot. Nineteen. Do you know their names?"

"He remembers their names, and so do I. Had he done what he was supposed to do, you would have been number twenty."

"Elishta, that's a lot," he repeated.

"The innocent die," I said, "There is no perfect justice, because there are no men as wise as wolves. Wolves say that it is easy to be wise when your belly is full. When your belly is empty, it is wise to fill it. Farm with all of your heart. You are not a uniform anymore. Show mercy when you can, and live in peace."

He turned his gaze back to me from the window. His courage returned to him. He was the coiled spring Jona remembered, again, even if he couldn't stand up to walk downstairs, yet. "I said I'd help you." He pulled a sheet of paper from a drawer near his bed and began gracefully scripting locations and letters of reference for us to his informants across the city.

I went downstairs and prepared his lunch myself. When I returned, he stopped to eat, and then picked up his quill again. "This might take a while," he said. Paper, then, from all over the tavern. By nightfall, a stack of papers was piled beside his bed, sorted by the numbers of guard posts upon hand-drawn maps. More marks in the maps indicated people and places to go. He gave us letters of introduction, too. People in the Pens wouldn't trust us, but they'd trust him. "Here," he said, "I'll stay here a while, but I got land waiting for me as soon as I'm strong enough to take it. I served twenty years. I got the farmland waiting for me."

Sergeant Calipari gestured at the man who had appeared behind me like a shadow from the hall. My husband had returned. "He don't talk much do he?"

"My husband?"

"Yeah," said Calipari, "is he all right?"

"He's been talking all along," I said. "Silence is a word to us, Sergeant."

"Can't be a nice word. What does he mean by it?"

I looked over at my husband. He turned away from us, and wandered into the hall. I knew what he was saying: these men who would have died instead of going to a church themselves; who help us because we saved, not because he wants to protect the people of the world from the demon children, and all those who protected the wicked from discovery.

I stood up from my chair, the papers under my arm. "He means to tell you whatever you wish to hear," I said. "You and he have much in common. We both hate this business as much as you do, in our way." I bowed to Sergeant Calipari. "You need to recover your strength. Spend a few more seasons here, maybe a year, even if you're strong enough to leave. There will be plenty of work here for a strong man when we're done purifying the place."

He laughed. "Burning it down, are you? Thanks for finding me, and helping me get healthy again. I've never been sick like that before. I don't think anything I ever had was as bad as that."

I bowed again. I followed my husband into the main building. It was early, and few people were in the tavern. Only the barman, and two hardened drinkers with nowhere else to go until their coins ran out.

My husband spread fireseeds across the top of the bar. Bellini cursed hard. He demanded to know what we thought we were doing, furious and terrified of what he knew we might do.

My husband pushed Bellini from the seeds. "Accept our help," he snarled. "We're trying to save your life, and keep your patrons safe."

In the city, the Guard Captain bows to us. The Bishops of Imam's faithful and the greatest Lords of the city would greet us as equals among them. In this stinking tavern, this sweating man screamed at us to stop saving his life, and the life of all his patrons here.

I stepped in front of my husband and smiled at Bellini. If I had the wolfskin on my back, he would have seen it for the threat it was. I gently pushed against Bellini's chest. He tried to punch my husband over my head. He hit only air. My husband was faster than men. He grabbed Bellini by the hair and threw him into the tavern yard. He tossed fireseeds across the man's back. I struck a match beside my husband, and tossed it at the thrown seeds, giving life to them. The lit seeds took root in Bellini's skin, blooming to life like firecrackers on a string. The flowers had long orange stalks, and petals of flame.

Bellini rolled around the sand to stamp the fire, screaming in agony. A fireseed was no worse than a bee sting, but there were a lot of them, and they hurt him deep.

We told everyone in the tavern to leave. They did. Someone helped Bellini to his feet, the flowers still eating into his back. They ran for the woods.

My husband and I cleared out all the people from the rooms, even Calipari. The building might not survive what we needed to do next.

My husband and I spread the seeds across the bottom floor, in the kitchen, and up the stairwell. We spread three thick layers of seed down the fourth floor hall and through the rooms. We didn't need a match. We stepped into the yard and waited. We handed around a flask of dandelion wine and waited for the heat to come. Under the glare of midday, the growing heat from the slate roof ignited the seeds on the fourth floor. The flowers bloomed from there, all the way down, feeding on the fuel inside the stain to burn bright and hot. The flowers of the fireseed didn't burn hot enough to ignite the building, but they came close in Calipari's sickroom. Wallpaper singed and peeled. Cheap wooden furniture warped and collapsed.

The burning flowers lived for only a few hours. After releasing their heat, the fireseeds' fruit congealed into the tips of the blooms like igneous pebbles. These would be swept through the building, slipping into every crevice. Many would be swept away into the yard. The wind would take them, and when the heat of high summer returned, the new fireseeds would blossom. Any taint in the tavern yard, no matter how small, would fuel the burning flowers. Someday there would be purity here.

We had not made a cure here. It was too late for that. Instead, we created the system of a cure. We would be here to keep watch, in the shadows of the woods, smelling for any sign of the stain accumulating in one place. Things would be better here someday. The people here would slowly get better. The fireseeds would blossom on this land for years to come.

**

The hard work was done. The local temples of Erin and Imam could take over, nursing the land and its people back to health. My husband and I returned to Dogsland, on the hunt for the bones of the demon child of a succubus that created Jona, the Lord of Joni. We were on the hunt for the immortal one, too old to know what demon had made him, or how many generations back it was. We were on the hunt for Rachel Nolander, the doppelganger's daughter that had escaped another death in Dogsland, a first generation demon. We took the skull from the church so it would stay near me. The Pens were not safe, even for us, but we found a room as close as we thought we could risk. We ate dinner in our room, with the wolfskins on our backs, and all the furniture pushed against the walls to keep it out of our way.

We spread Calipari's map across the floor carefully, leaving gaps where he left gaps so we could step between the pages on the floor. The skull was with us. I could touch it if I wanted to risk an infection. I could study it.

I did.

What is it like, to hold a million moments from another's life inside your mind? It's like living on an island, with two oceans beneath you: the ocean you see when your eyes are open is yours; the ocean you see when your eyes are closed is not. I had to swim in someone else's waters, and I did. For days I studied the maps, and I closed my eyes. My husband waited for me.

I'm starting to remember. I'm starting to see the shape of the memories.

Do you see the man and the monster, and do you see with our eyes into his life?

I'm starting to see it all.

Write it down. Write it all down.

Yes.

CHAPTER III

There was a tree. It was a big tree, which was rare for the city, and a willow, its thick leaves hanging in the heat like ribbons dangling from bound hair. Beneath those long branches, people took their rest in the shade. Near the tree, an old woman had set up a tea cart, slowly circling the trunk with the sun to stay in the tree's shadow.

That's what Jona remembered first about Rachel Nolander. There was this tree, and they were in the shadow of it. They had been trying to talk, and neither one of them knew what to say. Jona wanted to ask her about things that were true, but he couldn't ask her these things because they were too many people around, and he didn't know what else to ask her about. Rachel broke the silence.

"So… What is your life like? I mean, who are you?" she looked away, and said it again, softer. "What is your life like?"

He squinted. He knew he didn't look like a nobleman when he squinted like that, with his king's man uniform and skin as hard as tree bark from the days in the sun. She probably didn't believe him right away when he said he was a lord. She probably wouldn't believe anything he said. "I don't know," he said. "What's your life like? How are we supposed to answer that?"

"I have a way," she said. "I can tell you a koan, and it will carry with it my whole life."

"Senta stuff? I don't know anything about Sentas."

"There aren't a lot of us this far south. Street magic, mostly. No one takes it seriously except for us. I take it seriously."

"Tell me, whatever it is you can tell me."

"All right," she said. "This is everything you need to know about being Senta. There was this Senta renowned for wisdom. This Senta was so wise that she never uttered a word. A young student of our unities learned of this woman from his parents, who spoke of this particular Senta with great respect. The young Senta journeyed over mountains and oceans to find her. When he found her, she did not greet him. He asked her why she never spoke. She opened a cage where she kept a bird. The bird remained in the cage. It had a mirror inside of the cage, and a dish for seed, and another dish for water. The Senta that did not speak waited. Nothing happened. Then, she closed the cage door."

Jona waited. "That's it?"

"That's it."

"Huh."

"That is also my life before, I think. That's... I think that's all I can say about it right now. Do you understand it?"

"It means you've never spoken about it?"

"More than that. It's a deep truth of the way the universe really is for everyone."

"Is it one of your spells?"

"Yes. Watch." A small ball of ice grew in her palm. She dropped it into his tea with a splash. "If you understand it, you will know the spell, too."

Jona swirled his tea. "I guess that's my life too, before we met." He held out his hand, trying to make the ice.

Rachel laughed. "I guess you don't really understand the lesson. You must also comprehend the koan in a place beyond words. My mother raised me since I was very young to be a Senta like her. It took years and years of focus and meditation. Then, one day, the cold filled my throat, and I breathed the ice. Now I can feel the ice everywhere around me anytime I think about it."

Jona frowned at that. "I don't like all that thinking. Nothing makes sense if you think about it too long," he said. "If there's one thing you can say about the Imam and Erin people, it's that they don't want you to think too much."

"This is exactly why I do not think they are correct, Jona. Do not speak of the false breaking with me. The cosmos is still in unity."

"What about the Nameless?" said Jona, "They don't make sense. Do you believe in them?"

"We were born weren't we? Think about this," she said. "I don't care what anyone says about that. There is a place for us in the world. Dogs do not hate us the way people do. Do you think dogs are capable of comprehending the cosmic Unity?"

"Dogs?" said Jona. "I can't say I thought about it that way…"

"Dogs don't bark at us like intruders. We're just another person to them," said Rachel. "Now, tell me who you were before you were with me. Here is another spell, of powerful fire: Tell me your face before you were born. Tell me anything, Jona. Just… Let's not sit here staring at each other. It's bad enough people would stare at us. We don't need to do it to each other."

The silence filled his ears, full of things he could never say to her. He was human enough to know that he couldn't tell her the truth in the shadow of a willow tree, with tea and all these nice people sitting with them in the afternoon shade.

"Anything at all," she said.

He opened his mouth.

I don't know what he said. I don't think he knows what he said either, except that it probably wasn't completely honest.

***

Jona and some of his fellow king's men were down in a dive out on the other side of the Pens. The place stank of dead animals. The living animals smelled worse. People wandered in from a back room in a pink haze, muttering anything they could think about that wasn't about being right there, in the Pens, where the animal stink pressed through the cracks in the walls. This was the tavern where the blood-soaked butchers drank after a ship came in for slaughter, still covered in animal blood. To toss a few back, to pretend like they were just anybody. The only music was a round or two of song that the killers kept singing because it was the song of their life. They sang this song all day while they were shoving cattle and goats and sheep and parts of them up and down the abattoir. That's where Jona and the boys were drinking.

Jona, Jaime, Tripoli, and Geek were at a table at the edge of the bar, near the kitchen. Tripoli had a thing for the barmaid, and was waiting to pinch her as she passed. Geek threw raw eggs back like shots of whiskey and washed them down with a beer as black as tar and bitter as rotten fruit. Tripoli and Jaime were betting on how many eggs Geek could swallow before he puked it all up.

Jona placed his bet. The other king's men laughed at Jona's bet, such a low number. Geek could eat dozens more than that, they shouted. Jona let them laugh. He counted Geek's eggs carefully until his number hit. Then he swung his bat fast, smashing the egg in Geek's hand. Before anybody could stop him, Jona kicked over the egg crate and swung his bat hard onto the crate, shattering everything. Breathing hard, he stomped on the eggs that had tumbled out of the mess.

The other three guards just sat there, shocked. Jona had just smashed all the eggs over a few coins. They refused to pay up on their bet, at first. Jona sneered at them. Nobody said he couldn't keep Geek from eating any more eggs.

They were too appalled to argue with him. If they had been a bit more drunk, they might have tried to fight about it, but they were still sober enough to want to keep drinking. They weren't ready to be thrown out into the night.

Jona sneered like a rooster crowing over his kill. He laughed, counting their coins in his palm. Jona wiped his bat off on the barmaid's dress, just to rub it in more, right in front of Tripoli. Tripoli left. Then, Geek left. Jaime ignored Jona, and leaned into a cup like he was trying to fall into it and drown.

Jona got bored. The barmaid handed him one last drink, on the house, and told him to go smash eggs somewhere else. Jona didn't know what it was in the cup, but it was worse than the beer and the beer was awful. He walked off by himself. The soles of his boots were sticky with egg. He'd have to take them off if he went home, but he didn't want to go home. He was so mad after what he had done that he wanted to punch someone. He should've known destroying the eggs would've spoiled everything. He should apologize for it.

Tomorrow, he'd pretend to be hung over beyond belief, and claim that he couldn't remember anything because he was so drunk, even before the contest started. He'd been drinking all day. He'd lie and lie and lie. Nobody would call him on it, and nobody would believe him.

***

Long ago, before he could remember anything about anything, Jona's mother had cut demon wings away from his back. He told people that asked about his scars that he had fallen on a spiked fence when he was a kid. Sometimes he forgot they were there. He'd catch a glimpse of his back in a mirror and see the scars and part of him wondered if that was really his back, skin jagged like it was shredded with no memory of the pain. He could forget about them hidden under his uniform, forget about his blood.

Once he figured out that he could make people sick if he so much as spit on them, he never made anyone sick on purpose. People did fall ill sometimes, because everybody spits and people shared drinks and handshakes and people kissed sometimes if the mood was right and sometimes they might even try to make love and Jona couldn't hide among men without doing at least some of these things from time to time. His mother told him all the time to be careful. He tried, but like his lost wings, it was so easy to forget.

His life with the king's men had hardened him. But this was only the surface. Inside, he was formless, shifting into whatever place he found himself, trying to squeeze into the crevices like water down a mountain, tumbling through life.

The Night King found him before anyone else did. Jona had just broken all the eggs, and was walking around, looking for another tavern. He was alone in the night. He took one step, and he was sober. The next step, he was drunker than he thought he had been. Before he could take another step, he was so drunk he couldn't walk. He leaned into a wall. His boots stuck to the ground. For one brief moment, Jona thought it was the eggs, sticking under his boots.

A bag came down over his eyes, and hands took his arms at the elbows and held him up. They didn't say anything. They just took him.

***

The Night King's fellows tore the uniform off Jona's body. The only thing they let him keep was the bag on his face. They pushed him down a long, damp hallway. If he ever reached a room, he didn't notice. They pushed him to his knees. Jona leaned back against the men that had him. He could move a little, but he was still deep inside of the water in his mind. He was on hands and knees before he knew what he should be trying to do. The hands behind him yanked him upward into a kneel, and his head swum.

Someone leaned over him. A knife cut over Jona's chest. It didn't cut deep, but it bled. The blood was acid, and toxic. Someone pressed a stick into the spilling blood. The stick wilted against Jona's chest. It was pushed into his wound, and wilted before it could pressure any part of him, like being stabbed with a ribbon.

"I know what you are," she whispered.

Jona couldn't speak. His tongue felt as thick as a sausage. He tried to move his head.

"I could turn you in, and have you burned. You know that, don't you? Anyone could if they found out."

Her voice sounded like it was far away, but it was so close to him he could feel the breath on his shoulder. She was leaning over him, whispering into his ear. His limbs felt heavy, like sinking ships. He couldn't fight back even as he longed to strike out. The torturer pulled up Jona's hands with care, and placed something in them. The bag was peeled back from his head, but he couldn't lift his face up. He saw woman's hands, holding up his own, and what she had put into his hands. She had given him a doll, with long, white hair. An old woman. His mother.

"You need to prove useful to me," she said. Jona wanted to look up at her, but a hand grabbed his hair from behind, forcing his head to stay down, even if he had enough strength to lift it. "Be extremely useful, or I won't stop with you."

The clouds parted from the haze in Jona's mind. He knew exactly what choices he had. He took a deep breath, and moved his tongue. He found enough to speak his heart. "I will," he said, "Anything, just…."

"I'll be in touch," she said. The bag returned, and the darkness of it. Rough hands dressed him.

As if it was all a dream, Jona was back on the surface, dressed in a clean uniform in moments, with clean boots. The tiny doll weighed down his pocket like a stone. The cut on his chest had been sealed in wax and clean bandages. After the cut healed, it was like nothing had happened to him. He hid the doll in the huge, empty house where his mother wouldn't find it. Jona thought of saying something, but couldn't think of what to say. He had been found out, and he was going to be used because of it. He didn't know how or why, but it was so.

One night, Jona was walking home from a shift in evening

twilight, and a merchant stepped out of his shop to stop him, glancing around nervously.

"What?" said Jona. "You want something? I'm off duty."

Then he saw the doll the tailor held in his hand. The man gestured Jona into his shop with a nod, and handed him a scroll. *Night King's Man* was written in jagged red ink.

A smuggler was pretending to be a baker two districts over. The merchant gave Jona clothes for the job to wear, and heavier clothes to carry. The merchant didn't speak. Jona changed in a back room. The scroll had detailed instructions, including what to do with the paper itself.

Jona did as he was told. He cornered his victim as the man waited for a ferry on an empty street. Jona called out his name. The man looked up. Jona forced him around a corner and tied a bag full of bricks around the man's neck. He pushed back against Jona, but Jona was stronger. Confused, the man started to speak out against it, but Jona was faster than any cry for help. Jona pushed the man into the water. His face, going down, in a flash, was a pale mask of sudden clarity. His stomach churning, Jona waited to make sure the man didn't come up for air. When he was sure, he tore up the scroll and tossed it into the water.

Jona ran from the scene as fast as he could, slowing as he neared the merchant's shop, where he ducked into the back door, and changed back into his uniform.

The merchant didn't seem to care if the job was done or not. He paid Jona for his time with a blank face. He patted Jona on the back without a word.

This was the beginning of Jona's second life, when nightfall meant walking in shadows, following men and women, sometimes killing them. Before that, at nightfall, Jona did nothing at all. He read until he ran out of candles. He swung his sword aimlessly on the roof of his house until he ran out of moonlight. He let his mind wander until he ran out of darkness. When the sun rose, he pretended he had spent the night asleep like everyone else in the world.

Then, the Night King came, and filled the empty hours with blood, and hunting.

***

I pieced together some of the murders, but not all of them. They were so sudden. Most of the time all that lingered was the anticipation, and the way the knife felt in Jona's palm when it punctured someone else's skin. Jona remembered standing in a corner and staring at a door with a knife hidden in his shirt sleeve. He remembered trying to walk casually through a crowd, searching for a woman or a man or both.

There was one I studied closely, scenting at the place where it had happened because Salvatore went there before Jona knew to look for him. Jona was underground, pushing through the Nameless' illegal temple, the crowd jumping to the huge drums, other music somewhere beneath the drum, pushing into each other right at the edge of where the sewer fell into the bay. Their hair was all spiked and green from clumps of lime. They reeked of sweat, and lime. They were so ugly, in rags, and so proud to be ugly. They smiled with phosphor smeared on their teeth and laughed and laughed and danced ecstatically pressed into each other.

Jona pushed through the crowd, found his mark pounding the drums at the center of the sound.

He slipped a knife from a pouch up his sleeve.

Thrown, his knife went straight into the drummer's eye. The man's head whipped back. He fell backward, gasping. His trembling hands reached for the handle, too surprised to wonder from where it had flown. He tried to stand.

Jona raced up to the drum and leaped on top. It gave a little under his boots, but the leather head didn't tear with his weight. He tugged his bat from his back, and smacked the drummer's hands away from the knife. Jona clubbed the man in the head, knocking him back again, and jumped on top of him. He swung the bat. He kept swinging. Blood and bone, he kept swinging. Jona closed his eyes and didn't stop. It made him sick to think about it, and what he saw.

When he finally stopped, Jona realized that the drumming had long since stopped. It shouldn't have surprised him, but it did. No one had tried to stop him.

Blood and bone and brain crawled in the crevices that snaked through the stone to the sewer water. In that bad light, the water in the sewer was dark red, like death.

Jona turned to the Nameless' dancers. They stood still, looking at him.

"What?" said Jona. "Night King sends regards. Stay out of my way."

Was Jona wearing a mask? I don't know. Sometimes he covered his face when doing the Night King's work where people might see. Sometimes he didn't. Corrupt king's men were nothing new. If anyone recognized him, what could they do with the blessings of both the city's kings upon his deeds?

The crowd pulled back. Retracing his steps to the main sewer lines, Jona felt their eyes on him the whole way.

Jona now got most of his work from a carpenter that didn't mind speaking. When Jona got back up to the surface to report on the job, the wrong name slipped from his tongue. For a second, the carpenter was furious because he thought the wrong man had been killed. Jona described the man, and it was the right one, but the name was off. It was hard to remember everything he was doing in the night.

Home, in clean clothes, he came downstairs where his mother cooked breakfast. She hugged him hello.

"Long night?" she said, making conversation.

"I just went out and about. Didn't find anything at all. Didn't even look."

"Have fun?"

"Eh, not really," replied Jona. "It gets boring pretty quick when you aren't rich, and you have all night to remind yourself that you aren't rich."

"We're still nobility. Don't forget that when you're getting bossed around all day. Porridge?"

"Thanks."

He sat down to eat. She joined him at the table, but didn't eat anything. She never ate breakfast with him. She just watched.

Spooning the porridge into his mouth, he tried again to remember the dead man's name. It was on the tip of his tongue, but he couldn't conjure it.

Later that morning, Jona was working with Jaime in the Pens. Some weed smokers had been stealing goats, and smuggling the stuff sewn into dead animals. They wouldn't bother anyone if they hadn't stolen the goats first. Jona and Jaime found a man they knew had done it. They pushed him against a wall to get names out of him of anyone else helping him. The man was terrified. A name hit Jona like a brick wall.

"Grigora," he said, out of nowhere, almost under his breath.

"Who?" Jaime turned his head. He had the smuggler by the hair against a brick, names pouring from his lips like water.

Jona shook his head. "Sorry," he said, "this fellow I met last night, is all."

Jona looked out at the horizon, wondering where he was going that night. He had heard that Grigora had a few friends that had gone sour over his death, and the Night King was already making plans for Jona to take care of them, too.

When the smuggler's confessions were done, Jaime punched Jona's arm. "Wake up, Jona. Need you sharp."

"Yeah," said Jona. That's all he said to Jaime. If Jona had said the truth, he wondered who among the guard would turn him in and who among them were doing the same thing he was, working late into the night for the kind of people that they spent all day trying to find.

***

Jona sat with his mother's co-workers at the dress shop, all women as old as she was or more, and all of them chattering like Jona wasn't even in the room. That suited Jona fine. It was Adventday, when people visit neighbors, and they'd come to drink bad mint tea and talk about dresses. The dressmakers loved to come to the Joni Estate—what was left of it. They loved to see how a noble lady wasn't rich anymore, once proud and now making dresses with calloused hands from so many needle-pricks, and the special way the lips moved after years of pinching threads down. There but for the mercy of Imam, went all of the snotty children that wore the fine gowns they sewed.

When they finally noticed Jona, too quiet, one of the dressmakers asked him politely about his work with the king's men. He smiled. He knew the story to tell them. He told them about the time he beat a confession out of a young man just to keep one of the noble women that wore the fancy dresses happy. The noble lady had been offended by a brute because he had nabbed a purse from her coachman. Of course, the coachman was wearing his fat purse like a peacock's tail down in the Pens and expected his noble seal to keep him safe. This noble girl begged Corporal Jona, Lord of Joni, to beat the petty thief until he confessed to stealing everything he ever stole in his life. He confessed to so many coins, a fistful at a time. Calipari kept track in a ledger. Once it got to be enough, the guard could hang him. They carried the thief to the gallows with two broken legs, and a face smashed into meat. Beautiful girl, that one, with the bluest eyes and looks so good in a low-cut dress with her calves sealed in ribbons and she dances like a lark. Last time Jona crashed a nobleman's ball, she deigned to dance with him. She was a solid kisser, too, but he urged the dressmakers not to tell her fiancée about that. He might want to beat a confession or two out of Jona if he ever found out.

Jona took a long, loud sip of his tea in the silent room. He reached for one of the Adventday sandwiches on the other side of the table with his dirty hands, and sat back down with a deep slouch.

"I say something?" Jona grunted with his mouth full of food. Chunks of sandwich showed in his mouth when he talked.

The little old ladies touched red cheeks with pale fingers. When the conversation began again, the women talked about the last dress they sewed for the girl, and all the special things she had wanted embroidered into the hem, as if anyone noticed such small details but dressmakers.

Jona's mother shared a brief smile with her son, and poured more tea into his cup. "When are you meeting Lady Ela Sabachthani for tea, Jona?"

The dressmakers fell silent.

"Couple weeks. Wants advice about the crime in the districts. Wants me to tell her what she can do about it. Nothing to be done for it, is what I'll tell her. Burn the whole place down, and kick everybody out."

"She invited him for tea," said his mother. "He'll be going to nobleman's balls when the rains stop. He'll dance with the women who buy our dresses. Isn't he handsome in his uniform?"

The other women didn't say anything. Some of them put down their cups. One of them got up to leave. "Now you're just making things up," she said.

Jona poured more brandy into his tea. They couldn't afford sugar, so they had to use cheap brandy to take the edge off the cheap, bitter mint. The more he thought about it, the more brandy he wanted to add.

Lady Ela had tea with everybody. If you were of noble blood, you could count on it, eventually. The last time it happened, it took Jona five minutes to get politely shown the door.

***

Jona was sitting in on an interrogation with a candle maker whose tax ledgers looked funny to Calipari. He rolled his eyes while Nicola questioned the man. Jona had seen the books, but nothing worth all this interrogation.

"And the capital expense was…?" Sergeant Calipari questioned and questioned, waiting for some admission that hadn't come, yet.

Jona stared out the window past the heads of the two men. He wanted to go home, take a cool bath, open a bottle of wine, and pretend like he was taking a nap. That's what everyone else said they did after a long day at work.

Sergeant Calipari snapped his fingers. Jona nodded. He raised the hidden mallet from his lap up over the table in a smooth motion, and slammed down upon the candle maker's thumb before he could think to pull it away.

The candle maker screamed. He sucked his thumb in his mouth, whimpering like a child. His nail cracked and bled.

Jona turned back to the window again. He thought he saw a bird fly by, but it might have been anything blowing in the wind. He wanted to take a long, cool bath with that wine he just got as a bribe, and maybe afterward he could buy some better sausage with the money he kept hidden on the roof. His mother didn't know about the money on the roof, or where it came from. All she ever saw of it was better food.

Jona looked down. He frowned. The candle maker was still there, holding back tears and clutching his broken, bloodied thumb. He was listing all the names he could scrape from his head. Jona didn't listen.

Calipari carefully transcribed this new list of names. He'd give them to scriveners for warrants, and all the tax evaders would be arrested for their crimes, except for the candle maker. The informant was free to go, until an informant was needed again, or unless his crimes were too serious for that. Had Calipari told him he could go? Calipari went out to see the scriveners, and Jona was alone with the weeping candle maker.

He looked in terror at Jona.

Jona lifted the mallet. "What?"

"Please…" the candle maker was crying.

"Get out of here. Don't look back at me, or I'll crack your face, too."

The candle maker bolted for the door.

Jona went back among the cells. He wasn't sure if Calipari wanted the candle maker arrested or not, but Calipari wouldn't let the candle maker leave the station if he was supposed to be arrested. Jona, still unsure, left the empty room. He went back in the cells to check and see if the candle maker was there. Jona found Tripoli in one of the empty cells, and no sign of the candle maker. Tripoli was drinking. Together the two corporals traded a flask of cheap whiskey until it was empty. Tripoli fell asleep on a pallet.

For a moment, Jona thought about locking Tripoli in, on a lark. Instead, he returned to the main room with the scriveners to ask about what happened to the candle maker. Calipari wrinkled his nose at Jona's whiskeyed breath and ordered him home. Before he left, though, Jona showed Calipari where Tripoli lay asleep. Cursing, the sergeant locked the cell and kicked the bars. Tripoli didn't even stir.

Stumbling home, a chill of dread hit Jona. He shouldn't have shared the flask. He told himself it was all right, just this once, to share a flask. Tripoli'd be feeling ill a few days. When it had happened before, no one had died. No one would put two and two together as long as it didn't happen that much. It would be all right. Tripoli would be all right.

It was so easy to forget that he wasn't like these men who were his friends. He had to be more careful.

***

Jona snuck into most of the better dry season parties because it's what his mother had done to meet his father. It's how people met when they couldn't officially meet. His official meeting seemed like she was biding her time until she needed a king's man owing her favors.

How little he understood. Lady Sabachthani already owned the king's men. She already owned him, and he didn't even know it.

Jona's mother had bragged about the invitation to tea among the dressmakers, and had fluttered about the house to get him ready for this. His uniform was clean and starched. His hair was cut close and combed into place with lard to hold it down. If she could have personally, she would have walked with him all the way to the door of the parlor room of the third or fourth cousin, twice removed, that was chaperoning. The distant cousin had just been engaged to marry Ela's distant cousin, and Ela was visiting, nominally to celebrate the engagement. It was a ruse, and explicitly described as one on the invitation. Ela wouldn't meet nobles like Lord Joni in her own house, no matter what Jona's mother said to the other dressmakers. Lord Joni was unmarried, and so was she. Decorum still applied. But Lady Ela Sabachthani had tea at least once a year with every noble in the city, even Jona. She made up excuses about important issues, and found an excuse that merited a meeting in someone's house, for tea.

Jona wasn't one to get called Lord Joni much at all, unless he was getting mocked for it. He never understood what Lady Sabachthani might have wanted from him, and he was too afraid to ask her straight out.

This time, Ela had brought a basket, which she coyly set beside her unexplained. When the conversation slowed, she opened the basket to produce a tiny black terrier.

She put the little dog at her feet and told the dog to follow her as she walked around the room. It obeyed. She winked at them, and ordered the dog to climb on the wall. To the politely delighted gasps of her audience, masking the fear of Sabachthani magic, the dog walked up the side of the wall, stopping at the ceiling.

Flush with success, Ela then demanded the dog serve tea. It came down from the wall as easily as it had gone up the side of it. It jumped to Ela's chair, then the table. The little dog tried so hard to hold the teapot with his clumsy mouth, but clever as he was, he was still just a dog. The pot slipped from his teeth, and broke on the table in front of Ela. Hot tea spilled out.

Ela cursed like a sailor, and threw the animal back into his basket. Her face flushed.

In the silence that followed, Jona wondered why he had been invited, and why she had gotten so mad, and why he couldn't just go home right then. The room was silent, waiting for Lady Sabachthani's mood to shift. Jona only got more uncomfortable in the silence. He stood up. "It's just a teapot," he said, and handed her his napkin across the table. "That dog was walking on walls and you're mad over a teapot? I never saw magic like that before. Not even Senta do that."

Ela ignored the napkin. "Stupid thing did it on purpose," she said, kicking at the basket. "Parlor tricks like that... My father ended a war with one spell, and I have a retarded dog who can bend his weight up a wall."

The hostess didn't say anything. They were all watching Lady Sabachthani. She had the kind of power that made people patient.

"It's still impressive," said Jona. "I'll find a new pot."

The hostess looked up at Jona as if he had just confessed to murder.

"What?" he said, confused. "I say something?"

The hostess cleared her throat. "The servants will do that, Lord Joni. They're waiting for you to sit down so they can clean up."

The other guests smiled and said nothing, except for Ela. "I always liked that about the king's men: problem solvers. They don't wait around for anyone to do something. Not like us."

Lady Ela put the basket in the hostess' lap, and gave the dog one more command. She made it roll onto its back and pee itself from inside. The dog obeyed. Urine leaked out of the basket's seams.

Lord Joni was the only one laughing with Lady Sabachthani. The hostess, with the dog on her lap, smiled while her fingernails dug into her teacup. She wouldn't remove the basket, because Lady Sabachthani had placed it there. She pretended to enjoy it. Tea service was soon over. When Jona left, no one said good-bye to him.

***

My husband came back from the noblewoman's house. He said they had burned the cards Jona had left behind with his home's address. None had ever been to the house, and no one remembered the way. Lady Ela would know, but we couldn't approach her casually. The main city temple petitioned the Captain of the Guard for an address, but he found no record, and his search would take time. Jona's fellow guardsman had probably destroyed the records to protect his mother and the house she had left. The courts might have tried to take it from her.

Given enough time studying Jona's memories, I would be able to walk straight there from anywhere in the city. I just needed more time. In the meantime, Salvatore was a greater threat than an empty house and an old woman. Salvatore would try to run. The old woman? The empty house? They weren't going anywhere.

***

Jona walked around the Pens. He waved at a pinker he knew as he passed. Dellner was just a petty cutter that birdied his boss for a little reward money a Lord had offered. He did everything he could to pay for time at the underground hookahs. He'd confess anything, turn on anyone, as long as there was coin in it for time underground.

Dellner didn't respond. Annoyed, Jona called out Dellner's

name. Dellner didn't even look up. Jona waved Geek over from the other side of the street. Dellner didn't move a muscle where he stood. He leaned against warm stones, breathing while two guards shouted and waved their hands in his face.

Geek squinted. "How pink's your birdie? Never seen anyone this deep above ground. Shouldn't have let him walk around. Might walk into a carriage without seeing it."

Jona scratched his neck and shook his head. "He's so pink, he might as well be meat." Jona pushed Dellner deeper into an alley. Dellner didn't fight back. Geek followed. "Only a week ago he was our boy. He must've been living in a weed pit with the reward, puffing like he's trying to kill himself with it." Jona pushed Dellner harder. The man stumbled into a brick wall and scraped his head against it. His blood was pink. His sweat was pink. It left a stain along the wall. He stumbled and fell. Dellner's head rolled back and gazed up at the sky. His toothless mouth hanging open was pink inside.

"What should we do with your birdie?" said Geek.

Jona didn't answer. He leaned over and flipped Dellner over, making sure the man's face was in the mud. Jona put his heel to the back of the pinker's head, pushing Dellner deeper.

Dellner's body couldn't connect to an appropriate response. His arms lay limp in the mud. His face stayed in the mud. His chest heaved up and up, struggling to breathe, while his feet tried to walk away from the mud, as if they were planted on solid ground.

Geek said something, but Jona wasn't listening. "Hey!" Geek shouted, grabbing at Jona to pull him off.

He wasn't fast enough. Dellner's body was weak from the smoking the demonweed hookahs. His chest stopped shuddering. His legs and arms went still.

Jona stepped off the body. Geek stared at Jona, his face pale. Geek's hands were shaking. "What'd you do that for?!"

"Well…" Jona thought a moment before he spoke. "I didn't mean to kill him."

"We could have taken him to a temple! They'd have watched him until he came off the smoke!"

"I don't go for the temples, Geek." The body in the mud looked more like a muddy root than a man. Jona half expected a brown trunk to sprout from the back of the fellow's skull. "He didn't go for temples, either."

Geek said nothing about it later to Calipari. Nobody birdies on the king's men, least of all another king's man. Geek helped Jona push the body down a sewer grate, and if anyone was watching they didn't say anything. A bad interrogation was all, and these things happened, and everybody knew Dellner was nobody to nobody.

Lunch came, and Jona sat down with all the boys outside the guard house. The other guards looked at him without eating, waiting for Jona to leave. Jona snorted. He took his bread to the main room where Sergeant Calipari sat poring over scrolls while he ate.

Jona nodded towards the papers. "What are you doing?"

"I can't make figs out of this tax form from the... You know, that one..." Calipari's voice trailed off as he crunched numbers in his head, looking for the smugglers in the columns. The scriveners on the other side of the room tried to make conversation, but Calipari scolded them and they bent their backs to work.

Sergeant Calipari set his ledger down, and snapped a finger at Jona. "Hey, Lord Joni."

Jona formed a mask on his face, playing the role of the red-handed bully, too proud to show any red in his face. That's who he was supposed to be, he knew.

"Don't kill any more birdies, even in accident," said Calipari. "Don't be so cruel. You're a solid man day-in, day-out, but you aren't a nobleman when you're in that uniform. Even noblemen can only break and batter the ones on their own lands, and you got no lands left. The king's subjects are not yours to break and batter in the king's streets. Take pity on the pinkers. Nobody asks to live like that, even if they choose to go down to the hookahs."

Jona nodded.

"No one's reporting on it. I say let it die." He looked back down to the ledger and circled something with a quill. "There. Corporal, I'll break you myself if you ever do that again. I'll pull the lever when you hang. Clear?"

Jona nodded, and chewed his bread, silently.

Sergeant Calipari didn't look up from his papers. Behind him, the young scriveners were pale and shaking. One of them stood up to leave, until Sergeant Calipari cleared his throat. The scrivener sat down, and cut a new goose-feather. He held his feather over the page like he couldn't remember where he was.

Sergeant Calipari had just threatened to kill Corporal Jona, Lord of Joni, a king's man and nobleman. Jona heard it. They had all heard it. Jona knew he was supposed to be afraid.

Jona finished his bread, and went for a walk. He couldn't figure out why he wasn't shaken. He knew that he should be terrified, but he wasn't. He wasn't even angry.

The guard had hardened him, the Night King hardened him, but inside he was formless, still.

***

Out with the boys, this time Sergeant Calipari was with them. They were deep in the Pens, underground, betting on the cockfights. Jona wasn't betting. He stared down at the flurry of blood and feathers. He was bored by it.

Calipari came over and smacked him on the back. "Buck up! You're bringing us down."

Jona shrugged. "Guess I'm not kicking for this kind of bird," he said. "Going to go find me a better tail-feather."

The boys laughed and Jaime said he wanted to go, too, so Jona waited out one more fight. Then, Jona and Jaime went above ground and north of the Pens. Uniforms got deep discounts there. Jaime picked out a child, all soft curves and barely thirteen, and hopped up the stairs after her, laughing at Jona to choose well.

Jona never actually went upstairs with the girls. Instead, he sat with the madame of the establishment and shared a cup of tea, ignoring all the sounds from above, and all the people coming and going. The two talked about the madame's daughter off and married to a nice officer of a merchant ship, the girl now living right on the bay next to the port. They both knew her son-in-law was dead and her daughter was pushing mugs in a dive, pregnant from who knows who.

Jona talked about his quest for a suitable bride among the rest of the nobility as if he actually wanted to marry anyone. The madame gave Jona her motherly advice based on the news she heard from the noblemen that passed through her establishment. She mentioned upcoming parties he might attend to meet promising young ladies. This season there weren't as many parties to attend as usual, but still plenty of opportunities for an up-and-coming nobleman with such a fine uniform.

In truth, Jona wouldn't have come here at all except that Jaime followed him out after a brothel. In the end, Jona was glad for the conversation with the woman. People didn't really talk to Jona, with his uniform on. When Jaime staggered back downstairs, his eyelids dropping from the effort and the booze, Jona was disappointed that his time was up.

Jaime swayed around his boots, barely able to keep his feet beneath him. The proprietress frowned and put her cup down hard on the table. Jona shrugged. "Can't be helped." Jaime slapped Jona on the back and tried to say something, but when he opened his mouth, bile spewed out. Gobs of vomit splashed into the tea, and smothered the fine china. Jaime simply laughed.

Jona had to walk his stumbling friend home. Jaime couldn't make it without shoulders to lean on. But even drunk, he knew the way to the little house he had inherited from his wife's family. He pointed and mumbled the directions home. Jaime's wife had been waiting up for her husband to return. She and Jona didn't say a word to each other as he let Jaime's weight lean over to her. She was strong enough for him. She eased her husband onto the kitchen table sideways where he could puke and it could be wiped away without much fuss. She and Jaime had been married for fifteen years like this. From the windows, one of Jaime's sons looked down, barely thirteen and looking more like his father every day.

Then Jona was standing in a dark street all by himself, surrounded by these plain, simple houses. He wondered what it was like inside those houses in the daylight. He wondered what it was like on an Adventday afternoon, sipping tea and watching the kids while the good wife sews Adventday Caps with her sisters on the back porch, and people go around visiting everyone. He imagined the scene. It all seemed so normal, but the women had no faces, and the children were just small, formless, hands running through trees and grabbing at everything.

He tried to picture a child. Any child. He couldn't think of even one. He tried to remember the name of Jaime's son, in the window, but it came out all wrong—too much like Jaime drunk and smiling. He tried to think of any child in the world, and hold that child in his mind's eye.

He couldn't see anything. He couldn't feel anything. The black absence of feeling caught up inside his chest as if his heart had blackened into a stone. Jona sat down on a curb, and pressed his hands into his chest. He tried to breathe, but air wasn't coming into his chest right. He stayed there a long time, bent over from this pain—an ache in his chest like a scream that wasn't coming out. Not even tears came out.

It diminished, but didn't faded. He walked home slowly.

***

My husband scoured the city, sniffing through the trash heaps for the worst of the stains among the outhouses and drinking houses and all the places Jona might have sweat out a long night. He had lived here too long. He had been in too many of the buildings here. He had walked down these roads, pissed in the alleys, and wiped sweat away everywhere he went.

Jona was alone every night, when everyone else was dreaming. He never slept like people were supposed to sleep. He kept his heritage a secret, and he was careful about it, but it was too easy to make mistakes when he was passing among the king's men. He kept his true self hidden, like his blood, and no one gets close.

Jona's life ended at the edge of his skin. This made his loneliness a broken sail that hung always on his back, windless and rain-drenched. He walked with this sail hanging over him. His shoulders rolled forward, and his eyes gazed tight into every stranger in the world. *Watch out.*

That was Jona's life, before he knew there was anyone else like him. This was before he found out about Salvatore, the immortal—I think his name is Salvatore—and before he met Rachel Nolander. This is the life he wouldn't tell her about, under the willow tree, when she asked him.

There wasn't anyone else in the world like him, and he felt it deep inside, all the way back until before he was born, as the Sentas said.

***

This was the life Jona knew. And then Rachel Nolander, a doppelganger's daughter, came to Dogsland with her human half-brother.

They came on a ship.

CHAPTER IV

Rachel came to Dogsland on a ship. I had to think hard on it. I had to be sure so my husband could tell the Church of Imam, and the guard. They needed to find the smuggler's ship and burn it, arrest the smuggler and hang him. I had to search for every hint of her I could find in Jona's memory.

When the candle burned low, and her hand pressed into his bare chest, and the sun lingered on the western horizon and Rachel was about to get up, get dressed and slip into the night and Jona was about to get up, get dressed and slip into the night, just before then, they talked.

What is your face before you are born? she had asked Jona. He could ask the same of her.

Rachel had never had anyone but her brother to talk to about her life. The demon's mark couldn't be cut away from her skin. Her hands were human enough, with most of her arms. Her face and neck appeared human if no one noticed her tongue. Everything else was twisted from the stain. Her father was a doppelganger demon that had burrowed into the skin of Djoss' human father. Their mother was a Senta, telling fortunes and casting small spells for coin. Rachel hid her twisted flesh beneath Senta robes, like her mother had taught her. She practiced her mother's faith, though the Senta would burn Rachel just like everyone would burn her. Her brother raised her after her mother died, and he was a hard man that knew no way to raise a girl. The koans raised her, studying them focused her mind into a form that carried her into the world, and her place inside of it.

When I entered Jona's skull, I heard the coagulation of her stories inside of him, and saw her with my eyes, smelled her, tasted her. I saw deep.

This was his *Her.*

***

We came to Dogsland on a boat.

The sloop was full of garbage. The old man who sailed the little boat alone never tossed anything away.

Below deck, damp papers clung together tied up with strings and stacked. The paper attracted flies chasing the greasy remains of the food eaten off the paper. Clothes were folded loosely across every spare spot of floor. Old crates and empty boxes piled against the walls. The shifting waters knocked them over sometimes, never to be picked up again.

Beneath the rotten crates, people and things came to Dogsland, and back out again, where no inspector would want to look. He knew what Rachel was, and he didn't care. He was paid better for this than for the pinker's weed. Rachel's passage had cost almost everything she and her brother had. She had been found out. They had jumped out a second story window to escape the city. They had run to the seaport and moved fast to find a man who would take their coin.

Her brother, Djoss, stayed on deck to help with the sail and the rudder. They sailed for three days. Rachel sat alone in the dark. She felt the ocean below her rolling around. When she was bored, she snapped her fingers and watched the Senta fires flicker in the little cabin. She couldn't keep a fire inside a wooden hull with all that rotting paper everywhere. All she could do was spark a little. *Snap. Snap. Snap.* When she wasn't fidgeting from boredom, she crossed her legs, and closed her eyes, and her breathing drifted into soft syllables in her mother's tongue. She searched for the truth in the koans she had memorized since she was young.

After nightfall, Djoss came down below to bring her food and eat with her. They ate sea tack in the dark. It was hard, and tasted like pig fat and sand. They drank weak tea made without any boiling water. Fire left a smoke trail in the sky that could be seen and followed.

Rachel tried to say she was sorry she had been found out. Djoss wouldn't let her apologize. "People would never understand," he said, "and there's nothing anyone can do but move on."

"Run, you mean," she said. "Run for our lives before anyone can catch us."

"Something like that," he said.

"Maybe things will be different this time." She didn't believe that, but she had said it anyway.

The sloop faced fair weather all three days. The channel's famous storms were missing. The old captain leaned back in his seat. "Must be blessed by the Nameless," he muttered. "Not a cloud in sight."

***

We landed north of here.

On the third day, they reached Dogsland. The customs agent took one look into that filthy sloop, and curled his nose. He handed the Captain a slip of paper from across the bow, and rowed on to the next ship.

At night, the true cargo unloaded. Rachel and Djoss stood on a rocky shoreline next to abandoned warehouses. Djoss pushed the old man's sloop back into the sea, and waved. The old man didn't wave back.

Rachel squinted at the moon over their heads. She couldn't see any stars. The street lamps drowned out the night sky, their gathered light pushing against the sea clouds. The moon slipped out from behind the sky's curtain like a pale, bodiless belly. A bad omen, after all that good weather. Storms were coming back, and soon.

By morning, rain fell in sheets. The streets ran black with rivers of mud. The sewers belched a thick, green sludge that smelled like noxious death and fed the street rivers. Rachel and Djoss waited it out on an abandoned stairwell, where a crumbling roof held back the worst of the water.

"I guess we made it," Rachel said.

"Yeah," said Djoss, "You know anything about this city?"

"No," she said.

He frowned. "Me neither."

The streets were flooded. Anybody walking there was ankle deep in muddy sewer water. Dead rats floated past clinging to paper and small sticks. Something else floated past, in a wad of cloth. A doll or a dead baby drifting through the flooded street, catching on the ridges of wheel-ruts. Rachel closed her eyes. When she opened them again, it was gone.

She forced a smile. "We'll be fine," she said. "It's the biggest city in the world. Nobody will notice me here." Her hands were balled up into fists inside of her pockets. She kept looking down to make sure her sleeves were still laced shut across her forearms.

"It's not your fault," he said.

This far north of the main city, the buildings were still cracked and bruised from the war nineteen years ago. All the men and women here walking the streets were shipwrecks with feet. All these cracks and angles pushing through the floods, they sank in every step.

***

We did the best we could, but there wasn't much.

They spent weeks on the street, sleeping in doorways. The winter rain was ceaseless, and if it broke it didn't break for long.

In the heaviest downpours, the landscape blurred before Rachel's eyes. The mud, the cracked boards, and the faces in the street were all the same weary entity swirling its sea-beast tendrils like roots across the mud.

She closed her eyes again.

If they stayed on the street, people would notice that only her clothes had a shadow. Someone would step on her boot and discovered strange lumps that shouldn't have been there instead of toes. Sleeping in doorways, sleeping in abandoned buildings, sleeping in hovels and trash, she was always at risk that her serpent's tongue might fall out of her mouth where passing folks could see. They sought out shadows and hidden places in the night, but this was no guarantee. She tried to sleep face down when she could, deep in a shadow. They walked all day in between the sweeping storms, hidden in the crowds, and selling cheap illusions when Djoss couldn't find work for the day.

Everywhere Rachel went, she was afraid.

There was work or there was not, safe and unsafe. That was all to the ones like Rachel and Djoss, on the street. If anyone came near, they didn't stop to talk about anything that wasn't a job. Rachel and Djoss pulled back into shadows and corners and crowds and walked away.

We kept moving.

***

We came south. Djoss and I kept going where we thought there might be work, and maybe a place off the street. It wasn't fast.

Djoss and Rachel reached the edge of the warehouse district.

Down the street to the south, four men swung brickbats at each other. Three other men crawled away, crumpled in the blows. Blood was on the ground.

"A good sign," said Djoss. He smiled at the war in the middle of an avenue. It was the kind of thing that meant no one would be looking after them. "Yeah, we'll find a place down this way if we keep moving."

"I hope not."

"Hope so, you mean. Rowdy work's easy to come by, easy to keep."

"Djoss, please…"

He kept smiling. He led her down through the streets, south and south into the night.

Past the warehouses, a river curved through the levies to the sea. They crossed a ferry in morning twilight with the crowds of men on their way to work among the abattoirs. It cost almost everything they had left.

We kept moving.

A cock crowed in early light. Dawn pushed against the jagged rooftops.

Somewhere, birds were singing.

The walking shop-girls were already awake with their handcarts. Street boys played dice on a fat brick fence for the honor of skinning a cat they had found in a rat-trap. Warehousemen chewed on bread and sawdust sausages while they walked to work. A skinny woman puked into the sewer-grate. She cursed her lover's face.

Djoss bought an apple. Rachel snatched it from him before he could take a bite, and looked at it carefully. She shined it with her bare hands. He grabbed it back from her. "Get your own," he said, and bit into the apple. With a frown, he looked down at it. The apple was all brown beneath its red skin. He ate a few bites anyway, then offered Rachel the rest. It tasted like wet rot. "I'll get my own," she said.

"If you do, you're sharing."

She tossed the core into a ditch.

"No, Djoss," she said. "No, I won't share an apple with you."

Djoss blinked. They couldn't share anything if she bit it first. He knew that.

Behind them, a homeless man pulled the core from the ditch, stuffing it in his mouth. Rachel felt a chill move over her skin.

"Let's get out of here," she said, glancing behind her.

Djoss had seen it, too. The two walked faster down the street.

***

We found the Pens, and we stayed.

Djoss and Rachel were in a cobbled street lined with colorful shops. They sat down at a street café for tea and biscuits that tasted like they were both made from the same wet, brown paste, and watched people walking.

Rachel frowned because no one was saying hello to anyone. It didn't seem like a friendly place. Djoss smiled for the same reason. It was the kind of place he could find his brand of work.

Wind came up from the abattoirs, carrying the smell of animals kept in close pens and death. Rachel put down her tea and biscuit and tried to cover her nose. Djoss choked and held his breath until the wind passed. He nodded at her, trying not to laugh.

"Gotta be rowdy work around here. Smell it, can't you? Nobody come looking for us if it smells like that. Good folk don't bother looking."

"We'll get used to it," she said. "We just need to…" Her eyes were still watering. She waved her hand. Djoss took her tea from her and tossed the dregs from her cup. He dropped what was left of her biscuit and smashed it into the ground, stomping on it. No one could eat what she left behind. No one could get suspiciously sick. He hadn't done this since they came to the city. He was already planning on staying in this district longer.

***

Djoss fell in with some people when he was looking for work. It just happened. All that wandering, and it happened out of nowhere.

A butcher kept his pigs in a pen behind his shop. He wasn't a big enough shop to house his animals at the merchant exchange, to get them slaughtered in the big abattoirs. He kept them in his yard, killed them in his shop, and sold them here. Only sixteen pigs remained, rooting in their own muck, waiting for their turn beneath the knife. They were small. Poor shops like this one killed what came in, butchered it and ground it all into sawdust sausage.

Djoss stood at the gate when the butcher came out, clearing his throat. Djoss wasn't alone. Three boys were there, too, looking for work. They were probably brothers: tallest, middle-sized, and smallest with the same homemade burlap clothes. Djoss was like a tree beside them.

Everywhere's different. In the north, he'd have knocked on the door in front of the building and requested work in writing, with a sealed certificate from the city work council, forged. Here, in Dogsland, he stood back and waited. They made you wait to make sure you're serious.

Rachel waited in a nearby alley, watching from a shadow.

Three pigs went to their death in the shop without anyone speaking a word. The butcher was a small man, with ropy arms and crooked teeth. When he came out for the fourth pig, he sneered at the beggars at his gate. "You want something?"

The tallest boy spoke first. "Just looking for work. Anything you got."

"Got nothing. I do all the work here. You tell your dad he stinks worse than my pigs. I don't hire dirty people. Gotta have clean hands."

Djoss rubbed his hands together. They were nearly black from grime and calloused.

"He ain't our dad," said the middle-sized boy.

Djoss said nothing. He frowned down at his hands. There was

nowhere to clean them. The water was all muddy here.

"Hey," said the middle boy. "I'm hungry."

"Get out of here, all of you," the butcher growled.

"I said…" The middle boy squatted down, coiled and tense. He jumped the fence. His brothers followed. The middle boy darted around the butcher, making for the shop. When the butcher went after him, yelling, the other two boys leaped after pigs at the fringe of the huddled masses.

Djoss reached over the fence and grabbed the nearest child's earlobe, pulling up the tallest one. The youngest boy had managed to tackle a pig, and hang onto it. The middle boy came running out of the butcher's shop. His hands were bloody, but he didn't have any meat.

The butcher came out next, mean-eyed, a huge skewer in his hand. His face was so red that it looked like the veins on his skull were going to burst.

Djoss let go of the boy he held and stepped over to the butcher with his hands up. "Hey, don't kill the little bastard! He's just hungry!"

The butcher raised the skewer higher, trembling.

Djoss grabbed the man's forearm and stopped the butcher's strongest swing as casually as holding an egg over his head. Djoss was the stronger man, by far.

The butcher spit in Djoss' face.

Djoss laughed. "I'm on your side, pigman."

The youngest and the oldest got a pig between them and ran for it. The middle boy tried to catch another, but the pigs were too fast. He fell on his face. He got up from the muck, laughing, and dove again.

Djoss threw the butcher back against the wall and snatched the middle boy. He hefted the fighting child up like a sack. To the butcher, he said, "Be back with your pig in a minute." Djoss looked over at Rachel and shook his head at her not to follow. Rachel stood up and leaned against the wall across the butcher's yard to wait in plain sight of the angry man.

The butcher stepped over the fence.

Rachel snapped her finger at the butcher. "You all right?"

The butcher sneered at her. "I'm going to get my pig back. Going to the king's men for it. If that's your man, I ain't paying reward for what he stole. That was a grind, and I know it."

"Djoss is getting your pig back," Rachel replied. "Whether you pay him or not, you still get it back."

The butcher didn't say anything. He just walked off, looking for guards.

Rachel left, too, in a hurry. Farther up the street, Djoss carried the pig under his arm.

Rachel shook her head. "We go back, he might get us arrested."

Djoss looked up and down the street. There weren't any king's men, yet, and running would only draw attention. He pointed off down the street behind him. "Boys ran off that way, to this alley." he said, "Maybe got somewhere to cook it that way."

At the corner of it, peering down the long, narrow path between two buildings, the alley was busier than the street. After the buildings ended, it even opened up into a kind of yard, but what exactly was back there was hard to see from the street. There were people moving around, there, and sitting along the sides of the buildings, and moving around. A man in a red cloak stepped out from a doorway right at the front. "You going back there?" he said. "Yeah," said Djoss. "You stopping us?"

"No." He was ugly and thin. He smoked a pipe with pink smoke and watched from a doorway. "Don't cause trouble. King's men come looking for your pig, I might not stop them, if they want it bad enough."

Djoss nodded.

Past the alley was an abandoned shipping yard. People lived there in tents and old crates. Rachel scanned the crowd while she and Djoss walked around. She set her eye on a woman dressed in the same kind of home-sewn burlap the three boys had been wearing.

The woman stood up when Djoss and Rachel reached her crate. She must've had manners once, or else she wouldn't have pulled herself up from the mud. She wouldn't have curtsied. But when she spoke, her grace fell. "What do you want?"

Djoss smiled. He tried to be friendly. "You got three boys?"

She frowned. "I don't know where they are."

"We'll share this with you and your boys if you can cook it. We don't have anywhere to cook anything."

She looked with some trepidation at the stolen pig. It had clearly been a long time since she'd had anything that good to eat, but she never believed it would really be handed to her.

"Bring it here, then," she said. "I'll get the fire going, and we'll cook it up. You know my boys are going to be hungry."

"Everybody is," said Djoss.

"My name's Sparrow." She started piling wood upon large stones in the middle of her crate. She had gotten the wood from the crate, itself, burning her home to heat the cooking stones. "You from around here? Never seen you before."

"We came south from the warehouses," Djoss replied. "Looking for work."

"Plenty down here for a man. Nothing for me." She had stones placed around. "Here, take this pot to the river. Got to boil the pig."

Rachel placed her hand on Djoss's leg. "Wait." She pulled a chunk of ice from the air and placed it in the pot. It was faster than river water.

"Don't need ice," said Sparrow. "What good is that?"

"I'm not done," said Rachel.

She snapped her fingers and concentrated on another koan. *Snap snap snap.* Fire picked up in the wood. She pulled it from the air all over the ice, feeling the heat in her fingertips. Flame licked across the ice. The fire took to the wood, too. The ice melted quickly, and the heat rose up into the water from the stones. Soon, the water was steaming like it was about to boil.

"Don't say thank you, or anything," she said.

Sparrow cut the pig's throat. She bled it out into the boiling water. It trembled in her arms, but died soon enough. She hacked up the pig as best she could without a knife. It was hard to break the tendons loose from the bones. "How'd you do that?" She tossed pieces of the pig into the pot.

"I'm Senta."

"What's that?"

"It would... take a very long time to explain."

Sparrow poked at the meat in the pot with a stick. "Yeah, and if it was worth knowing you wouldn't be here with me, would you? Not if you knew anything really good."

CHAPTER V

*I*t happened so fast. Out of nowhere, we were making friends. We brought a pig we stole. We shared it. Got introduced to someone who could help Djoss find work. Djoss makes friends. I don't really make friends. Djoss just reaches out his hand and I don't want to talk to anyone.

Sparrow's kids came through when they saw food in the pot. They didn't look at Djoss and Rachel. They were smart enough to know when they should shut up and take what was allowed to them. When they got meat, they ran off with it, hiding from even each other to keep what was theirs in their mouths like wild dogs scavenging. Djoss, Rachel, and Sparrow weren't so uncivilized. They didn't run away anywhere to eat. The good meat got eaten as fast as it was boiled through, but there were still edible bits left, and some organs, boiled soft in the pot. Sparrow's kids were coming back, loud and rowdy. They wanted more. Sparrow smacked the first hand reaching for the pot. "Ain't yours," she said. "You want work you bring the pot over to Turco, see if he wants any. You remember me you get any coin from him."

"We will," said Djoss.

The pot was still too hot to carry. Djoss peeled his shirt off and wrapped a hand in it. It had been a long time since Rachel had seen him without his shirt. He looked like the side of a tree. His skin was pale and flaking like bark, and he had lost weight. His muscles bunched like knots under his ashen skin. He looked strong, but not healthy.

First, he carried the pot towards the alley where they came in. He saw a big man, bald with burn-scars all over his head and his ears cut off. Rachel went with him.

"Hey," said Djoss. "Looking for Turco. That you?"

The man slowly reached a hand into the steaming water, and pulled out the pig's head. He bit the animal's cheek like a slow turtle eating wet grass, never taking his eyes off Djoss.

"I guess you are Turco, then."

The man in red lit a match in an open doorway, to the side of the alley's entry way and pulled on a pipe. "Not him." His bright red clothes looked like they'd been cleaned sometime this year. No one else's clothes looked like that. His hands were clean, too. He stood up from the open doorway. He didn't bother closing the door. Past him, Rachel could see people sitting in the dark, but it was impossible to see what they were doing. "This for me?" He stood up and looked into the pot. He grimaced. "It's disgusting. Who made this?"

"I don't remember her name," said Djoss.

"Sparrow," Rachel said. "She has three boys."

"Her boys need it more than I do." Turco pulled on his pipe. and blew a colorful smoke ring. "Who are you?"

"I'm Djoss, and this is my sister."

"You going to be living in our little neighborhood too? When I saw you coming in I figured you were looking to settle down in one of the crates if you could find room for it. Thought I'd have to come find you later. This is our place. Keep the king's men back because of the good stuff. Cost some folks plenty keep it alone." He pointed at the men inside the building. "They don't pay for it. You'd have to pay me to live here."

"We don't have any money."

"Dog doesn't have money, and he stays here. Sparrow has no money, and she stays here, too." Turco smiled at Rachel. "You mind getting your hands dirty?"

Djoss held up his hands. "My hands are dirty. I can bounce

anywhere. Stevedore, too, if that's what you need."

Turco handed the pipe up to Dog, who took a long drag. His eyes rolled back in his head.

"What's with him?" Djoss said.

Turco shrugged. "Got his tongue cut out. I don't know his name. I always call him Dog because he follows me like one. Let him borrow my pipe."

The pipe went back to Turco. Dog went back to eating the pig's head. He chewed on one of the ears after he finished the cheek.

"What is that? It doesn't smell like tobacco."

"The pink stuff. Demon weed. Good stuff."

"Does it have anything to do with demons?"

"No," Turco replied. "Just call it that. Want to try?"

"Djoss, don't…" said Rachel.

"Sure," Djoss answered. "Bet I'll be working with it soon enough."

Turco held out the pipe. Djoss took it in one hand. The fire in the pipe was low, and he needed to get another match to light it. He breathed it in, closed his eyes, and exhaled.

Rachel wanted to scream.

"It's good," Djoss said. "It's real good." He pulled the pipe from his lips. He was smiling. He gazed into the burning leaves inside the pipe.

Rachel wanted to smack it out of his hands.

Her brother handed the pipe back to Turco and coughed, laughing. He leaned over and put his hands on his knees. He coughed a little more.

Rachel smacked his back. "Are you okay?"

I'm…" he started to laugh. "I'm fine. You should try this, Rachel."

"No," she said. "And don't ever touch that again. Whatever it is, it can't be good."

"Think it's any worse than eating this pig?" Djoss reached his own hand into the pot. Even with his callouses he had to move quickly, and he was clumsier after the pipe. Sparrow hadn't had anything to cut through the stiff bones, and whole ribcage cooled in the pot, the bones still joined to the spine. "Hey, you got a knife, Turco? Want to cut this up a bit for us?"

Turco pulled out a long knife from his boot and took a rough, hacking blow at the backbone, knocking some of the boiled meat loose. "You want work, too?" he said.

Rachel tightened her fists. "I'm not doing anything for you, Turco."

Inside the room, she heard someone singing. They were off key. People were laughing, there.

Turco took a lazy drag from his pipe. "Too bad. Your brother'll have to work real hard. Come back tomorrow. Sunrise."

***

You know men like that are only friendly when they want something.

If they pay us for it, and they help us get off the street, Jona, what were we supposed to do? Turco was taking a cut of Djoss' pay. I knew that. He took a cut of mine, too, when he helped me find work. But at least there was work. We didn't have anything before that. We stayed there a while, too.

How was it?

Horrible. Just horrible.

When night came close, Sparrow pulled a stolen canvas sail over the roof of the crate. Turco and Dog slept at the head of the alley, near the room. Rachel could tell where they slept because their bodies left a pink smear on the wall that melted with the dew. Rachel knew better than anyone the danger of stains left on the ground.

Rachel stayed with Sparrow while Djoss disappeared for hours with Turco and Dog, and her boys ran wild.

The two women didn't talk much. Rachel didn't want to make a spectacle, so she kept her Senta tricks to herself.

Instead, she sat quietly, and looked out at the dark waters. She searched inside of herself for meaning in the koans, calming her breathing with her eyes closed. *What is my face before I am born?* The understanding of the fires came easily to her. The understanding of the winds and the ice as well. They were koans of the division of things. Insight into the Unity koans of the dreamcasting came to her rarely, if it ever came. When it did, it was never good.

***

My husband said he found the crates where Rachel had stayed, and the stink she left behind.

They have nowhere else to go, I said.

What else can we do? Her stain lingers there, where she sweat it out. The secret corners where she hid when she needed to squat away from people's eyes. The only way to reach it all is to burn everything.

These people don't have anywhere else to go.

We'll bring them blankets. We'll bring them blessed apples and dandelion wine. We'll try to help.

We'll burn what little homes they have to the ground.

They will rebuild there, when we're done.

I want to go home.

Soon.

***

It was just horrible, Jona.

Sparrow looked over the woman in her crate. "You and him been together long?"

"Ever since I was born," said Rachel. "He really is my brother. You don't see the resemblance?"

Sparrow snorted. "No. The boys like him. He's not like Turco. He's not mean like them."

"What was your husband's name?" said Rachel.

"I don't talk about the dead," said Sparrow, scowling.

"Why not? What's bad about remembering…?"

She shook her head. "Hurts me to talk about it. You see how my boys are growing without him around? You see them, don't you?" She didn't linger in her pain. She was numb to it. She was numb to all of it by now. "Can you teach me how to make ice? I could use that. Keep me cool on a hot day."

"It doesn't really work like that."

"Thanks for nothing."

Sparrow left to bathe in the river. Rachel washed herself as best she could with all her clothes on and a stone to scrape away the mud. It was better when Sparrow wasn't around.

Rachel closed her eyes, searching the black center of her heart for the woman's fate. She saw nothing at all. She wondered, in her heart, if this void was a kind of truth, too.

Turco came by every day, and so did Dog, and sometimes they brought someone new. Sparrow asked Rachel if she wanted to make a little extra money for something easy and quick.

Rachel could never do that, even if she needed the money enough, with her scales. Rachel left. She walked the city streets alone, wondering where Djoss was. She searched for him until she got tired of walking. If she had to run, he was nowhere to be found. She didn't like that.

When she returned, Sparrow was sitting calmly like nothing had happened, staring at the river, a few more coins for her sons. Her boys brought food. Djoss came by with what he had bought with what he had earned.

Days passed slow as mud. Nothing was good. Nothing was beautiful. Rachel slept with her face to the walls of the crate, and both hands pressed up against her jaw. If her tongue spilled out of her mouth as she slept, even this miserable place would be no safe harbor for her and Djoss.

***

I was so glad to get off the streets. You've never lived like that. You'll never understand it unless you do.

The third week, Djoss came back to the crate with a busted eye, and a large bag of oranges. He handed the oranges to Sparrow and her sons and gestured for Rachel to get up. Rachel touched his eye, gently. "What's this?"

"Turco got me a job bouncing," Djoss replied. "Already got a place to sleep tonight off the streets. It ain't much, but it's indoors. We could take a bath." He looked over at the other people in the crate and dropped his voice. He had been so happy, and now he was ashamed of their fortune. "Get in out of the rain."

Rachel looked over at Sparrow, who lay staring at the rotten walls of her crate, pretending not to notice them.

The boys' faces were already smeared in orange juice. The youngest one had tried to eat the peel. They didn't listen to a word.

Sparrow didn't look away from her wall. "So that's it, then?"

"Thanks," said Djoss. "I'll be around sometime."

Sparrow was silent.

***

Jona, what do you do about the lost ones living in crates and alleys? Do you do anything?

No.

Does the king do anything?

Nothing. Why should we? What would we do if we could?

Down in the alley, past Turco and Dog, Djoss kicked a bucket of rainwater over. "Why do people just wait to die like that?"

Rachel shook her head. "We have to take care of us," she said, and hugged him. "Come on, and let's see this room you found. I can't wait to take a bath."

He led her to a bakery deep in the Pens District, where men and women walked to work every morning to the abattoirs. Rent was cheap, and the people lived their lives as best they could with closed windows.

To get to their room, Djoss and Rachel had to walk through the store. It smelled better than anything they'd smelled since they got to the Pens.

Djoss waved at the baker and pointed his thumb at Rachel. "This is my sister."

The baker grunted at her. "Rent's due again next week," he said. "I leave stale bread for the tenants. First come, first gets it. Put some water on it, and it softens right up. Tastes bad, but costs you nothing." He handed them the first of their bread, wrapped in old paper. It was heavy as a stone.

In the room, Djoss bathed while Rachel stood facing the wall, waiting her turn. There wasn't a chair to sit in and she was tired of sitting on the ground. Using a clump of soap he had stolen, Djoss washed his only clothes as best he could in the bathwater. He put them on wet and left the apartment so Rachel could take her bath in peace.

Rachel bathed in the same, cold, dirty water, running her hands over the scales down her stomach and legs. She barely needed soap to keep clean. She just needed to shed the dead scales and burn them every now and then. When she was done, she poured the water out in a corner of the room, careful to keep it from splashing. The mud floor had no foundation, and the bad water melted into the black as she sat naked on the countertop, waiting for the poison to seep into the ground. Her Senta clothes stretched over the space beside her to dry a while. She couldn't risk using a koan to dry them with fire, tainted with her stain as they were.

She let her tongue stretch out from her mouth for the first time since the journey on the boat. Her tongue fell down past her chin. Her face tasted like dirty soap. She pulled her tongue back down her throat, where it coiled up like a spring. Some of her earliest memories were of her mother teaching her to talk without revealing herself, her long tongue coiled up in her throat, using just the tip of it to sound out words.

A rainstorm swept the streets outside. She was inside, and her clothes were drying, and she was dry next to them. Djoss was at work, earning money to pay the rent and buy food instead of stealing for once, or working for Turco doing who knew what.

It was a home.

***

What's it like, changing towns like that all the time?

I'm scared everyday of my life, Jona. Every single day, I'm terrified. It's like a bad song in the back of my head that's always playing. I don't even bathe naked if I can avoid it. I keep a towel or my clothes or something over the tub that's big enough to cover me if someone walks in.

You're naked now.

I've got a blanket. I've got you. What's it like for you?

I don't know. I guess I'm not afraid. I don't look different from other people. I run for it if someone makes me bleed. I try not to let people notice that I can't sleep. People don't really notice if you don't talk about it. They're too busy sleeping. I guess I'm not afraid.

I wish I knew what that was like.

What what's like?

To live without fear, Jona. I'm terrified.

You don't act afraid.

The seed of my life's flower has landed here. It is my responsibility to bloom. I'm always afraid, but I try to bloom. I live with it, so I get used to it, and I ignore it as much as I can. I just stay careful, and I never let fear rule my life.

You're scared right now, here with me in a locked room?

I'm terrified, Jona. And I'm happy. Why does everyone talk about only feeling one thing? Nobody ever feels only one thing at a time. I feel lots of things, all at once.

Just because you don't, that doesn't mean nobody does. I only feel one thing.

What's that?

I have to go soon. There's someone I have to see.

That's not a feeling.

The feeling is I hate him. I'd kill him if I thought I could.

Don't kill anyone. Don't even joke about it.

I can't kill him. I'll see you tomorrow.

CHAPTER VI

Jona looked out the window past his mother's shoulder. He let his fork linger in mid-air, half a piece of chicken hanging like a wilted crescent moon.

"Are you all right, dear?" She had eaten her small portion already. She always said that she really wasn't hungry. Jona didn't fight her about it. "Jona, dear," she repeated. "Are you all right?"

"Hm?" Jona set his fork down, and glanced away from the window. "Oh, just thinking about tonight."

"Any big plans?"

He lied. "I was trying to make some in my mind."

"Well, be careful out there," she said.

"I will, Ma." Outside, people were walking like they were going somewhere important.

"You could just stay home and read a book."

Jona looked back at his mother. "We can't afford that many candles, Ma."

She winced. She had spoken from a different time in her life, long lost to her. "Still, you could just stay home," she said. "There's always something to do around the house, even in the dark. You could go to the roof. There's plenty moonlight most nights. Don't need light to hang laundry."

Jona shook his head. "Not if it rains."

"Wear a jacket," she said, her voice quavering slightly.

"I will, Ma."

She pointed her finger at him, sternly. "Be home before dawn. I hate going to work not knowing where you are," she said, "It worries me."

He laughed. "I might not make it home tonight, Ma. I might go straight to work if I'm near and out for muster." He stood up and stretched his arms. He hadn't taken off his uniform since the last time he washed it. The sleeves were spotted with brown blood stains, and the whole thing reeked of sweat and rain.

He would need to change clothes before he left, if only because the smell might give him away from the shadows.

Killing people was easier than shadowing them. He didn't have to change his clothes when he was killing people, and it was over quicker. He simply found his man, did the job, and went off into the night.

***

Jona stopped below his mother's window and listened to her breathing in the dark. She didn't snore when she slept, but her breathing was hard enough to hear outside her open window. She breathed in dyes and the floating remnants of threads all day long with the dressmaker's. Her lungs were heavy from the work, she had said, but none of her fellows were that bad.

Jona looked up past the eaves of his ancestral manor. It wasn't particularly impressive these days, but it was larger than any of his fellow guardsmen's houses. He wondered why his mother never rented out any rooms, like in the house where Salvatore lived. He wondered if it was because of him.

The laundry lines nearby fluttered with clothes. One nice thing about keeping the house empty was that the laundry could dry up on the roof, where no one could see his clothes slowly fraying due to his tainted sweat.

Jona left his mother's window.

He had a mask, but it was too early for it, and it was too hot until the stones let go of the sun's heat. Tonight was going to be hot, too. It would only be worse underground.

Good, decent people were still walking in the late twilight. Women kissed men beneath parasols. Horses pulled carriages over cobblestones. All of this had been the Joni Estates, once.

A light drizzle strolled with him. It sounded like polite applause on the brim of Jona's hat. Rain kept people's eyes down. That was good. Jona made his way to a sewer grate out beyond his father's lost lands, where the underground waterways were older than the buildings, and dropped down into the darkness. There were plenty of grates along this line, and he could see well enough to move from one patch of moonlight to another, counting his path between the grates along the walkway beside the flow of putrid water. It had rained most of the day, and the water was high, sometimes splashing under his boots where it rose over the lip of the walkway. Mice, clumped together in the dark, looked like a living carpet scurrying away from Jona's boots.

Jona hated the sewers.

When he had counted five grates, he turned. He counted out another seven and turned again. The lines broke at the rivers, but there was always a way for city workers to cross the rivers without paying a toll. The sewer lines spit out rowboats left for workmen piled pell-mell just inside the mouth of a grate where it spit into the water.

The sound of the underground drums reverberated from the deep edge of the underground, then faded out as Jona walked on. He had to stop and check the numbers on his map. He miscounted once, and had to retrace his steps until he could hear the drums again. Up out of the sewers in an alley, Jona walked with a crowd of net-weavers to the edges of the decent neighborhoods, where buildings bowed a little and alleys smelled a little better than where Jona was coming from, and the cobblestones emerged like islands from a black sea of mud.

It would have been so much easier if he could have just crossed a bridge, paid a toll, or ridden ferries across. The first night, he hadn't even bothered changing out of his uniform.

***

"Salvatore," the man had said. A carpenter with tools in his belt and sawdust all over his sleeves walked Jona into a half-finished room, where he had pulled out instructions from the bottom of a tool box: maps through the sewer lines, places to stand. All of it mapped out, moment-by-moment and late into the night. "This hard working fellow like Salvatore's gone crazy over a girl. He needs someone to scare him off, but it isn't as simple as killing a man."

"How can you map his life out like this? Doesn't he get sick of doing the same thing every day?"

"Yeah, but..." The carpenter pursed his lips. "He's... well, he's not exactly like you, but he is kind of like you. He's been living a while. Too long, maybe. It's a mess. Heard we're sending you on it."

Jona realized he had been holding his breath, and unclenched from the shock. "You said, he's... like me?"

"Yeah."

"I didn't know there was another one."

"Ain't any more than you two," said the carpenter. "That's all there is. Just you, and him. Imam might notice him with what he's doing. That's bad for us and our interests. Ought to just... Night King said let you take this over, prove yourself. Been working hard. You earned a chance to use your head."

Jona looked at the carpenter's face. It was blank. The man lived a lie. He could be lying, now. "If there's any more like me and Salvatore, I'd like to know about it. I won't do anything. I just want to know. That's all I'm saying."

"I'll pretend like you didn't say that."

"Please."

"It'll be hard to get Salvatore off this girl. His head is... well, he seems normal enough, right? But he ain't. Aggie, his girl, can't know you're there. She'd break under a whip, and where'd we be then? Imam all over us. Salvatore burning alive over some girl, and we're gone to ground. She goes missing, they start sniffing around, find the stain of his blood? Best to keep it quiet. Focus on the man, and don't let her know you're there. Salvatore drops her, she'll forget about it soon enough, and go back to praying. Girls sneaking out give it up soon as they got no reason, too. Salvatore's a mess. He's a good boy for us, but his head's all wrong. Needs to find himself a new girl won't get us in so much trouble."

"Okay," said Jona.

"This is a soft job. This is you proving to us you're more than a knife."

"Okay."

"When you think about it, it's a gift. I wouldn't have given it to you. I think she likes you. I think she knows what you want."

In the notes, it was written out how much Salvatore was handing over to the fence, and how much money he made for the Night King. One week of theft was more than Jona made all year at everything he did, including the bribes.

For the first few steps away from the carpenter, Jona considered taking all this information to Sergeant Calipari. He had ample evidence of a thief at work, with deep connections to the Night King. He could get the carpenter from the handwriting, if it was the man's handwriting. If not, a few hours with Geek and Tripoli taking turns would clear everything up. What stopped him wasn't the doll hidden in his house, or the Night King's reach—but that he never knew another like him.

**

Following and watching and always thinking what it could mean—what did any of his actions and gestures mean—Jona kept close to Salvatore's heels a while.

This is his *him*.

When night comes, we will take to the streets of the city, and see if we can find the demon child, the immortal.

***

That first night, Jona had to follow the maps. By the time he got anywhere, he was too late to do anything but scout the scenes of Salvatore's life. In a week or two, he'd figure out enough wrong turns to know the sewers better than the streets above.

Salvatore ate the same thing in the morning, from the same shop. Every night, he went looking for the woman he loved. Every night, he planned his caper, he met up with his girl, he burgled someone, and he fenced what he stole with the Night King's man underground. Then, he took his girl out on the money. He spent everything he made, every night. When the landlord demanded money, Salvatore'd do a quick job before he met the girl. That's what the notes said about him. There wasn't any mention of his heritage.

If the notes were right, Salvatore wouldn't be in his room when Jona got there. Jona was still wearing his uniform that first night. He didn't need to ask anyone's permission. Inside, everyone was either sleeping or out. Jona slipped his boots off at the front door and carried them so he could walk softly up the stairs. He found Salvatore's room unlocked. Jona stepped inside, closing the door behind him. He lit a match.

Salvatore was well-aware of the uselessness of locks. He kept his precious things well-hidden, instead. Salvatore slept in a hammock, and it was the only thing visible in the room, which was only just bigger than a closet. There wasn't even a candle to carry the match fire. The heat crept close to Jona's fingers. He blew it out. He poked around with his hands in the hammock in the darkness. Just rags. He pushed on the cloth, testing how well it was tied to the wall. It was nailed strong. Jona sat in it. Then, he laid down in it.

He tried to imagine talking to another demon child. *What do you know about being like us? What do you know? Because I don't know anything except people get sick sometimes, and they'd burn me alive.*

It was the first time he had ever thought about what to say as if it could be a real thing, with words and a face and someone talking back.

Jona left fast and quiet.

***

Salvatore smiled while he walked down the street, because he had a girl. If someone stopped him and asked him why he was smiling, he'd just shrug, and grin. "Nice day," he'd say, even in the middle of a thunderstorm.

Once he passed beyond his district, where people might know him, he slipped into an alley between a draper and a wool merchant. From the alley, he had to slip behind a pile of empty crates and down a tiny stairwell to a cellar door, leaking water. A single slit on the third brick from the top hid in the shadows of the brown stone.

Salvatore slipped a coin into the slit. The lock clicked open. A hidden gear turned, and the cellar door opened inward, into darkness. It was a temple to the Nameless, fathers of demons. It wasn't much of one.

Salvatore walked through pitch black until the end of a long hallway, counting his steps with his hands in front of him. He turned a corner and did the same. He did this every night. He did it in his sleep. In the distance, he heard the echo of the drums. He wasn't stopping there, until he had something to sell there. He just moved faster underground than above, where carriages and people and ferries slowed him down. He jogged along familiar paths.

When Salvatore turned a few more black corners, he stepped up to the street-level again, into a new alley, faster than if he'd gone through the streets. He was next to the ferry now, at the Silence Tavern.

Silent, it wasn't. Wild, disorganized music tumbled from the windows. Bouncers tossed drunken men into the streets, where the men could fight each other away from the mugs and tables. Women who had finished working for the night told filthy jokes arm in arm, laughing and laughing and drinking on their side of the tavern.

The bartender was a man so short he could walk barefoot atop the bar to serve the drinks and stand at eye level. He only had half his thumbs, and the mugs he carried were as dirty as he was. He spilled a lot.

Salvatore raised his hand, and the bartender walked over and planted a drink in front of him. Salvatore placed a pure silver piece in the man's open palm.

"I got a drink you won't believe," said the barman.

"That so?" said Salvatore. He sniffed the mug in front of him for hints of urine. He put it back down on the counter without a sip.

The small man kicked the mug away, spilling over the bar. Other patrons shouted. The bartender ignored them. "You running out tonight?"

"Maybe," said Salvatore. "I'm thinking on it."

The bartender turned away from Salvatore long enough to grab a fresh mug, pour some wine into it. "Got a helmet you wouldn't believe either." He placed the new drink in front of Salvatore. "It's just a helmet. Looks like nothing."

Salvatore lifted the glass to his nose for a sniff. He frowned. "I'm not in for that. I like a sure thing." He set the drink back down on the counter, untouched.

"Now, listen, it's not like that. You know those big insect-looking things up by the Sabachthanis? Those things he built?"

Salvatore leaned back, folding his arms. "I don't cross Sabachthani, and I especially don't cross those," he said. "Cut me up like nothing."

"Listen, with this helmet… I did it myself three times just for the fun! All the house guards wear the same kind of helmet. They got no head to think with. They just see a helmet. Easy."

"Easy?"

"So easy, you wouldn't believe it," the barkeep said. "Bet he'd get robbed everyday if it weren't, well… You know… Sabachthani's stuff. Some of it don't sell for any price. You want in?"

Salvatore nodded towards the door at the back and got up from the chair. He left the wine where it was.

Jona slipped into Salvatore's place from the crowd. He grabbed the abandoned wine and sniffed it. He thought it smelled fine. He threw it down before anyone could stop him.

Jona ordered another drink. He didn't know what to do. He figured it would all be over as soon as Salvatore went after Sabachthani's house, and Ela sent her dogs after him. He was supposed to improvise about the girl, and he didn't know what that meant either, or how to do it. He knew how to drink, and he was good at that.

The next night, Jona waited in the shadows in front of Aggie's window. By then, he'd seen her coming in and out of the window of her cell a few times. Jona didn't think anything would happen this night, with Salvatore chasing Sabachthani's rich goods the night before, he would have faded into the house defenses, mysterious and dead. When Salvatore arrived, Jona didn't believe it right away. He couldn't imagine anyone trying to steal from Lord Sabachthani. What had happened that Salvatore was still here, and still alive, with only a helmet to protect him? Later on, he saw the helmet come out and he thought more about it.

Salvatore never used it, Jona realized. He was smarter than that. When Aggie was ready to do a job alone, Salvatore would put it on her head. Until then, he just kept it, hidden with his tools.

This was the first time in all his nights of watching Salvatore that Jona hadn't wanted to grab the man and shout at him. Staying out of Sabachthani's house was the first smart care the thief had ever taken regarding his demon blood. He should never have gotten involved with this girl, a novice of Imam, who grew sicker every night they kissed.

***

My husband and I walked the convent's walls, the skin of man upon us. We kept to the alleys and shadows. We poured holy water where we thought we might have smelled the stain.

We lingered into the night to see if Salvatore might return to his lover's window, even after she had died, because he was forgetful and a creature of his habits. We stood where Jona stood all those nights he watched.

I saw with my eyes.

We waited together the first night. Then, we took turns for two nights. Then, we stopped. He wasn't coming back for her. He couldn't even remember her name. We hadn't expected him to arrive, and invested no more hope in it than that.

He must have found a new window by now, forgotten all his nights here.

***

Jona watched from the shadows.

Salvatore walked past the convent as the vespers crowd dispersed. He waited until the lights were out.

All good novitiates had washed their faces and gone to their pallets. The bad ones kept themselves awake in the dark, waiting for their chance to slip into the night.

Salvatore slid where a building's shadow fell on the stones of the fence. He pulled himself over in one graceful leap, then moved across the marble courtyard by hugging the stone fence, and the shadows it made from the streetlamps.

He climbed the fence where it met the other side of the building, balancing on the stones with the soft soles of his boots, and pressing his stomach against the wall. He jumped up along the convent wall with an arm stretched out. A hook appeared in his hands like a silver bird's beak, and bit at a brick windowsill. Salvatore hung there a minute, like a black flag at half-mast, then a second hook swung up from his wrist to a windowsill. A rope tumbled down to the ground from the back of the hook. Salvatore climbed up to the windowsill he had hooked. Placing one hand upon the ledge, he unhooked the teeth of the grappling hook with the other. He pulled himself up, then threw the hook again, to a new windowsill, near the top of the building. He snagged it on his first try. His girl was waiting for him at a windowsill.

Jona frowned from the sidewalk. Salvatore looked like a thief at a convent's walls. How could Salvatore stay out of trouble? How long had he been doing this? There must have been bribes. Someone had bribed the guards, but it would take a single open window, a single sleepless night, and someone would scream murder and then nothing could stop the guards, not with all the witnesses—not gold, not connections, not even Imam himself.

CHAPTER VII

Wh*at is it?*

I see with my eyes into the novice's window. I see her life the way Jona never could. She didn't deserve to die.

We will avenge her. Anything we can use?

No, but it's a start.

Tell me what you know and we will find the patterns in them. Salvatore wasn't after nuns. There was something else about her. There are women like that in the city. The temples can watch for them, see if any are stained.

Lonely women, who long for more than what they have, and are full of fear and energy…

***

Aggie kissed Salvatore as soon as his face breached the window. She gestured for him to drop down to the ground, then climbed out herself, and slid down to join him. She wasn't as graceful as he was. Salvatore flipped the rope to loosen the grappling hook, and held out his cape to catch it. The metal hooks snagged on the cloth like falling into a hammock, and as quickly as they landed they were back into the hidden places in his clothes where he kept his tools. The next thing he did was hand her boots. Anchorites didn't wear shoes. She'd need them in the sewers to keep her feet clean enough to fool the nuns.

Once underground, Aggie grabbed Salvatore's arm to stop him. Then, with a small proud smile, she produced a small votive candle she had stolen from a devotional. She held it out in the moonlight from the sewer grate. Salvatore reached forward in the dark and lit the candle with a match. The girl looked like she was waiting for him to kiss her. When he didn't, she slowly placed the candle in the driest spot beside her feet.

Salvatore pulled the helmet from a pouch under his cloak, and placed it on Aggie's head. "What's this?" She tugged the helmet off and grimaced at it. It wasn't fashionable.

Salvatore smacked the helmet with his blackjack, knocking it into the air. She struggled to catch it, and missed. It clattered onto the ground. Salvatore had already jumped into the darkness past the candle light, into the sewers.

"Wait!" she shouted.

Aggie picked up the helmet, and the candle. She moved slowly, protecting her fragile light from breezes and movement.

He turned at the edge of the light. He was laughing.

Underground, and above ground, and over a ferry, and Jona watching behind them.

Jona wanted to stop them both, grab Salvatore by the collar and shake him, yell at him: *We can't live like that! We just can't!* And yet there Salvatore was, a demon child with this beautiful girl, running through the night, not a care in the world and no one at home with breathing as thick as oatmeal.

Jona walked on, behind them, back in the darkness, jogging and counting the grates like in his map. He had learned the ways well enough in time. The sewers ran under the streets, and because he knew the streets he knew the sewers fast.

***

Aggie stopped to vomit in the middle of a street. She leaned over the gutter and her body convulsed. She wiped it off her lips with the back of her hand.

Salvatore touched her back. "You okay?"

She spat it all out, then leaned into a wall to catch recover strength. "I'm chewing too many redroots," she said. "It's staining my teeth. Have to stay awake, though."

Salvatore ran a his sleeve over her face. "If you're sick, they'll let you sleep all day," he said. "They'll bring you gruel in bed, right?"

She forced a smile. "That only happened once."

Most nights Jona followed them, the girl threw up.

***

I know what she was doing, with the redroots, and everything else she made Salvatore buy for her. In the girl's mind a woman could lose a baby if she ruined her body. If that didn't work, there were places she could go. Salvatore would know. He'd probably done it enough times.

She wasn't pregnant, though. She was too naive to know pregnancy, which Anchorites were never really taught or shown, and the demon stain made it hard to get pregnant, as sick as she was.

The nuns had never taught her the ways of flesh. She was just getting sicker and sicker. Her stomach didn't grow. It hollowed out.

***

Jona couldn't touch the girl, because he was told he couldn't touch the girl.

Aggie was given to the Anchorites when she was five. The nuns watched her all day. They probably knew something was wrong, but they didn't know she was out in the night. She was beautiful. I saw her tumbling from a window on a rope in Jona's memories. I saw her running with a candle in her hand, trying not to drop it in the darkness. I saw her weak and frail as a bird, her stomach upended. She looked up at the man she thought she was dying for.

I wanted more for her than her life gave to her. I wanted so much more for her that I could shout at Jona—grab him by the collar and shout at him. His memories are all I have. They are not a man; they will never change.

***

Before Aggie wore a helmet and worked alone in Sabachthani's estate, Salvatore took her dancing, where they could rob rich men. He brought her dresses he had just stolen from shop windows. They barely fit, and they'd have to pin the dresses together. They danced at night parties to which they weren't invited, and to which they showed up very late. Aggie smiled and leaned back in a rich man's arms. She whispered with a thick accent about vast holdings in far-off lands. Most of the rich men knew she was lying. They assumed she wanted money. She did. They did not expect to be drugged for it. They drank too much wine, all of these men. She had a handkerchief inside her glove. Salvatore wasn't far if something went bad.

In the dark, Aggie looked down on those men. She said, to Salvatore, that she liked to imagine her father asleep the same way, beneath her. She couldn't remember what he looked like, or his name. For all anyone knew, the man with foul breath and wandering palms was the father that bought her a place among the Anchorites.

She watched the men's eyes while the drug spread through their blood. Their eyes glazed in surprise, then fear, then something else, and then they rolled back in the head like they were dying. She wiped their rancid kisses from her lips. She wondered if these men had daughters.

She sifted through their clothes for money, while Salvatore took anything else he found worth taking that was small enough to hide in his clothes. Sometimes, if the light was right from the moon, or maybe a candle, she'd catch a glimpse of herself in a mirror before they escaped, and stop to stare. They didn't have mirrors in the convent.

Watching them from shadows and windows and rooftops, Jona considered telling Aggie all about what it was really like to never sleep and to live all day and all night, and to live out among the thieves. She didn't know anything. He didn't say anything. He didn't do anything. He watched for days.

***

Redroots don't work forever.

"What's wrong?" said Salvatore.

When a novice slept in dark corners, a whip woke them. Aggie was caught asleep in a corner, and she was whipped. Welts lingered on Aggie's shoulders for days and days, that kept her awake. Aggie couldn't protest, or the whipping would get worse. Her blue eyes smoldered into the corners of her face. The whippings got worse and worse. She threw up all over the floor. She ran a high fever, and spent days healing in bed afterwards. Salvatore took her to an inn after he had made enough coin to pay for it picking pockets at a street puppet show. She wasn't in any condition for dancing. He ran warm water over her back. He tried to touch her. She pulled away from him. He didn't know what to do. He tore up clean sheets and got them damp with water. He placed them over the welts in her back.

"Do you have any scars?" she asked.

Salvatore sat quietly with her. He said nothing. After a long time, he spoke, quietly. "You'll get better soon. You're young. You'll heal fast."

She placed her head in her arms. "You don't ever tell me anything."

"What do you want to know?"

"Do you have any scars, Salvatore?"

He thought about that one. He looked at his hands, and what parts of his arm were in the open. He didn't see anything. "I don't think I do. Are there any on my back?"

"No," she said. "No scars. Nothing at all."

"Is something wrong?"

It was her turn not to answer a question. Salvatore seemed to like it quiet.

Jona had been horrified to see Aggie emerge from her window with blood all over her back hours ago. He pressed his ear against the thin wall and couldn't think of anything. If he knew how to find the carpenter, he'd grab him and shake him and shout at him: *What do you mean improvise? What does that even mean!?*

The room next door was quiet a long time. Near dawn, Salvatore woke Aggie up and helped her dress. She said she wanted to go home and to sleep a couple nights.

"When will I know to come back for you?" said Salvatore. "Do you even want me to come back for you?"

"Don't say that," she said. "Don't say that, just… Three nights. I'll sleep. Come see me, then."

***

Aggie apologized to Salvatore for being so sick. She had to stop him because she was choking on her own blood. She ran naked to a window. She leaned out, and blood spilled from her lips with vomit.

People in the street cheered for her, naked in a window and puking. She paled. She fainted. She hadn't even noticed the people in the street. She hadn't seen Jona standing in a window across from her, waiting for any chance to do something, looking in at them, and listening.

Salvatore dragged her into an empty bathtub, and washed the blood off her body with a pot of tepid tea. He'd have to send down for water, and he knew she wouldn't want anyone to see her like this, all bloody.

When she came to, she cried. She leaned into his arms.

"I don't know what's wrong with me," she said, "I'm so sick all the time."

Salvatore wrapped her in a blanket. He kissed her temple. "Everything's going to be fine," he said, "It happens sometimes to everyone. It's nothing."

And Jona, with his hands clenched, hearing it and not believing it from the next room, or outside their window, or anywhere he could see or hear, their constant ghost. I see it all in his memories, all those nights he followed them. He wanted to do something, but he didn't know what to do.

***

The Mother Superior, in her written deposition to Calipari after the girl was burned, didn't even suspect.

When she heard footsteps and hushed whispers in the night, she rolled over and touched the keys on her nightstand. She thought the girls were sneaking into the kitchen for a snack. She had been right so often that she didn't consider all the possibilities the night held.

***

Inside the convent, new little girls cried loud at night, screaming for the mothers that had given them away. Jona heard them in their rooms, weeping and calling out for their mothers. No wonder the king's men avoided this place at night.

Salvatore and Aggie never lingered or paused because of them. They stayed quiet until they slipped underground. They never reached out a hand to any of the other girls there.

Jona couldn't ignore the screaming, frightened girls.

During the day, when he was working on the streets of the Pens, Jona was followed everywhere by the animals crying out like the girls in the convent. He wanted to let them all out, to start a stampede of girls and animals all over the city, freeing them all to go home to their mothers. Jona wanted to do something big like that, something raw. He wanted to smash everything up.

Calipari saw it all over Jona's face, and made use of it. He arrested a smuggler on flimsy evidence, and sent Jona into the room alone. "Don't come out until you're right in the head," he said. "I want full confession. I want him in a prison cell or hanging. Get your hands dirty."

Jona ground his teeth. "I'm fine."

"Then do your job."

Inside the interrogation room, Jona sat down across from the man. He sat there, and waited. He stared at the man. The man stared back. Neither one spoke a long time. When the man opened his mouth to start speaking, Jona's fist met his jaw.

This went on a while, but all that came out of it was the confession. Jona emerged as raw as when he walked in. Calipari tried it again, and when that didn't work, he decided to just ride it out. All things passed, eventually.

***

I don't know where they were, but Jona was near and listening to them.

Salvatore asked Aggie what she remembered about her father. She told Salvatore that she remembered that her father always smelled like wax and roast beef. She thought that he was very fat, too, but who could really remember? Was she sad about it, Salvatore asked.

Aggie's eyebrows creased. "He's the one who gave me away, isn't he? If it's not one cage, it's another. I'll walk for the veil, but I'll slip out the door and no one will ever talk about me again. We'll get a little place all our own, in a new city, and we'll be together forever. If I hadn't come to the convent, I wouldn't have that, right?"

"Right," said Salvatore. He ran his fingers through her hair.

***

Jona in the shadows, peering through cracks in the cheap walls, watched Salvatore's hands moving gently over her long hair. It was all Jona had ever wanted. He wanted to hold someone beautiful. He wanted to stroke her hair.

***

Aggie talked a lot about her past. She was trying to draw out Salvatore's life, and she used her own as bait. Salvatore listened. He was a wonderful listener. Jona listened too, when he could get an adjoining room or a place near an open window. If the carpenter asked him what he was doing, why it was taking so long, he'd say he was looking for an angle. That's not what he was doing.

On seventeen occasions, Aggie was whipped in front of the whole convent and brought to tears. She was told to offer her pain up to her savior. Salvatore frowned when he heard this. He asked her about happiness. Aggie shrugged. "Who can remember that? It isn't all bad, but it's mostly bad. We're raised to be terrified of the world outside our windows. We think everything outside is rape and murder and theft and wickedness."

"Isn't it?" said Salvatore. "I do my best, but I'm only one man."

She didn't laugh. "It's not so bad out here," she said. "Every year another group of girls stand in the aisle and bow their heads, and swear the oath of the Anchorites of Imam.

"Except some of the novitiates walk out just before the ceremony. Instead of walking up to the altar, the girls just… just leave right out the front door.

"Matrons warn us about the girls that choose this path. Evil is all that waits for us outside the heavy doors. Men will stab us with knives of skin. Wicked women will attack us in their petty jealousy. The weight of children will destroy our bodies until death. Only in Imam, sanctuary. Only inside four safe walls, true serenity."

"It doesn't sound so bad," said Salvatore. "Really, it doesn't. It sounds peaceful in there."

"You try it, then."

***

"Peace is boring," Aggie shouted into a mug of wine. Her eyes dropped.

"I've had enough," Salvatore bellowed back. "Are you ready to go?" He had his hands over his ears. The drums were so loud.

"I'm trying to tell you something!" she screamed. "Listen to me!"

"I'm listening!"

"Peace is boring," she shouted, "Promise me we'll never have peace!"

"I promise nothing!" he said. "Ready to go back? It's late!"

She peered down at her mug. "Wait," she said, and took the last of her wine in one messy chug. "Yes."

***

"Growing up, the Matrons wanted me to sing all the time because it kept me out of trouble. I didn't mind singing. I got to stand and look at all the congregation members. I got to see all these people. Once, I told one of the older girls this, and she smiled at me, and it was a key opening the door.

"'Don't tell me you've never been out there. Tonight wait for me to knock on your door three times. It'll be real soft, so don't sleep. I'll go without you.' That's what she said to me. I thought she was lying, or playing a joke. But it wasn't a joke. Once we were on the street, the older girl told me to watch for the blue on the eastern horizon before morning services. That's when we had to be back and to sneak back into the convent. Then she shoved a fistful of redroots into my hands. I dropped them. My hands were shaking too much. She didn't stay to help me pick them up.

"Even after the locks were changed, because of that girl… Other ways out than doors. We can get out if we want to. I want out, Salvatore. Please, get me out."

***

My husband is asleep. I want to nuzzle his neck, but it would wake him up. Instead, I lean over the maps on the floor. I burn one candle, and look at the maps.

Calipari never drew the sewers. If we were going to find Salvatore, we'd need to search underground. I drew out all I could from Jona's memory but it wasn't enough.

My husband had spent all day underground, running from one manhole to another, sniffing his way through the dark.

He told me that he couldn't find anything. Salvatore had lived a long time, and he probably had been hunted before us. He was keeping away from us.

Keep searching, he said. *Anything at all, just keep searching. We'll find them all.*

CHAPTER VIII

*D*joss... *Well, he's the only family I've ever had. Can we talk about something else?*

A door opened and closed. Rachel didn't sit up in the hammock. She knew it was Djoss. She didn't want to look at him.

"Hey, Rachel," he said.

He sounded tired. He'd been gone for two days.

"Hey."

"Been good?"

"No," she said. "Where were you?"

"Don't be angry," he said. "We need the money."

"Just tell me where you were."

"I had work. Then, Turco wanted some help with something. When I got done, I had to go back to work. You could have come down and seen me bouncing."

"Djoss..." She sat up. She forgot what she was going to say when she saw the blood. His lip was cut. He had been sliced along his arm.

"It's nothing," he said. "Rowdy work. Bouncing."

"Let me see."

"No, it's fine. Barely bled."

"Did you rinse it in wine?"

"Of course not. That hurts!"

"To heal the blood of men we must use the blood of earth."

"No."

"You were gone for two days and you come back bleeding. Let me pour wine on you, for luck, like in the koan."

"No."

"Please, Djoss? I want to do something. I've been here waiting forever. There isn't anything for me to do here."

"Then go out," he said. "Get a job. We need the money." Djoss threw a bag of coins on the ground. "That's all we got in the whole world unless you got something."

She leaned back in the hammock. "You're sleeping on the floor."

He sat down on the floor. "You've been sweating on the hammock too long," he said. "I couldn't use it, anyway. Tear right through to the floor if I got on it."

***

I got really bored.

The baker above them shared a cot with his wife next to the yeast buckets on the main floor. At night, he dreamt of growing larger and larger like a loaf of bread until he pressed against the doors and rolled down the road. Rachel dreamcast in the koans, of her face before she was born. Inside her meditations, she watched the baker's bread rising and rising until it sunk down into the basement and crushed them with all the cockroaches and that sickly growing smell of yeast. It was easier to focus in a quiet room, alone. It was boring, though. It was lonely.

Rachel snagged all the old bread from the stairwell. Djoss was asleep in a corner away from the oven's lingering heat from above. He snored lightly. She set the bread on the floor inside the doorway and closed the door quietly.

She walked up the stairs again, and looked into the baker's shop. It was empty. All the bread had been baked and bought. All the money had been moved into the back rooms. She could walk around, if she wanted, and lean on the counter as if she were a customer, or a baker, or anyone else in the world. If she had the courage for it, she could step outside the shop.

She went back down the stairs. She opened the door, and slammed it behind her.

Djoss woke up with a start and shook the sleep from his head. "Hey," he said, fighting a yawn, "can I get some of that bread?"

"Yeah. Sleep well?"

"Oh," he waved her off with his hands, "I was just resting my eyes a minute."

"You were snoring."

"That was my stomach," he said, reaching for the bread.

***

Tell me something about yourself, Jona. I'm tired of talking about me. Tell me about you.

At night, I'm lonely a lot. I don't like the nights when I have nothing to do.

Lonely… Yeah, I can understand that.

Djoss finished most of the bread, even as stale as it was, saying he said he had to go to work.

"Where do you work that they make you work like this?"

"Turco's got me on a thing."

"Where?"

"I'll be back," he said. "Just stay here. You'll be fine." He stepped out the door, and closed it behind him. She was alone again, with nothing to do but hide and wait in the dark, living off whatever Djoss brought to the room and their landlord's cast-off loaves.

Three cities ago, she and Djoss had jumped out a window to escape. Soldiers kicked at their door. The soldiers heard Djoss and Rachel jump with a feather mattress clutched below them to break the fall. They landed hard in the street. Djoss had to splint his wrists for a long while after they got out.

Rachel thought a lot about how to escape. The basement below the bakery had six tiny windows, too dirty for anyone to see through. A little sunlight pushed through the filthy glass and it was day. The sunlight sank into the shadows, into nightfall.

Rachel paced the basement a bit to walk off her worry. If that got old, she sat on the hammock and used a kitchen knife to carve the leftover stale bread into little shapes, dogs and swords and children carrying flowers all crude enough to be indistinguishable from each other. They just looked like oversized crumbs. She tossed them into her chamber pot.

When Djoss finally came back with a cot so he wouldn't have to sleep in the mud, she set it up for him in a corner. It wasn't bought new. She put the four legs of the cot inside dented pans filled halfway with water. Bugs couldn't climb up the sides of the bed if they couldn't swim.

She fished the larger silverfish and roaches out of the cans every couple days and burned them in a pile in the middle of the mud floor. It took a long time to burn them because they were so wet, but she kept snapping her fingers at them, pulling the koans out of the air, and snapping at them more.

There was nothing to do but study the koans she had memorized. She reached into her quiet self for the core of the Senta. She searched for the gaps in the walls where insects moved. She asked herself the first question of the dreamcasters.

What was my hand before I was born, for my hand is how I change this world?

Where would the creature's spirits fall onto the floor, and when?

Rachel's inner eye reached out and dissipated against the walls. She leaned back in the cot and closed her eyes. She couldn't see the future. She couldn't see anything.

***

Our ways are probably not for you, Jona. I did the best I could studying all the koans my mother made me memorize. Telling fortunes is good money if you can see into the visions. Easier than cleaning.

Rachel saw nothing for a long time. When something came to her it took a long time to become recognizable, and it felt like a dream. Swirling images pooled together into her father standing over her in a dark room. The demon inside of him was smiling at her.

Rachel woke up from her meditative trance alone. Sweat covered her, slowly devouring at the canvas she wore, nibbling at the leather.

Outside, she heard the rain falling. Rachel lay back in the cot and stared at the floorboards above her. She watched a single black spot crawl out from the cracks in the boards. The black spot walked along a crack, furiously traveling cross the wide expanse of wood.

Rachel imagined what it would be to be an insect on a vast open plain of wood. She trapped the creature in Senta ice when it finally reached the edge.

She tried to find dreamcasting again for a while, but then she was hungry. She stretched.

Djoss would come home later, and everything would be fine because he'd bring something new and then the baker would give them new leftover bread.

***

I'm always afraid, Jona. I want to be somewhere where there aren't people, and they never come, and I can live in peace.

Djoss came home late, exhausted. He said hello when he came in, tossed a bag of dried fruit in Rachel's direction, and then collapsed onto his cot to sleep.

Rachel waited until he was snoring. She wanted to know where he was when she went out. If anything happened, they could run together as long as she knew where he was.

She opened the door. She stepped into the hall, and left the door open behind her. She climbed up the stairs to the main store. She smiled at the baker.

He nodded at her. "Thought the big fellow might've eaten you."

"I don't go out much."

"Rent's due next week," he said, "You can pay now if you want."

She didn't have enough money for that.

"Djoss'll take care of that later. I just wanted something fresh for a change. Do you have anything fresh?"

Back downstairs, she watched Djoss' chest rising and falling. If she could concentrate she might be able to see into his dreams. But she didn't want to know his dreams. She wanted to know his life.

She thought about waking him up just to talk to him. He rolled over in his sleep. He had a bite mark on his neck.

She cocked her head, and leaned closer. She sniffed his clothes for perfume. Prostitutes wore perfume. He smelled like rotting meat, not flowers. It could have been from a fight. It didn't look like it came from a fight.

She decided to say nothing.

Another night alone and the next night and the next night and her life was a lump of pain in her gut. She started to buy bread everyday because she liked to pretend she was friends with the landlord, but she didn't have friends.

Djoss had friends. He came home after long time spent with friends, and she was his secret ghost.

***

It felt like forever. I don't really know how long it was. I was too afraid on the streets, even when I knew no one was looking for me here.

When did you finally go outside?

I did when I was ready. Djoss didn't push me. He did, in his own way, but not really. He never brought me anything to read, or anything to do. He wouldn't even bring me cards to shuffle and practice divination. But he didn't push me, either. He just didn't help me. I couldn't live like that forever without help, you know. One day, I went upstairs and bought bread and I walked out into the street. I walked around the block. It rained. I didn't have an umbrella. The bread got soaked. So did I. Then, I came back. Djoss didn't even notice.

The next day I did the same thing. Then the next. Then I went to the tavern and danced with a stranger. Then, I got a job.

I always wondered what it was like for other people like us. I spent so long never talking to anyone about it.

It's nice just to talk, I think.

CHAPTER IX

J ona had jumped one of the walls. He was on the other
side of it, deeper and darker in the shadows than
the two people in the street, who were just a little
movement in the dark. If he didn't know they were there,
he wouldn't have pulled their shape from the shadows.
Two large walls blocked off two different noble estates on either
side of the alley. Past the walls were trees. Noble estates were
the only places in Dogsland where two trees' branches touched
each other. Salvatore and Aggie could hide in those shadows a
long time before anyone would notice.

Salvatore carried the helmet with him tonight. He placed it
on the girl's head. "There's two of them. They look for these
helmets," he whispered.

"Who? Why don't you do it?" She whispered louder, "*Where
are we?*"

"You'll never believe until you see them. Lord something-
or-other made them. They're illegal, but he doesn't care. Why
would he? He's rich!"

"Lord who? Who is he?"

"Someone important," said Salvatore. "I don't remember his
name. He does magic. The real stuff. Not Senta tricks. Be careful.
Anything magic, you leave it. Can't sell magic. Gets people in
too much trouble."

***

Tell me his patterns. Do you know them?

I can smell his life, and I can see with my eyes, but some things are still unknown. I can guess, but that's all I can do.

Memories are never more than a guess, anyway. Do you think any of this has been completely true?

Some of them he heard from Salvatore. Only the emotions of them are true, the way people feel about things. Everything else is just a dream. Aggie spoke to Jona before she was burned, too. She confessed all her sins—all he wished to know. A dream of a dream... Unreliable, but compelling to me.

***

Below the bay all the city heretics came together. They tore their clothes and spiked their hair with green lime and ugly was the new beautiful, where they were pounding big drums to echo deep. They weren't digging, and they weren't hurting anybody. My husband and I might go down to scare them off before we leave. It's almost better to leave them there, without a reason to dig into the ground and bleed. It was just a place to go to dance and to be strange.

We know that Salvatore and Aggie had met down there, from what Jona learned from Aggie, herself, when she was waiting to be burned alive in an empty prison cell. Salvatore was among the heretics every night, when he was done stealing for his supper.

She had been brought there by an older man who left her at the edge of the throbbing push of bodies. It was only her third week sneaking out of the convent at night and she was already underground. These things happened in cities; beautiful young women wound up in places they couldn't have anticipated. Aggie stood next to a giant tambourine on a stand, rubbing her hands along her arms. The lime that had been smeared there must have been itching her. Salvatore saw her standing there, so beautiful, and so scared of her own daring.

He knew what to say to her, how to say it. He knew how to thrill her into abandon.

That's what I think happened.

I will walk among the dancers tonight, and search for him. I will wear the skin of man, and be smeared with lime.

Take a bath before you come home. Wash your hair.

I will.

***

Nights came and into the sewer darkness they went. Aggie held his hand, and tiptoed in her new shoes through the black tunnels, cupping a votive candle against the breezes in the dark if they stopped to rest.

Hold out your hand behind your back, and there was someone's purse. He needed her just to walk along with him and hold out her hand when he touched her wrist. He'd slip something there from the other side, where she wasn't holding his hand in hers. *Tell him anything you think he'll want. Tell him you love him. Just get him back here. One good hit, he'll go down. It'll be fun. Be someone else for a while. Be anything but a convent girl.*

***

Not even Jona, Lord of Joni, who had attended to the Lady Sabachthani's whims for an occasional cup of tea, had seen the guardians of her estate before. Salvatore probably had, in this life or another, but he wouldn't remember them well unless he felt something for them. He didn't seem afraid of them.

Their silhouettes were a nightmare of spikes and curling steel armors, praying mantis things the size of carriages. Only a powerful master of magic could build one of them, much less keep two at his front gate in open defiance of the law. Lord

Sabachthani would never have dared such a transgression beneath the eye of a dutiful king, but he had used magic to stop the terrible war and that meant something to the city, and to the king beyond just laws. If the king had been paying any attention to his lands, he probably would not have approved the guardians, but the old king had long ago withdrawn from the world, no son or daughter to mind his lands or the men that ruled them. What Lord Sabachthani did was between him and his money and no one who wanted his money suggested anything else about it.

In the daylight hours, the guardians trudged like weary oxen from their post back to a grove inside the estate. At evening twilight, the sleepless juggernauts creaked and groaned from their place among the birds. They stomped across the grass to the main gate, where they stood at attention, waiting to kill.

Sabachthani lives in Dogsland, not in my forest. Let him do whatever the King and Imam allowed. The forest was patient. All these walls surrender to our children and our trees, eventually.

***

Salvatore and Aggie stepped into the streets sideways, clinging to the shadows of the stone fences. Salvatore looked both ways down the street. The lampposts wore fog cloaks. The lights hung alone like ghosts.

Salvatore went first to draw any eyes that might be watching. He strolled down the middle of the street, walking back the way they had come. If any people were watching for trouble, they'd see Salvatore, not Aggie. If any guards were stalking the night, they'd follow him into an alley and search him hard. They'd find nothing, and by the time they were be done, Aggie'd be underground.

Aggie adjusted the helmet on her head. She slipped down the street, up against the edge of the wall.

She had no idea how dangerous this was, and Salvatore had sent her alone like it was a game.

Aggie crept up to the abominations at the gate. She reached out a finger to touch a bladed spike. The creatures didn't move.

Jona watched her from a tree across the street and back a bit from the wall. He had climbed inside a neighboring estate where he thought no guards would see him. Any guards at this estate were human and tired enough not to notice one man in a shadow of a tree. Thieves didn't come to the noble estates much. Jona watched her, and he didn't know what to do if the magical guardians attacked her.

Aggie closed her eyes. She took one gentle step past the gap in the wall. There wasn't a gate here. There was no need. The mechanical monsters stood in the entrance, blocking everything. They didn't move an inch for Aggie. She had to slide sideways to get through.

Salvatore yawned, and leaned against a fence across the street. He pulled out a two-inch cigarillo laced with redroots. Thieves of the city in the north marked the hours on a job by smoking. *Maybe our demon child was from the north, maybe that was where he had fled from, and returned to.* Two inches was just enough time for a good thief to pull in and out of a big house like this one.

Aggie ran through the shadows of the yard, between the willows and the magnolias. She pressed her back against a wall. She shoved open a window with a tiny wedge from her pocket. Inside the window, purple drapes caught the night breeze. A long, black hallway yawned open before her. She looked both ways, then jumped inside.

Jona considered leaving her here, and grabbing Salvatore and dragging him into the sewers again for a solid beating for sending Aggie into Sabachthani's all alone. Jona didn't move. He had grown accustomed to waiting, though he didn't know what he was waiting for, exactly. He knew he was going to have to do something, soon.

Aggie was gone a long time.

Salvatore smoked everything he had. He rubbed his hands, expectantly, glancing up and down the street.

Aggie snapped her finger at Salvatore from behind him along the nobleman's walls. She had a thick wicker basket under her arm and a smile big enough to see beneath the helmet on her head.

Salvatore exhaled, and smiled with her. He pointed to the sewer grates. They went back underground, where they could talk in peace. Jona went down, too, through a grate one block down. He crept up to them kissing in the dark.

"I didn't see you leave," said Salvatore. "I feared the worst."

"Used a different way out, got spun around a bit. Lots of locked rooms inside. I found one with a keyhole big enough for my fingers to get in. I didn't even need to do anything to pick it. I found something heavy in the center of the room, on this pedestal," she said. She swept her helmet from her head. She put it down on the ground. Her hands were still trembling with excitement. "I actually…" She held the basket up. "I don't know what it is. I couldn't see."

Salvatore took the basket from her arm. "It's heavy," he exclaimed, surprised.

"I hope it's magic," she replied.

Salvatore hefted the basket in his arms. "Better hope not," he said, "If it is, we dump it here and walk."

"Let's open it!" She closed her eyes. "You do it. I'm afraid to look."

"Yeah. Got a candle?" Salvatore slipped the lid off. He lit the candle and held it out over the lip. "It's… "

"What?" She opened her eyes. "What is it?"

"It's a thing… it's… kind of like a dog, but there's metal all over it."

Salvatore leaned over and studied the creature. He pulled it up by its metallic scruff, and turned it in full candle light. The front half of its body was more metal than animal. The back was still recognizable as something like a dog.

The dog, if it could still be called a dog, ignored them both. The creature inhaled slowly, exhaled in a puff. Whenever it exhaled, a small golden powder spilled out from its snout, like a mold. The basket's insides were thick with it.

Aggie reached in to pick the creature up. It remained still as a statue. She held it up with one hand. It was no bigger than a terrier. "What...?"

"Shh," whispered Salvatore, "quietly. Oh, I hope you didn't hurt it."

She frowned. "Is it a dog?" The skin was missing in places. Naked bone and muscle showed in ridges along its bloodless haunches.

"Put it down, Aggie."

She laughed, confused. "What is that supposed to do? What kind of magic is that? What's it for?"

Salvatore gingerly extricated it from her hands. He placed it in the basket and put the lid gently over it. "Aggie, we need to dump that. It'll be our death when Sabachthani finds our soul stink on it."

"That doesn't make any sense."

"Magic makes no sense. Drop it. We need to run before it does anything. If it does anything." Salvatore took a deep breath. Thieves did not live as long as he had by being reckless with magic. "Better thieves than us have hung for less," he said.

"Let's at least dump it in a house in the High Streets, scare someone."

He shook his head: *No.*

"We should get someone in trouble with it," she said. "I know who."

"If you plant it it's their heart on a plate. Things like this... People who make them... No, Aggie."

"We need to go back to the convent. Take me back." She picked up the basket. "Take me back, Salvatore."

"Who could you possibly hate so much you'd have them killed?"

She creased her eyebrows like little hammers. Her lips curled. "I'll show you."

"Who is it?"

"I'll do it whether you come with me or not," she said. "If you come with me, you can see who."

Salvatore sighed. "*Who is it?*" he repeated.

"I hate her so much." She stomped her foot. "I'll leave you here and do it myself. I wanted something dangerous. When you told me there were dangerous things, I went looking for one. Lord Sabachthani might destroy her. I want that. You've seen my back."

"Aggie…"

She left him. She stepped into the darkness just like he had taught her to step. Her feet, thieves' feet now and not a nun's awkward gait, stayed forward on the balls. Her toes turned in a bit to keep her step solid and silent even in darkness, leaving no footprints, and no sound. The helmet was a sparkle in her stolen candlelight.

Salvatore reached for her.

Jona's hand caught Salvatore's sleeve. "In over your head, Salvatore?"

Salvatore whipped around.

"I'm here to help," said Jona, sneering. "You know who sent me. Your friends are worried about you messing with this girl."

"I have friends?"

"Productive little boy. Production falls, and they find you trying to mess it all up."

"We're not friends. If we don't stop her, do you know what she's going to do?"

Jona nodded. "You don't get to love pretty girls when they might get you found out," he said. "Don't you know what's in your blood? You're lucky people look after you. Lucky you bring them so much good stuff."

"Who really sent you?" said Salvatore. "Sabachthani?"

"It's time to let her go," said Jona. "Just let her go. You've done enough. I'll walk you home. I'm thirsty. First round's on me. Come on, Salvatore, let's go."

Salvatore looked down the sewers. The light of Aggie's candle flickered in the distance. He frowned. "I'll forget her, right? That's what you mean. Then, I'll find somebody new as soon as I forget her, and it'll be like all this never happened."

Jona smiled. "Other girls are all over, and they aren't in convents."

"Right," said Salvatore. He flipped a backfist at Jona's skull.

Jona snatched his wrist.

The blackjack slammed into Jona's knee from Salvatore's other hand. Jona fell to one knee. He grabbed for Salvatore's cloak. Salvatore flipped the cloak off in Jona's hand.

He should have expected the blackjack in the other hand. He was too distracted by the chance to finally speak to Salvatore, standing so close to someone else like him, after all that watching from afar. He wanted to get Salvatore alone and talk about how he lived, and how he should live, and how their life came to be at all in this world.

Jona's pride hurt more than his knee. He should have remembered the blackjack.

***

When Salvatore caught up with the girl, she was already at the gates of the convent, struggling to figure out a way inside. She had wrapped her cloak around the basket, and had knotted the cloak over one shoulder like a cheap sack. It swung in the air, heavy enough to throw her balance off.

She frowned at Salvatore and pointed to her window. He reached for the basket, but she pulled away. She pointed up again. Salvatore shook his head, but he had his grappling hook out with his other hand. He let her go first, carrying the basket in her cloak, then climbed up the wall behind her. He held his hand out to push her up into the window. She turned around and glared at him like an angry child. He pulled his hand away from her.

***

Mother Superior remembers the girl who bled of Elishta after the king's man breached her halls. She said that the church of Imam wrote us to ask for fireseeds when the girl was arrested and thanked me for them. They couldn't just burn the convent down.

They should. Salvatore was in her room, right up until the end. The Temple is sure of it. I'm sure of it. He would have gone to her room, and tried to save her from herself.

They want us to share the thief's knowledge with them, when we find it. They want to know all about how he ruined their girl.

When the time comes, we will not share. They had their chance.

***

Inside the girl's narrow room, as she had told it to Jona later, Salvatore placed a hand on the basket.

"I'll scream."

He pulled gently at the basket.

She took a deep breath.

He took his hand away. "Please don't be this person," he whispered. "Don't hurt anyone like this." He held his hands up, like surrendering.

She took the basket into the hall. Salvatore knew exactly who she was going to try and destroy with this thing, and it would never work.

Salvatore looked at the space in the doorway where she disappeared. He leaned out the window at the world outside the convent. He smelled the air like an animal searching the wind, and all the night city and the humid lamplight and the fog and the people walking up and down the dark streets and the people moving in and out of windows.

Salvatore looked back into the darkness where Aggie had disappeared. If he left her, he'd never return. If he stayed, he'd never leave her until the end. If he stayed, he'd try to protect her and damn them both.

If he left, he'd forget her face in a couple months, and then he'd forget her name, and then he'd find a new love.

He looked to the pitch black doorway, then to the window, and back into the black.

***

Jona watched Salvatore descending alone from the window. Salvatore left his hook where it was on the convent wall. Maybe he wanted to give the girl one last chance to change her mind, or escape.

In the street, he looked around for signs of his stalker, gesturing to his collar. He wanted his cloak back.

Jona came out to him with the cloak under his arm. He held it out.

"Thanks," Salvatore grunted.

"You done with her?" said Jona. "We need you to be done with her. You could get a lot of people hurt."

Salvatore turned and walked away. Jona tried to quicken his step to catch up, but Salvatore kept ahead. Soon, they were running, Jona chasing Salvatore through unfamiliar streets.

Jona slowed. He didn't have anything else to say, or to do. Salvatore ran on alone.

That must have been his life, mostly.

***

The carpenter raised his eyebrow and shook his head, incredulous. "You sure that was enough?" he asked. "That was a light, light finger. You always seemed like a heavy, then you're so light."

"Salvatore isn't going back."

"She still had the... whatever it was?"

"It's all her, now. Salvatore's not around to take it."

The carpenter shook his head. "You took too long on it. Go on, then. Hope it don't come back and I'll tell what you did to the ones that care about it. My advice is stay on your man. Isn't going to end well between us if you don't get smarter. Be back to blood soon, off the sharp stuff, I bet."

Jona waited.

"What?" said the carpenter. "You want something?" He picked up a mallet. "You better not."

"I want to know what your name is," said Jona. "I want to know what the point of all this is. Why do I do what I do? I can't figure it out. None of the people seemed to matter, and nothing I do for you makes sense."

The carpenter put down his mallet. He smiled. "Thought you were gonna ask for money," he said. "Get out of here, demon. Best advice is don't ask questions. Stay on your man. Watch out for him."

The next morning, Jona was early for muster with the king's men. He sat with a night shift scrivener and the night shift desk sergeant. Jona helped them cut the dead wax from their candles while he waited for his crew.

Finally, Sergeant Calipari came in, piles of paper in his arms. He placed them on the table, and started to flip through them.

"You're in early. Weren't out with the boys were you?"

"My ma needed help with something," Jona said. "You go out?"

"I went home right after work and wrote Franka a letter. Went to bed."

It was like nothing had happened, and all of the nights were unreal—dreaming of being dreamless, and nothing else. Better that than all the killing and stalking in the dark.

A hammock in a dark room, swaying gently, and a girl in a window, letters to a woman on the edge of the city—all these things were equally unknown to Jona. He tried to wrap his head around them. He tried to nod like he understood it and figure out what people had said before he had to speak again, but inside it was like fish seen through water. He darted his hands in to snatch at a normal life only to feel it slip from his grasp, a silver glimmer darting away. He had done what he was told. He'd always do that. It made his head hurt to think about what Salvatore could have been doing right then, what was happening to Aggie in her convent, and if the temple nuns had found the demon stain or the magic wherever the girl had hid the basket with a Sabachthani's dog.

CHAPTER X

When's the last time you did any... you know, Senta stuff?

Yesterday, I managed some dreamcasting. It's how we see the truth beneath people's lives, like the way dreams are true with what they say, but never in how they say it. Sorry, I guess you don't know about that. It's like dreaming. We're wide awake. It's real, but it's not real. It's hard to explain without a koan.

Which one is that?

What were your hands before you were born?

I don't get it.

Hands are the thing that make you a man, Jona. Without them, what are you?

I don't know. What is that supposed to mean?

It's dreamcasting. It's one of the koans that reveals the truths of the world. I was meditating on it, then I went walking around, looking for signs it might be working, and I went into this butcher shop, and I asked him for the best sausage he had. He handed me the closest sausage to his hand. He didn't seem very enthusiastic about it.

I asked the butcher how he knew which sausage was the best.

He told me that every sausage was his best.

Then, I saw him having the same conversation with his sons about which one of his sons was the best, and then I saw his sons having this same conversation with their sons, forward and backward in time a thousand generations.

Are you meditating on me right now?

Oh, I can never concentrate naked.

***

Fear becomes normal, like walking with a limp. You have to walk. I went out with my brother. Rachel double-checked her clothes for holes. She re-tied the lashes at her sleeves. It would be too easy to leave the edge of a scale out, black and shining like a dark coin. She wouldn't even feel it.

Sentas, strict adherents of a disciplined faith, cover themselves up all the time, no matter where they are. They wear long, flowing pants or dresses, and always rugged boots. They wear two long leather strips, stained red, that cross over their chest. This is supposed to symbolize the Unity. Rachel's leather strips fanned out, ragged and frayed, from her belt to her boots.

In these clothes, Rachel could hide everything but her face, her hands, and her hair. Seeing her on the street, no one would bother her. She kept away from the kinds of places a good Senta might go for coin: rich houses, opera halls. She kept away from temples and the men of law. Her clothes had a shadow.

People didn't seem to bother looking closely at her behind the Senta leathers. They just saw her clothes. Uniforms were like that.

Djoss stretched, and flipped the dust off his cloak. "Ready?"

"Check me," she replied, "can you see anything?"

"No," he said. He wasn't looking at her. "Let's go."

"Djoss!" she said, "Check me!"

He sighed. "Nobody will look at you out there."

"Just check me out, okay?" She pulled her hair up over her head so she could see her whole back. Djoss found a place on the collar where her cloak had pulled it down. No scales were showing, but he flipped it up just the same.

"See," she said.

"Nothing was showing," Djoss huffed.

"This time. We need to think about replacing my clothes soon. It's been a while."

"I'll ask around," he said. "Turco knows people."

"I don't trust him."

"He's been honest with me so far. He's not a bad fellow if you gave him half a chance."

"Be careful," she said. "I don't know what I'd do without you. If you get arrested, or killed…"

Rachel's sweat ate through the cloth eventually, and she wore one layer of rags to take the brunt of it. In the heat of Dogsland, sweat leaked out like tears from her scales day and night. She had gone through the rags beneath, replacing them again and again with Djoss' help. Replacing her Senta leathers, unlike just rags, would be hard if Djoss wasn't around. Sometimes, a good Senta might dreamcast too much of the truth of her life. They'd know.

Rachel hadn't been outside the building in weeks. She was hiding out, sweating out the fear of all that time spent sleeping in alleys, with the sound of boots stomping through the street late at night, and men with bats chasing her and her brother away if they weren't hiding enough, looking hard at them, after anything that could be used against them—a tongue or a glittering scale, for instance.

The streets smelled worse than the muddy basement room. Households emptied their chamber pots in the alleys between the houses, sending waste flowing through the mud in a vast delta of silt and filth towards the sewer drains. Somewhere, below the mud, there used to be cobblestones. Mud and piss and rain crawled to the salt flats south of the city, where land melted into the ocean like wet, frayed silk.

On the streets, men wrapped their boots in full spats. Women wore their skirts to their knees to keep the fringes from the mud, and long boots with cloth bindings covered their legs.

The wealthy all carried parasols because it would rain soon, and when it wasn't raining, the sun was hot, hot.

Djoss' shirt reeked of sweat. Rachel kept close to him, and the acrid stench of his body drowned out the rest of the city smells.

Djoss waved at a vendor with a huge conical hat. "That guy's totally off," he said to Rachel. "Talk with him a minute and he starts babbling about how the king's coins are reading his mind. He won't accept local coins. Only foreign ones."

Further down the road, Djoss took a left. "It's easy to get to the pub," he said, "You just hang a left right there at the crazy guy, and straight to the river. When I'm not out with Turco's crew, I'm there."

"How do you hide what you carry for him?"

"Meat," said Djoss. "Heavy, but it makes you move faster on account of the weight. Sell of chunks of meat if I can. Sew it up and keep walking. Gets lighter as I go."

A left into emptiness, a vacant street where the only sign of life was a lamp-lighter's cart. Rachel and Djoss walked up an empty hill for two blocks. At the top of the hill, a few cobblestones poked up through the mud that wept down the rest of the road along the sides of the hill. River sailors passed the night in a string of inns and pubs and cheap brothels at the bottom of the hill. The hot baths were more popular than the girls.

Djoss led Rachel down the other side of the hill to a pub that squatted on a high wall over the river dike's edge. Disheveled men slumped in sleep along the benches lining the river's edge, pissing off the piers when they woke up.

He was working tonight, and needed to stay near the door. She walked in alone. She pushed for room between two drunk women, and raised her hand for service.

She turned around to see where Djoss was, but couldn't see the door past the swarming crowd. When she turned back to the bar, the harried barmaid was in her face, impatiently waiting. Rachel ordered a single drink and looked around the bar for a place to sit. She wanted her back to a wall, so she could watch everything.

A bartender pounded a bell three times. A cheer went up, but there didn't seem to be a reason why. Rachel sat down where she could. She raised her hand at the tavern boy when he came by lugging bowls of soup, and paid him quickly.

Rachel searched for some kind of silverware. She saw none. She looked over her shoulder. A man nearby was slurping from the bowl in his hands. He managed to do it without spilling a drop on his shirt.

Everyone was shouting over the music, so the musicians played louder, and it all escalated. Rachel had to shout to get the barmaid back. She gestured at her bowl of soup for silverware.

The barmaid shouted. "No more spoons!"

Rachel didn't want to spill it all on her clothes. She picked up the bowl carefully. She tried to figure out how to maneuver the soup into her mouth slowly and carefully. The brim of the bowl flattened out at the edge, and it made drinking it precarious.

People stopped talking to watch two fighters bounced. Djoss pushed through the crowd to bounce them. He got them both in his arms, a giant next to these brawlers who stilled in Djoss' shadow. He got his arms around their necks and dragged them into the street. He looked like he was half horse, dragging those two smaller men.

Rachel leaned to the man on her right without looking at him. It felt daring to talk to anyone after so much time hiding. "What do you think they're fighting about?" The man wasn't paying attention to her. He was talking to a woman on his other side. She touched his arm. "Hey," she said.

The man turned her way, frowning. "What is it?"

"Hey, what do you think those men were fighting about?"

"I don't know," he grunted, turning from her. The woman he'd been talking to had disappeared. He turned back to Rachel. The way he moved, he must have plenty to drink already.

"This your soup?"

She picked up the bowl gently. "I guess so."

"I've got a spoon, if you want." He reached back into his pockets and pulled it out, holding it up to her. She shook her head. "Thanks, but I don't want your spoon," she said. He'd probably want it back. He probably wouldn't wash it. He might use it right there, where it might make him sick right there.

"How about a handkerchief?"

"No, thank you."

"You're going to need it."

"Am I?" she said. She decided that she didn't like this man very much. She looked around for her brother. She didn't see him. She leaned closer to the stranger anyway. "I'm here with someone," she said. "I don't see him, but I'll use his handkerchief if I need it."

"That fellow, is he here where you need him?"

She laughed. "He works here."

"Good for a man to work where you can keep an eye on him."

"I've never been here before."

"My name's Salvatore."

"I'm not telling you my name."

"You should," he said. "It's polite."

"It isn't polite to push your name on someone who doesn't want it," she said.

With a recklessness she didn't feel, she picked up the soup bowl and threw it back like medicine. Soup spilled on her face and a little on her collar. He held up the handkerchief for her with a smile. She accepted it, unsmiling. The handkerchief smelled like soap. This wasn't the place for those kinds of handkerchiefs.

Rachel did a mental check for her money. She didn't have much, and she still felt it in the crease of her clothes. She put the handkerchief into the pocket where she kept her coins.

"I'm keeping this."

She slipped the coins out from underneath the handkerchief, and hid them in her palm. Then she reached down to adjust her boot, dropping the coins down inside, where she'd feel them against her heel all night. Her scales and claws wouldn't chafe.

Salvatore smiled lazily. "Want to dance?"

"Yes," she said. "But I can't. I don't know how."

He laughed at her. He pulled her arm, and she let him drag her up from the bar to the center of the crowd. He was a drunk enough that he kept laughing too long even if it wasn't so funny.

Rachel let him spin her around the room. He had a stiff back, but he was light enough on his feet to keep her from falling back into anyone. She clenched at the feeling of his hand against the small of her back. She hoped he wouldn't notice the strange clicking of scales beneath the cloth. She hoped he wouldn't step on her toes, either, and then she might have to explain the bumps where her talons hid in her boots.

Salvatore spun her around, and threw her backwards in a deep dip.

He was handsome enough for one dance, and he hadn't stepped on her foot, yet. Rachel kept one hand on his back, and the other trapped in his palm. His skin reeked of smoke and soap, and his hands were too clean. The song ended. She gestured with her head to tell him to stop.

He led her back to their seats. Her soup bowl had disappeared before she could drop it on the floor to try and break it. He bought her a new drink. She thought about leaving.

"Why?" she said.

He grinned. "No reason."

She was thirsty enough from dancing to want it. She didn't want to make a scene with this man, whom she would be leaving as soon as she was done with the drink. She wanted to be polite, so she could leave without a scene. He stared at her. She drank fast.

She cocked her head. "So say something."

He laughed. "I never know what to say."

"Don't just sit there like a snapping turtle," she said. "It's uncomfortable."

"I'm trying to think of the right thing to say. I think I got it. Your eyes are like two bright shiny coins. You dance like a silk ribbon." He bought her a fresh drink. Her mug was gone to the dishwater behind the bar, and she thought maybe her soup bowl would be all right there.

"I do not. Be careful what you wish for…"

"I just might get it?"

"No," said Rachel, "Let me finish. Be careful what you wish for when a woman's involved, because she'll probably get what she wishes for instead and you won't like it."

"What is it that you wish for?"

"Better company." Rachel pulled her chair away from him. "I'm leaving." She stood up, and walked to the front where Djoss stood glowering at everyone. She handed her glass to him.

"Hm? Oh, thanks." He tossed the glass back.

She walked out the door, and waved over her shoulder to her brother.

"You just got here!" he called out to her.

"Be safe," she shouted.

Alone, Rachel walked carefully along the way her brother had shown her. The odd merchant was still open, shouting at a man nearby. Rachel went to the back side of his cart and slipped a jar of pickled eggs from the display, holding it to her side while she walked away.

She turned down the road to the bakery, cradling the eggs. She couldn't remember if she liked pickled eggs or not. If she didn't like them, she could give them to Djoss. He ate anything. They'd both gone hungry too many times to care much about liking the food they had.

Inside her room, with the door locked, she listened to the sounds of the night. A voice cried out a woman's name, and someone pounded on a building wall. Then it was quiet again.

In the morning, she decided she was going to find Turco. She needed to get out, get working, like her brother did. The fear remained, always, but it couldn't be the only emotion she allowed herself to feel.

***

Jona had seen it all that night. He never told her about that. He had watched her, with Salvatore, not knowing who or what she was—who she was going to be. Jona thought a Senta ought to know better when a demon child was touching her hand.

Salvatore was a fool for pursuing someone that might see through him, but Salvatore was lost in his own habits and loving a woman who didn't quite fit among the people in the room around her, in the taverns of the night, or the secret temple.

Jona followed Salvatore out of the tavern, into the street. He watched the thief walk up the same road after her. Watching this, disdain swelled up like an acrid belch from Jona's heart. Salvatore had already forgotten Aggie.

Salvatore was at the baker's door. He was reaching for the handle. Jona shouted Salvatore's name. Salvatore turned, startled, and Jona shook his head.

The thief slammed the wall with his blackjack —then took off, running.

***

The second time Jona saw Rachel, she was walking through the Pens, stopping at every servant's door and asking for work. She looked familiar, and he couldn't place her right away, in the daylight and a crowded street. How much love begins with déjà vu?

Jona waved off Tripoli, and said he'd be back in a minute, he thought he recognized someone. Jona ran a little farther down the road. He saw her walking up to a man with a long moustache loitering at a red door. That red door wasn't the kind of place Jona would go without a whole crew behind him, ringing bells and enough solid evidence to arrest everyone inside.

The red-dressed man in the red door smiled like he knew her, but that's always how these things were. Jona had seen these sorts of greetings. In a city street, anything could happen. A man could stand with a giant slab of meat on his leg on a street corner for hours. People could be running from nothing and everything. Tiny sparrows could be walking around among the legs of people as sure of step as if they were six feet tall. Jona saw a beautiful woman he thought he recognized in Senta leathers talking to some street gang's watch-out man. It was so normal, but it was so strange. She didn't like him, but she talked to him. He wouldn't leave his place casually, because he was the watch-out man, but he got up for her and walked her down the street.

Tripoli saw it, too, and took up step after Jona even though he'd been waved off. The two king's men nodded at each other. Watch-out man walking anywhere got their attention, and he wasn't leading another troublemaker. The crowd parted for them, but the two they followed didn't seem to notice. Jona and Tripoli walked along behind the pair a while, watching from a distance.

The watch-out man wore nothing but red. He was easy to spot in a crowd of so much dirt browns and burlaps. He walked her to a door. It was a brothel door. Sentas didn't work brothels, and if she was a working girl, she was overdressed and not wearing any rouge or powder.

Tripoli shook his head. "What do you think that's about?"

"Don't know. Don't like seeing watch-out men walking around like that. Don't he care for what his people think?"

"Probably nothing. His sister or something."

"Don't see Sentas here much," said Jona. "Never seen one with a watch-out man."

Jona felt the tickling of memory in the back of his mind. The tavern had been dark. The street had been dark. He had been too busy watching Salvatore to get more than a passing glance. Come daylight, she could have been anyone to him. She didn't have to be anyone.

If he had gone further, he'd have seen the Senta in a broom closet, going through the brushes and the rags. Then, he'd see her pulling sheets from a line. Turco took a cut of her first few weeks' pay.

That's the story of her day, when she tells him about it. She worked a few nights, then moved on to a new brothel. Then another, when she thought the hallways were too bright during the day, and wanted to work at night. Her shadow was harder to miss at night. She stayed at that one a while, but Turco found out and he was taking a cut of her pay because he got her the job in the first place.

Everybody needed another maid. Anyone who could would get more coin working in the bed than cleaning it, and it wasn't so hard to lie back and encourage a man.

By the time Jona remembered who she was, she had long since drifted into new jobs, and there was no finding her without raising people's attention about it. She wasn't with Salvatore, Jona knew. She was just a woman in the street, with a life as mysterious as anyone's.

CHAPTER XI

Sergeant Calipari had his feet up on his desk, and a page torn out of an accounting book in his hands. He didn't look up when Jona drifted in from the street.

"Corporal Jona Lord Joni," said Calipari, "You're late."

Jona grunted and snatched the page from Calipari. "What's this?"

"Nothing, if the fellow I took it from is honest. A few missing digits, though." Calipari leaned back in his chair. He shook his head at his Corporal. "You need to get more sleep. You look like you were out all night."

"Got drunk," said Jona. "Threw rocks at ships. What'd you do?"

"Franka's boy came in town working for a fellow with some new horses. I took him to the dog fights. Kid lost big. I lost less," Calipari said with a smile.

"What's going down today?" Jona gestured at the empty desks. "I don't see the scriveners."

"They weren't late. Got them on the rounds like anybody. Get the privates some experience for when they rank up to corporal. Sunshine's good for their health."

Jona scoffed. "That's a bad idea, Sergeant. You think they all come back in one piece?"

"Maybe. Lieutenant wants us to head to Lord Sabachthani's place. Trouble with some noble. You're a noble, he says, so send you. Small stuff. Ain't worth his time."

"You'd think he'd be falling head over heels to help her."

"You'd think," said Calipari. "I heard she requested you personally. You making friends, Lord Joni?"

Jona sat down. He didn't like anything about being requested by Sabachthani. "I had tea with her once or twice."

"Big favor," said Calipari. "She collects."

"I may be a lord, but I'm just a corporal. Can we at least get the Lieutenant?"

"Huh, right, let me just ask him real nice…" said Calipari. "Nobody wants to get closer to Sabachthani than they have to. I'm coming with you. Nobody's ordered me on it, but you can't handle this by yourself."

Jona believed this was a set-up, but he couldn't prove anything. The carpenter would think nothing of throwing Jona to the wolves. Sabachthani was more dangerous than wolves. Perhaps it was an accident of his time with Lady Sabachthani, but that was even worse. He didn't want her attention. Either way, Calipari's presence should have been a relief, but under the circumstances it worried Jona more than any conspiracy against him by man or bad luck.

***

The doorman bowed and spoke into a tube that sank into the ground at his feet. He pressed his ear against the tube until vague sounds emerged from the tube that sounded almost human. The doorman bowed, and waved the two city guards up the main door.

Jona tossed the fellow a coin. The doorman winked, and slipped the coins into a hidden pocket. Bribing the doorman was how Jona snuck into the parties during the dry season.

Calipari hadn't even seen it happen. He was busy trying to sneak a peak at the monsters hidden in the willow grove. They were barely visible behind the trees. A trail of mud was trampled down in the grass where the heavy things walked back and forth to the gate.

In the yard, there was a conspicuous absence of birdsong.

Calipari looked up at the house. "Do you think it was a servant?"

"Maybe," said Jona, "We'll see. Do you know what got stolen?"

Calipari shrugged. "Nope," he said. "Bet it was a servant." He gestured with his thumb at the willow grove. "Bet it was those things."

"You want to handle that hanging?"

Calipari chuckled.

Jona stretched his neck straight. He twisted his natural scowl into a big, fake smile. "You ready to introduce yourself?"

Calipari smiled, too. He and Jona pulled little cards from pockets, printed with name, rank, and station house. Jona's was grimy, and bent in the corner. Calipari's was clean and white. Jona reached up to the main door and grabbed the knocker. The knocker was carved like whale's open jaw and Jona pounded its heavy tongue.

The doors swung inward. A butler bowed. "Guardsmen?" he said. "From the king?"

"Sergeant Nicola Calipari, by your request." The sergeant held out his card in one hand, offering the other for a shake. The butler took the card, and ignored the hand.

"Lord Joni," said Jona, his own card out and hand extended. The butler shunned even his card.

The butler turned to Sergeant Calipari. "My Lord Sabachthani is indisposed. Perhaps the Captain could come calling tomorrow."

Jona snatched the butler's hand and forced a quick shake. He shoved his card into the man's lapel. "I was requested by Lord Sabachthani himself, and I'm here." said Jona. He'd explain this to Calipari later. You can't let the help push you around—they're only the help. If you're worth anything it's *your* right to push.

The butler turned to Jona. "I was addressing the commander."

Calipari barely hid his laugh behind a frown. "I'm no commander," he said, "I'm just a sergeant. The estate asked for some king's men, and we came. Can we help you, or not?"

The butler gestured into the entryway. Jona and Calipari stepped inside.

The butler left the two in the drawing room and disappeared. Calipari made to sit down on a giant leather divan, but Jona stopped him, pointing to the window. From here, the insect leg of one of a guardians could be seen jutting out from the willow grove.

The seneschal entered from a door behind a bookshelf. To Jona, he looked no different from the butler: an older man, with the sniveling air of the courts about him, and no title or wealth to justify his behavior. When the talking started, Jona ignored it. Seneschals were nothing worth talking to. Calipari didn't know that, nor did he realize he was being patronized by the proud seneschal.

Jona looked out the window at the yard, waiting for anything.

A pack of dogs ran across the grass like a yellow cloak blowing away in the winds.

Jona shivered. Not one of them had made a sound.

The seneschal could be stalling, hoping to get rid of them. Lady Ela, Sabachthani's daughter, might come down at any moment. The house staff had their own political maneuverings.

Jona and Lady Ela had last danced together when Jona sneaked into her last ball. Ela had heavy feet, and she tended to get lost in her own dress. She didn't like to talk when she was dancing. She let Jona call her just Ela when no one was looking. If they ever found themselves alone in a crowded room, she liked to ask him about the people outside the walls of the Sabachthani estate, where the rest of Dogsland lived.

He told her about the criminals he met, and the criminals

he let walk away. He told her about the love affairs of men and women who do not have palaces.

If Jona were richer, he might have gone so far as to call her a friend. As things stood, they only spoke when Jona had crashed a party to which he wasn't invited. Sometimes, she invited him to tea at someone else's house to show off how merciful she was to the less fortunate noblemen. This was the first time he had ever been in her home with her permission.

The seneschal and Calipari were still talking and none of it mattered. The seneschal was trying to stall them until the masters of the house were truly unavailable. It was his job to get rid of people, even if they were requested. Lots of people were requested. If anyone else was visiting and they were more important, it didn't matter what was stolen or what was wanted from the king's man. Calipari didn't even realize it. Jona could linger, and let this problem fester, face it another day. He could let the seneschal push them both into the street in an hour. Or, he could face this problem directly. The carpenter had liked Jona better when he had a hard touch.

Jona coughed loudly, and snapped his finger at the seneschal. "Stop wasting our time. In criminal investigations, every minute counts. How exactly can the king's men help Lord Sabachthani?"

The seneschal held his breath. He paled. "No need to be rude, Lord Joni," he said. "My Lord Sabachthani requests your assistance with the theft of a dog."

"His *what?*" said Calipari.

The seneschal told them about the dog that was found in an Anchorite convent.

Jona scoffed. "So the dog ran away," he said, "and some nuns took it off the street. So what?"

The seneschal nodded. "Yes, perhaps. However, the dog's basket turned up in the convent as well," he said, "and this basket wound up in the Mother Superior's room."

Jona looked out the window. "Imam's flock was never much

for your fellow after that valley in the war," he said.

"How do they know it's *Lord Sabachthani's* basket?" said Calipari, "Can it be proven that the basket found in the convent is the one that went missing?"

"Of course," said the seneschal. "I'm afraid I know nothing else."

Jona stood up from the divan. He walked slowly over to the window. He turned, and stared down at the seneschal. He was tired of all the posturing. "So your master asks the assistance of the King, but cannot even bothered to send anybody down that knows anything?"

"*Corporal* Lord Joni, my Lord Sabachthani is indisposed."

"What about the Lady of the house? Any noble asking king's men to do their dirty work for them ought to do it face-to-face. Ain't that the law as it is written?"

"No need to be rude…"

Jona dragged the old man to his feet by his lapels. Then Jona smashed his knee into the old man's groin and threw him onto the floor.

Jona turned to Sergeant Calipari. "Just the help," he said. "He's useless to us."

The seneschal gasped for air, his face twisted and red.

Calipari stood up from the divan. "Lord Joni, I hope you know what you're doing. I don't think that was called for."

"Well, I think it was, and I'm the one they asked for. They demand I show my face, then refuse to look me in the eye? That's rude. I'm still a nobleman, and they know it. If Lord Sabachthani doesn't like us questioning his staff to our satisfaction, then he had better speak to us directly," he said. "My throat is parched. Let's go find the kitchen and see if we can't get some tea. If our host was treating us with respect worthy of the king's finest men, we'd have been offered tea ages ago."

"Jona, I hope you know what you're doing…"

"Don't mind about the help. They're pushing us around because they think they can. No way to let them treat you.

I can't remember where the kitchen is, but it's around here somewhere."

The seneschal had crawled on his hands and knees to the door, in too much pain to stand. He got his hand on the door knob, but struggled to open it.

The two soldiers walked off in no particular direction, away from the injured servant. Calipari stopped the first maid they saw and asked her for the way to the kitchen. Apparently, it was on the other side of the house. They moved in that direction.

Calipari whistled. "Your place anything like this?"

"No," said Jona. "We sold all this furniture and stuff."

In the kitchen at last, the two men drank very expensive tea sweetened with golden sugar a soft, warm brown like expensive molasses. It was the first time Calipari had ever had sugar like that. He reached his hand into the huge bag of sugar and cupped out a handful, then licked it from his palm, amazed.

Jona watched, curiously. It was the kind of thing a child would do. He didn't get any sugar around his house, but he knew enough not to do that.

"This all going according to plan, Lord Joni?" Calipari raised an eyebrow.

"I think we're about to have the friendliest meeting with Lady Ela Sabachthani we'll ever have in our lives, and then we will never be invited here again. If she's really nice to us, it means she's going to garnish our wages for that sugar."

"It's worth it," said Calipari. He ran his tongue up his palm.

***

In just a few moments, Lady Ela Sabachthani arrived in the kitchen, smiling as widely as her lips could bend. She was as beautiful as her money, in a fine dress and a face painted like her own portrait made in skin.

"Gentlemen!" she said. "My Lord Joni, it's been too long since I've seen you last. I simply must throw another party. How is your mother?" She kissed Jona on each of his cheeks, leaving a trail of white powder acrosss Jona's face from the powder on her cheeks.

Jona bowed deeply. "My mother probably sewed your dress, my Lady," he said. "You look absolutely marvelous this morning. It's a welcome change from all the vagrants and foreigners I deal with all day." He kissed her palm. At this, her smile fell into something real.

Sergeant Calipari bowed just as deeply, but she ignored him.

Jona didn't let go of her hand. "I'm so glad you took the time to meet with us in person," he said. "Your staff didn't seem to have a clue what actually happened in your house."

Lady Ela poured herself a cup of tea, took her hand away to stir some sugar into it. "This is not an internal matter," she said. "Someone from outside the estate—from your beloved city, Lord Joni—entered our home, and stole one of my precious dogs. This individual then took my dog to an Anchorite convent. The dog was discovered by the Mother Superior of the convent, in her room. The animal has already been returned to us. Our internal investigation revealed that an outsider was to blame."

Jona nodded. "Still," he said, "you must understand our skepticism. Why risk so much over a dog?"

Her laughter was like crystal bells ringing. "That is your concern, not mine," she said. "My father and I thought nothing of it, except that we believed the king might like to know our thief was stained with the stink of demons. It would seem perhaps a demon's child is loose in our fair city."

"Demon?" said Calipari. Now it was his turn to laugh. "Elishta's been sealed a thousand years. The Nameless were driven underground. Now they're stealing dogs and running around a convent?"

Ela didn't look at the sergeant when he spoke. "You are the investigator, my Lord Joni," she said. "And you... whoever you are." She took Lord Jona's hand and pulled him closer. "As for me, many who fear demons fear my father as well. I don't want to know anything else about this whole mess."

Jona bent his head. "Of course, my Lady."

"Lord Joni, I appreciate your attention in this matter," she said. "I love to know a man will come when I call him."

Jona smiled, as gracefully as he could. He didn't like the implied comparison, but she was right. He was her dog, as was anyone. Her father was a powerful man, and she, a powerful woman. He kissed her hand again.

She shook Calipari's hand, and paused. "Sergeant, you appear confused."

Calipari nodded. "I am, Lady," he said. "Dogs usually don't go quietly."

She nodded. "We cut out their tongues, first. They can still vocalize a little, but it's hardly all we do."

She disappeared into the depths of her house, leaving the two men alone in the kitchen.

Calipari drained his cup. "Well," he said, "good tea."

"Our welcome is wearing very thin," said Jona.

Jona felt sick. How had the Sabachthanis been able to determine that the thief was demon-stained? He wanted to climb out the window and run. But he wasn't one to live his life among the harts and boars of estates, rooting through the roots or trash heaps for food, always vigilant. He was not a dog, running for his life. Not yet. He snatched Calipari's tea cup and threw it hard into the rubbish bin, along with his. They both shattered.

Calipari grimaced. "She do something to you?"

"Yes," said Jona. "Let's go."

Hunters were coming. They were always coming for men like Jona and Salvatore. Hunters like my husband and I.

***

Sergeant Calipari wanted to check the convent's borders before going in. Nothing looked obviously suspicious. "Tell me this, Corporal," he said, "how does a demon child enter an Imam

Temple that accepts no visitors? Do they walk through walls?"

"Temple has doors, even if they're locked. Windows, even if they're high off the ground."

"Still, follow me a bit," said Calipari. "If you were going to bust into this, how would you?"

"Keys," said Jona. "I know what you're saying. Inside job."

"Either that or a stupid job," Calipari replied. "Demon was bright enough to get into Sabachthani's estate and this convent. There anybody you know works inside both places? Musician? Delivery-man?"

"Not this far apart. Not a demon child, neither," said Jona. "Someone with the stain would stay clear of any place they still want to hunt them down. This is all mixed up. We could be a message from Sabachthani about something, but what I don't know," he went on. "I wouldn't put it past Sabachthani. Our time's nothing to her. Imam flock won't even let Lord Sabachthani into a poor man's temple after what he did to the red valley, nevermind what else he does. We get in there and send a message for her. King's not going to live forever. People got to get ready for it."

"Lord Joni, you may take sides in all that stuff. I don't. I'm a king's man in the Pens and nothing else. If it turns out we're messengers for Lady Sabachthani, we'd best be good ones, and pay all respects to Imam while we're there. I like my neck where it is."

***

Jona yawned. "You almost done?"

Calipari stayed down, his nose on the floor, kissing the fourth of the white marble Stars of Imam. He stood up slowly, and finished with a bow to the altar before returning to sit down next to Jona.

"Feel better?"

"If I'm about to push some anchorites around, I'd like to pray about it first."

"You think Imam has it out for you?"

"I don't think Imam would mind grinding me down for less. Same thing I think about Lord Sabachthani. I should have hung back on this one. There's a reason none of the officers want in."

"If Ela sent for me, she wasn't asking for someone to bow and scrape. She doesn't know you from anybody. She knows me. She asked for me."

Calipari rubbed his knees. "You're going to make me bow and scrape a lot more, I know it…"

The first floor was a commoner's temple to Imam. Above it, anchorites that lived for their death in whole floors full of girls, all the rooms as quiet as tombs. The fourth, Jona knew, had cells for the girls, with windows open to Imam's stars, though it was hard to see any stars through the city's lamplight and sea clouds.

Jona looked up at the ceiling and tried to make out any sort of noise. There was nothing.

As they waited, a nun came out from a door behind the altar. She stopped to kiss the heavy stones and the bells before she came to the rails that separated Imam's chosen from the people of the city. She frowned at the two king's men. She waved her hand for them to approach, and to be quick about it. Her impatience was like a stone anchoring her flowing, black robes. The two king's men sat before her.

"There is no need for you here," she said. "The wicked lord has his abomination back."

Calipari rubbed his hands along his pants legs. "The thing is… All due respect, Sister…"

"We will take care of what happens here. Our girls belong to the stars. They are not to be bothered by earthly things."

"Sister, with all due respect… More trouble than us in the world, and we are the ones trying to do something about it."

The nun folded her arms.

"The thing is, the Sabachthani say that there's demon stain on it. Whoever took the basket was of the Nameless. Demon children coming into your convent is serious business. Merits a bit of an investigation if it's true."

"He would know after what he did to that valley."

"He *would* know," said Jona. "So, we want to know if anybody saw anything, maybe talk to them."

"I have already learned everything. This matter was taken seriously." She paused. "One of the older girls mentioned seeing something in her daily confession," she said, grudgingly. "She had assumed it was a nightmare, but it must have been your demon."

"What did she see?" Jona asked.

"A black form crawling over her, as if in a dream. The black form had a basket on its back. She described the basket in great detail. She had never seen its like before, nor could she have seen it. It is promising sign for an anchorite, to show signs of prophecy so young."

Calipari pursed his lips. "This... black form had the basket, and she can describe it in great detail? Does she know anything about the person carrying it?"

"I'm afraid not."

"May we speak with her?" said Jona.

"I'm afraid not."

"Would you mind if we spoke with her in your presence?" said Calipari. The nun merely pursed her lips in response. Calipari tried again. "Or we could ask you the questions, and you could take them to her. We could hear her response from behind a curtain or something, or you could come back and tell us if she needed to be in another room?"

The nun turned away without explanation. She went back behind the altar, to the stairwell there.

Jona and Nicola looked at each other. Nicola cocked his head. "Was that a yes?"

Jona stood up to leave, stretching his arms over his head. "You really want to question the girl like that?"

"Of course not," said Calipari, "How can we separate them if they show up? The girl'll be back behind the rails."

"You honestly think they're coming back?" said Jona.

Calipari sighed. "No. Whatever we were supposed to do, I hope we did it."

"Probably right," said Jona. "Lady Ela Sabachthani won't like it, but there's only so much we can do, when we can't go question anyone. I'm going to get something to eat. All this walking around the city makes me hungry."

"Don't think I'll be eating anything for a while," said Calipari. "Whole thing makes me sick."

Jona knew exactly what he needed to do to get to Aggie before someone else got to her. Jona did not hesitate. He jumped the rails, and strode quickly past the altar to the stairwell that led up to the silent halls of the novitiates, perhaps the only man to walk that ground since the day the convent was built.

Sergeant Calipari's head dropped into his hands. He tried not to laugh. Lady Ela Sabachthani had requested Jona, and she knew him well enough to know what that meant. Perhaps that would be enough to protect the king's men from the complaints to come.

***

Jona climbed the stairs up to the second floor, then wound his way through the choir stands to reach the next stairwell up. Curiosity being what it was, he peered out the door to the third floor. It was all hallways, with closed doors. He wondered what the rooms might be. The Matron Mother might be breaking Aggie with a whip or even testing her body for signs of the demon stain, in her blood or in her sickness. On the fourth floor, where he knew Aggie's cell sat, he saw the old nun in the hall, the girl standing abashed beside her. He swaggered up to them.

"What's taking so long?" he said, eyeing Aggie. She glanced

up at him quickly, then returned her gaze to the floor. She knew what a king's man looked like.

The old nun reeled with shock and shouted and struck at Jona with every mean bone inside her body—he was a horror and a shame and the king would know of this blasphemy and Imam would frown upon it. She pushed at Jona. She was used to pushing girls, not king's men. Jona's body was hard as a stone wall. He walked forward unhindered.

He smiled at Aggie. "You want to get out of here?"

She said nothing, only stared down at her feet, pale, while the old nun kept shouting, pushing against Jona. Other girls emerged from the doorways to the cells, horrified to see a man standing in their holy hall. Jona gently pressed the old woman against the wall. The old nun was crying, now. He turned his head to Aggie. "You the one saw the basket?"

She nodded and took a step back. She was about to run.

Jona placed his free hand on her wrist like a vise. "I'm a king's man, and I don't answer to anyone but him, not Imam, not anybody. I tell you to do something, you do it. I want to go somewhere, I go. Now, you're coming with me," he said. "You're coming or I'll ring the bells down on this building, and all my boys will come through swinging bats after you, busting up the place and anyone who tries to stop them. You're coming." The hall around them was a riot of screams and tears and recriminations.

The old nun tried to grab at Aggie, but Jona had one hand on her, still, to push the old nun back. That's exactly what he did. He shoved her, and she fell back into the hall.

When Jona got back to the bottom floor, Sergeant Calipari was praying again. He clearly didn't want anything to do with whatever Jona was doing. When he saw Jona pushing through with a girl in front of him, he jumped up, looking around nervously. Novitiates crowded silently against the balcony like scared birds.

"What are you doing!?"

Jona said it before he could think about it. "She's under arrest. You hear that, girl? You're under arrest. Let's get you out of here."

Jona felt sick to his stomach. Jona had to protect Salvatore instead of the girl. He didn't know how he was going to do it, yet. He was acting, not thinking. He was all steam and gritted teeth. He didn't know what to do but keep doing something until Salvatore was safe. If he didn't keep Salvatore safe, the Night King wouldn't keep Jona safe.

CHAPTER XII

My husband pored over my notes. He was patient with me, even if what I had given him was an indulgence and could only help us find small pockets of stain. I had given him notes from Rachel's wandering.

It's nothing we can use, I said.

We don't know that, yet. Better to know too much.

We see too much; we know too much. I hate that about cities. Too many smells and small gestures screaming truths they'd never admit to Erin or Imam or anyone else.

I see you.

I see you. Jona's memories wrap around a feeling and won't shake loose, I have to pick at it. I have to pry.

Memories wrap around feelings. You share a feeling with him, and it hardens it. Write it out, if only to finish with it. It won't hurt us to know too much. Salvatore has been alive a long time, and can live a little longer, still.

If we could have found them out sooner… If anyone had…!

"I know."

That's all he said of it. He returned to my notes, and Calipari's maps, and letters written to temples about supplies and lingering stains. Salvatore eluded us, still, and Rachel seemed as if she had never existed outside of Jona's mind.

I wrote it all down, even if it amounts to nothing but my own peace of mind.

***

Arresting Aggie got her away from the other nuns, out of the convent, and into a closed carriage. It didn't open her mouth. She looked ill. Jona and Calipari sat across from her, ready to block the doors with their bodies. She faced the front, and looked from one man to the next. She didn't know what was going to happen to her now. Nothing had ever prepared her for this. She watched, in daylight, from a carriage window, a street that she had seen from the convent's windows in daylight. She said nothing.

Jona winked at Sergeant Calipari. "So, how long you been busting out of this convent?"

She said nothing.

Jona laughed. "I can tell you've been busting out at night. The nuns don't see it. I do. You've been chewing redroots. Your lips and your teeth got the stain of it. Someone give them to you, or do you buy them by yourself?"

She got paler, if that was even possible. "I…" she took a deep breath, "I buy them."

Sergeant Calipari raised his eyebrows. He cocked his head, and nodded at his partner. Jona never had a reputation as a clever fellow. He was a brute force kind of guy. For the few moments, Jona saw this sudden praise in his sergeant's face, and he forgot what he was really doing. Then, he remembered what he was about to do, to protect Salvatore.

"Your secret's safe with me," said Jona. "If I was in there, I'd bust it down brick by brick. How do you leave?"

"Some of us stole keys," she said. The convent girl facade melted away. She slouched, crossed her legs, and leaned against the door. "I'm stamped. Got any redroots, now?"

"They're illegal," said Calipari. "How many girls?"

"What?"

"How many sneak out?" Calipari pressed.

"Everybody does it sometimes," she said. "Even the matron mother."

Sergeant Calipari laughed. "You got a fellow?"

"Yeah," she said.

"Only one?" said Jona. "We'd love to meet any fellows you got running around with a convent girl. Maybe he's buying your redroots, and you didn't even know he'd be in trouble for it."

She had to think about that. Her mask cracked a little before it came back. For a moment, she looked like a novice again, instead of some tough kid. "I got me a few fellows," she said. She didn't know what would happen to Salvatore if she said anything, so she was playing tough, saying nothing. Jona knew the name would eventually come out. Calipari could break her down if he had a chance at it. And then it was all over.

She looked Jona boot to face. "You like to dance?"

"I do," said Jona. "Look, we had to arrest you, and I'm sorry about it. We needed to get you away a while, ask you some questions. No other way to do it. Want us to process you, too? Keeps you out of the convent a few nights."

"I'll pass."

Jona and Calipari glanced at each other. Calipari was trying to hide a smirk. Jona nodded, slightly.

Calipari leaned forward. "You go out last week?"

She laughed. "No," she said. "You?"

"When'd you last sneak out?"

"I don't remember," she said. "It's been a while."

Calipari snorted. "Funny, you admit breaking out but not the other night. Girls getting out are smarter. Know better. A fellow in your bedroom is a reason to scream for help. You just went back to sleep. That's what you said to the matron mother, isn't it? Help us make this whole stupid thing go away, or we keep riding this carriage to a station house."

"Keep riding. Imam's flock won't abandon me."

"Imam know of your redroots and sneaking?" said Calipari.

"I'll get whipped," she said. "That's between me and them.

Doesn't involve the king."

Calipari scratched his head. "Jona, this is a lot of trouble over a little thievery. We should just test her. Only thing matters to anyone is the demon blood."

"How do you test for demon blood?" Jona knew exactly how. He had hoped Calipari was clueless, so Jona might have a chance to devise a plan before anyone could involve the girl.

"I know how," said Calipari. "Of course we'll have to get some blood from her."

The girl curled her lips, and crossed her arms. "Now you're just trying to scare me. You can't hurt me like that. Imam'll..."

"We don't need anyone's permission," said Jona. "You're in the hands of the king's men. We could cut your throat and throw you from the cabin and no one would even find out you were dead." Jona pretended to yawn. He smiled gently at her. She really didn't understand the men who could invade her sanctuary, drag her away, who would hang her if she earned it, maybe even burn her alive. She seemed to believe they might cut her throat, the way she was looking at them. Of course neither Calipari nor the king would allow that. Calipari chimed in. "We could kill you now and say you were fighting us."

Jona touched her nose with his outstretched finger. "We'll take your blood, girl. We'll take anything we want in the name of the king."

She looked out the carriage. Her fingers clenched against her own skin. She was hugging herself, covering her body with her arms. "Can we just get this over with?"

Sergeant Calipari leaned back. He pushed his leg all the way across the cabin, as if in a slouch, to block the door on his side. Jona took his lead and angled over a little, to get better cover of the door on his side.

"Personally don't like to rough up the pretty ones," said Calipari. "My man Jona has no problem with anything like that. Just this morning he slammed a seneschal over one little remark. Old guy, too. Couldn't fight back. Servant to a mighty lord and still nobody can do a thing about us once we set our mind on it, and the king likes us that way."

The girl looked out the window. She said nothing at all. The carriage rolled down the road.

"Say something," said Jona.

There was nothing.

"You're protecting someone, and it's going to get you hurt. Lord Sabachthani knows for a fact someone with a demon stain did it. Some demon child took his dog."

Again, nothing.

Jona balled up his fingers. He leaned in close to show his fist to her. Before she had time to think about what it meant, he popped his knuckles into her nose. It broke. Blood spattered from it. "I'm doing this for your own good," he said. "The sooner you talk, the sooner we can get whatever you're protecting and do the same to him."

She held her breath. She held her nose. Blood spilled over her white knuckles.

Sergeant Calipari frowned at his partner, and pulled out a dirty handkerchief. He pressed it into her nose. "Lean your head back," he said. "Come on, lean your head back. It'll help stop the bleeding."

Her trembling hands clutched the handkerchief against her face. She breathed again, in little gulps like gasps. She was crying. She clutched at her nose and curled into the corner of the carriage. Calipari gently reached forward to tilt her head back. He held her nose a while. She cried.

Jona didn't do anything. He put his boot up on the seat across from him to block the door with his leg. He wiped his fist off on his pants, then leaned back with folded arms.

He needed to ride her fear all the way to the moment where she might give up Salvatore, then keep her from it. He needed to do this for his mother's safety, and his own.

He should have felt awful about it, and he did, but he knew he was supposed to feel more awful than he did. His disgust was like a crust of ice melting as soon as it floated to the surface of him, gone in moments.

***

Sergeant Calipari opened the carriage door for the girl. "Come on inside," he said, gently. "Need you inside right now. We'll knock you out and carry you if we have to."

They wouldn't have to. She was broken. She obediently stepped out of the carriage. Jona held the station door for her, Calipari following right behind. Blood was all over her face, and all over her robes.

Sergeant Calipari led her by her arm through the empty station house to the interrogation room. He closed the door on her, leaving her alone. Calipari didn't turn around right away. He stayed at the door, holding the knob, and breathing slowly. Finally, after a long pause, he turned to face Jona.

"Why'd you hit her like that, so hard, so soon?"

"Not so insolent now."

"Not so talkative, either."

"We have to test her blood, anyway," said Jona. "We got plenty of blood. We find no stain, she'll be scared enough to tell us any other girls sneaking out. Nice open wound for us to work loose."

"Yeah, well, hand me some fresh paper from that desk." Calipari pointed to an empty scrivener's desk next to the doorway, its occupant out playing corporal in the Pens.

Jona turned to reach the paper, and came back around into Calipari's fist like a brick wall falling down. Jona's nose cracked, broken. Sergeant Calipari pushed Jona's hands with the clean paper up against his bloody face like a handkerchief. He got some fresh paper for himself.

"Stay out here," said Calipari. "I'm going to set the girl's nose in a minute. I'll come back out for yours when I'm done." said Sergeant Calipari. "You can wait a while, like she did."

Calipari's hand had streaks of Jona's blood on it. If there was a candle nearby it might catch fire. If he rubbed it on a handkerchief, the cloth would be moth-eaten by the end of the hour, and ash by the end of the day. The paper was already falling apart in Jona's hands. He tried desperately to keep the blood from his jacket. He had a couple spare uniforms his mother had sewn to hide how fast he went through shirts, but they were all at home.

Jona laughed through the blood and the shooting pain. Every day was another day he could be found out, killed for his blood, burned alive for being alive. "Go wash your hand," he said, to Calipari. He wanted to scream it. Then, an afterthought, struggling to find a reason the Sergeant would do it. "You don't want the girl to see the blood on your hand. She's already scared."

Calipari wiped his hand off on the fresh paper and tossed the crumpled sheet into a rubbish bin. "Keep laughing, I'll break your jaw, too," he said. "And don't pretend like you care about that girl, or I'll break your jaw." He was so busy glaring at Jona, he didn't seem to notice the paper falling apart in the bin.

With the scriveners out walking patrols, there was no one else at the station. If Calipari didn't notice, Jona'd be safe, and Calipari was about to go into the interrogation room. Calipari wasn't going to be rummaging around in a rubbish bin staring at the blood eating through all the papers there, melting everything to ash. But if someone else came in…

Jona stopped thinking because he realized he was being lectured, and he was going to have to listen hard if he was to going to get Calipari out of the room.

"You're a good guard most of the time," said Sergeant Calipari. "Ain't the first time something's gotten to you. You've gone too far. You've been working too hard. Take a couple days. Plan something with your ma. Or a girl. Something. Just get it on my desk by tomorrow morning, and I'll approve anything that says you're gone a few days with no pay."

Jona's nose had stopped bleeding. The clots had melted into his skin around the wounded places itching with a burn even as the clots closed the wound. His wounds didn't just hurt; the acid burned him a little, like a bad rash. He wiped away the blood with the paper he had. He didn't have much time to hide it, and Calipari was standing right there. Jona folded it up into a ball. He shoved it in his mouth and let it settle there. It didn't taste good. It didn't even taste like blood. It tasted like smoke and mercury. Jona glared at Calipari when he did this. Then, he swallowed the limp, wet, fading mass whole. He reached up to his nose, and pulled the bone out from where it was snapped. Then, he pushed it back close enough into place. It made a horrible crackling and hurt worse than the punch. Jona's eyes welled up. He clenched his jaw and felt pain all the way down to his toes. He grabbed a handful of paper for the blood coming. He held all the pain back. He held it all into just a glare. "Go wash your hands, Sergeant," he said, calmly now. "You'll scare the girl, you walk in stinking of my blood. Don't want to contaminate your tests with my blood, do you?"

Sergeant Calipari winced. "You good to walk around a while?"

"I'm good, Sergeant."

"Go get something we can use, a plant or something. I'll hand out that handkerchief she used, and you can use that, right? Demon blood kills plants fast. That's what I hear."

Jona nodded. "That's right, Sergeant."

Calipari dipped his hand in a cistern full of water at the side of the room. He dried his hands, and picked up an empty trash bin from beside a desk. He held it up to his chest, pressing one hand into his guts. He threw up into it. "Must be getting too old," he said. "Eating blood, you sick bastard…" He put the rubbish bin down and wiped his face clean. "You still here? I need a plant."

"I know," said Jona. "Making sure you're all right."

"You're the one busted his nose and I'm the one sick. Get out of here."

The two men looked at each other, neither one moving an inch. Finally, after a long moment, Jona moved towards the door. Calipari went in to talk to the girl. When Calipari was inside the room, Jona picked up the rubbish bin with Calipari's vomit, and the one with the smoldering papers from his bloody nose. He rushed outside, hefted open a sewer grate, and dropped them both inside. He thought about changing the water in the cistern, but that would take too long. Instead, he'd just have to get a plant. He'd pollute the plant before anyone came to use the cistern, then before anyone could, the whole place would have to be purified.

Calipari was too good at interrogations to be left alone with the girl. Jona had to hurry. When Calipari came into the station house with the bloody handkerchief from her, Jona was still running after a plant. Calipari was about to leave the handkerchief on a desk and go back in to talk to the girl, when Jona ran back in, with an apple in his hand. He held it up to Calipari. "Got this," he said.

"Will that work?"

Jona shrugged.

Calipari handed Jona the handkerchief. "If it's clean, you tell me. Then go home," he said, "I'm sick of you."

"You got it, Sergeant," said Jona, saluting.

Sergeant Calipari disappeared into the room.

Jona spit on the apple to start its rotting. That wasn't fast enough. Jona wiped it against his sore nose, where some thick, partially-clotted blood oozed onto it. The apple withered where the blood touched it.

Jona put his own blood upon the handkerchief, just in case. He only put a little bit, to let the cloth melt a little, like a cavity in a tooth. When it looked good, he walked into the interrogation room. The girl was abashed and staring at her hands. Calipari was silent, waiting for something to happen.

Jona placed the apple on the table with the searing wound facing Calipari.

The sergeant took a deep breath. He looked up at Jona, confused. The two men stepped outside again.

"We're testing her again," Calipari said.

"Yeah," said Jona. "You were the one grabbed her nose, when she was bleeding. I just punched her once. You stay here. I'll get the plants. No one else comes in. Keep it contained."

Calipari did not appear to be listening. "I want to be sure," he said, to the apple.

Unspoken in the room was the promise of the wooden stake, and the fire around it. Jona was going to kill this girl. He was doing it, and it was turning out to be easier then he ever imagined.

Jona, in the street, found onion plants for sale in pots. He took three in the name of the king.

He looked down at the doomed plants. He wasn't even sorry about these three little onions. He knew what he was supposed to feel for the girl, and it was little more to him than what he felt for these onions.

If he was a normal man, he'd be trying to save her—because she was beautiful, because it wasn't her fault, because all she wanted was freedom in the night. He wanted to feel like someone who would try to save her. He wanted to feel something about her that wasn't about himself.

***

I tried to keep her safe, Salvatore. I didn't plan it, but it worked out this way. Just me trying to do something. I'm just not smart enough. What's going to happen to your girl is my fault, you know.

What girl?

You don't remember her?

Maybe. Remind me what her name was?

Aggie, and if we don't do something to save her…

Wait, the convent girl, right? She was a good kid. She didn't know what she was doing. She never did. If she's in trouble, we should do something.

That's what I'm saying. I'll try to fix this, okay? You can get her out, and take her away for a while. I figure, we help her out, you and me. She'll figure out what you really are, eventually, but she won't go to anyone about it on account of being an escaped convict. Then, when she dumps you, she'll be free of everything, and she can be happy somewhere new.

I want to help. I'm sorry about what happened to her. I really am. What can we do?

I'm trying. Get out of my face. My nose is killing me. I want to break your nose, for this.

Not with my blood. Stay out of my shadows, for once, blood monkey.

***

Jona dropped some of the blood from his abused nose onto the dirt around a fresh onion plants. The plant browned very slightly at the edge of its leaves, but it didn't die right away. It would take time to get into the roots of the plant. Jona spit on it, for good measure. His spit was toxic, too, just not as toxic.

In the room, Sergeant Calipari put a few drops of drying blood from the girl's busted nose onto the onion plant. They waited, and watched the plant. It didn't happen quickly. It browned at the edge of the leaves, and slowly spread from there. The root sickened and melted into a dead paste. The plant collapsed.

Calipari cocked his head. He stood up, but he didn't seem to know where he was going. He sat down again. "Imam tests the girls, doesn't he? Anchorites test their girls?"

"Apparently, not," said Jona. "Want me to get another plant?"

"Yes."

The girl's eyes were like saucers. She rubbed her stomach. She seemed to want to curl into it. What was happening was not clear to her. I imagine it would be like finding out she was a fish, and everyone knew it once they looked at her in the right light, while all this time she thought she was a person. It would take a long time to sink in. The fact that it was a lie only made it more difficult.

Jona returned to the main room, where he had set the remaining plants on one of the scrivener's desks. He pulled the same trick with the second plant and brought it back into the interrogation room.

Sergeant Calipari was slumped in his seat. He seemed almost as defeated as Aggie did. He didn't want this for anyone. He never wanted this in his jurisdiction. "Anything you're not telling us?"

She struggled to find words. There were none. She closed her mouth and stared down at her stomach.

Calipari took blood from the girl's finger this time, pricked with the edge of a dagger. The blood fell on the plant's center stalk. They stared at the plant, waiting for it to wilt.

Nobody breathed.

The fringe of the flower curled first, and then the edge of the leaves, and then everything in the plant withered unto death.

Jona exhaled first. He leaned against the closed door. "If we find any more like you, we'll drag them in here and burn them just like we're going to burn you," he said. "If anyone hid you, or helped you, they burn, too. Whether you understand it or not, that's the way things are." She wouldn't betray Salvatore if she didn't betray him right now.

She shook her head, white as death. "No," she whispered.

"I can't believe I'm saying this," said Sergeant Calipari. "Take her to the cell farthest back. Keep her separated. Put up signs. Put up warnings. Keep the building closed down until we can.... I need to get a message to the Captain."

Jona wrapped bindings around the girl's hands. Would they test her again? Would it matter? As soon as Jona let the carpenter know what had happened, the Night King would speed things along. Aggie would be isolated. Her demon-stained blood was too dangerous to allow in the presence of anyone who hadn't yet been exposed. Calipari's testimony would be enough to stand in court, if it ever came to it, and Lord Joni's sworn testimony as a nobleman wouldn't hurt. But it never came to that. Demon children are not considered human. They have no right to trial. She'd burn as soon as people got tired of trying to find out how she managed to hide so long. She'd never say anything.

"And Jona," said Sergeant Calipari.

"Yes?"

"Don't... touch her," he said. "Burn the plants."

***

That night, Sergeant Calipari couldn't sleep. He told me this himself. Calipari held a pillow in his arms the night Aggie tested true, and he imagined it was Franka, off at the edge of the city in her tavern with the son that looked to Calipari like a father. It made him sick what he had encountered that day, like running into an invisible wall. He ran a fever for three days. He coughed up blood. When he was well enough to walk, he spent hours at the temples, drinking blessed things, and sweating out the stain. He thought it was from the girl. All the station house was washed in holy water. The carriage was burned, with the clothes the men wore when she bled inside the carriage. The nuns burned her sheets and clothes on the tile roof, and the cloth popped and snapped with the wicked stain she had carried home from her nights with Salvatore.

Calipari never wrote to Franka, out where she worked beyond the city walls, to tell her that he had found a demon's child. When he felt better, he burned his own sheets, and the mattress. He had a priest come through from Imam's temple to clean the room for good. The king replaced everything, and paid for the priest. Reimbursement for Calipari's expenses came with a royal seal. The handwriting under the seal was clean and precise, like a woman's trained script. It was probably Lady Ela Sabachthani's.

The more Calipari thought about it, the less he liked it.

And Lord Joni, who had damned this girl to spare a demon's child, was home a few days, feigning illness. When the priest came from the king, Jona took him up to an empty room of the house, one never used anymore. Jona said he had quarantined himself there, and had already burned everything. The priest of Imam cleared the stains away from the room with holy water, not fireseeds. He didn't realize how old and deep the stain ran. Even after one purification, flowers placed on the floor rotted in an hour. The priest scrubbed the room, floor-to-ceiling, in holy water. He offered to clean the whole, huge, empty house. Jona shook his head. He said they couldn't afford it, and the king wouldn't pay for it. He said he had been careful, and had planned for that, and had confined himself only in that one room, while his mother burned everything that came out of it. Jona promised to lock the room shut, never use it again until they could afford to get it really purified.

That lie reluctantly accepted, Jona went to a tavern, and then another, and then another. He pissed in the middle of the street. He lit matches and burned his own puddles of urine, like spilled kerosene. People thought it was a magic trick, like those the Sentas pulled. They cheered for it. But Jona didn't have the face of an entertainer. If they got a good look at him, they stopped cheering and walked away.

Jona, sobered up when he found Salvatore at the next tavern. Salvatore was dancing the jewels from a teenaged girl's neck. Jona pulled the thief away, into an alley. He told Salvatore the bad news.

Salvatore couldn't remember Aggie's name. He remembered she was a nun. He remembered that he cared about her. He couldn't remember anything else.

CHAPTER XIII

Days passed, and weeks, and maybe more. Memories do not keep good calendars.

Jona and the boys were in a dive hidden between the troubled warehouses north of the Pens waiting on this great band of musicians was coming through. The band never showed, and instead a troupe of drunk actors claimed the stage, singing lewd songs with perfect pitch and close harmony. Men had thrown their glasses or spilled their drinks or spewed their drinks because they were laughing so hard.

When the show was over, the crowd lingered in the bar by the stage, and the boys drank like gutters. It was Geek, Jona, Tripoli, and the two young scriveners full of sand after their first real action in a uniform, a day Calipari sent them out patrolling. The scriveners were chattering about this thing in the Pens the other day, and trying to talk tough about taking down brick-batters that wanted to smash a fellow's skull until the privates cut the handles off their brick-bats with swords and smacked the fighters with the flat of the blades and one of the fighters bought it when he tried to get on top of the private, but the kid had stuck his blade in the fellow's belly and he wanted to stand up to tell the story, to show it was just like this, how he had killed someone evil in the name of the king...

Jona stood up and glared at the private. "You think you're so tough, why you pushing a quill all day instead of walking the Pens?"

The private looked up at Jona.

"You so tough?" Jona grabbed the private by his shoulders and shoved him back away from the table. "Tough boy. Let's see you take me down. I won't pull nothin' but a fist. We'll see who wins."

The private didn't move.

Geek placed a hand on Jona's arm. "Let them have their day in the sun, Jona."

"Yeah, one day in the sun? Two? Me and the other boys are in the sun pushing meat around every day when those kids're pushing quills. Don't be acting all rowdy when you're nothing."

Geek stood up next to Jona. He tapped Jona's shoulder.

Jona turned. "What?"

Geek smiled, grandfather-like. He was a big, soft guy, with lots of muscle beneath his weight. He knew his way around Jona's moods. He smiled, and raised his hands in surrender. But he wasn't giving up to Jona. He was pushing Jona back. "Don't you think you should find somewhere else a while? Plenty people we don't need working in the morning you can throw around instead of our own people."

"What are you talking about?" said Jona. "They're just getting on my nerves."

"I'm asking you nice," said Geek. "You start this with him, and he's out for a week with busted everything, and you know Calipari'll make you take his desk once he finds out."

Jona looked over at his boys. Everyone was eying him like he was ruining a perfectly good evening. And he was. He nodded. "I'm going somewhere else because I'm nice, and because Geek asked me nice," said Jona. Then, to the scrivener he had thrown back, he snarled, "If you touch me, I'll break your arm off. What's your name, anyhow? You're new."

"Pup's my name," he said. "It's what people call me, anyhow."

"Well, you watch it, Pup. You're nothing after one day in

the sun."

Pup was smart enough not to respond.

Jona had drunk plenty to get this angry, and after being this angry he wanted to get drunk to get more angry. He stumbled into the street. He looked up and down the road, and he didn't see a thing. He saw the same things over and over every night. He saw people moving and milling and hopping in and out of the taverns and theatres and animal pens and shops and secret backroom casinos along the trouble at the stinking edge where the warehouses met the Pens. He'd seen them all. He'd done them all.

Jona didn't know what he was going to do now. He didn't have a job for the Night King, hadn't for a while since Aggie was condemned. He wondered if he could volunteer for anything, see if the carpenter needed someone killed tonight. But showing up drunk would only get him killed, and volunteering for more was not the way things worked with them. He was their blood monkey, and that was all. Like a dog, he obeyed, and did nothing more.

So Jona was bored. He didn't want to drink. He didn't want to gamble. He didn't want to steal. He didn't want to talk to any of the people he knew. He didn't want to do anything.

He wanted to find something new—a new tavern, a new restaurant, a new play, a new anything.

He wanted—but he wouldn't admit it to himself, or even realize it—to fall in love.

***

Jona was alone, putting one foot in front of the other, and looking for his birdie in one of the local gangs so they could go drinking and Jona could make the birdie sing without a fist for a change. He couldn't find him. He didn't know if the fellow was down in the pink pits sucking Demon weed from a hookah, or if he was already drunk somewhere else.

He looked up at the moon hung like a silver earring on a veiled face. He stopped where he was and leaned against the nearest wall, watching all the people walking somewhere, so intently. He had nowhere to go. Nobody looked over at him—their eyes stopped at the uniform. His face might as well have been a black mask.

As Jona lingered there, a gorgeous carriage turned into a nearby alley, headed toward the brothel that way. The bells had all been wrapped in black cloth, and the noble insignia was obscured with drapes in an attempt at anonymity.

Jona recognized the carriage. Lord Elitrean's son was shameless... as long as everyone pretended they didn't know his name. Jona, feeling wild himself, decided to grind the young buck's horns down a bit. He wanted to do something that wasn't boring. He wanted to do something new. He thought he wanted this. He thought it would be a quick laugh, and maybe a lecture later. He didn't realize this night, this impulsive act, was going to lead him to the thing he had been seeking without knowing it for weeks, months, maybe years.

Jona jogged to keep up with the carriage. The coach stopped back in the brothel's rear entrance. Lord Elitrean's son disappeared before Jona could get there. The coachman smoked a cigar and leaned against the vehicle. He knew he was in for a long night tonight.

Jona walked up to him. "Whose carriage is this?" he barked, "You, tell me whose carriage this is!"

"This is nobody's carriage," said the coachmen. "Owner ain't here."

"Yeah?" said Jona. "You steal it so you can smuggle?"

"This is a lord's business," said the coachman, "and if he wants to keep the carriage black, then it's black."

"How I know your 'lord' is no smuggler pretending when his family crest is covered up like this?"

The coachman shrugged. "You want me to strip the drapes, I strip the drapes. But Lord Elitrean's son will just put them right back on and come down on you like a knife. Don't be complaining to me when he does."

"Give them to me," Jona snapped.

The coachman did as he was told.

Inside the brothel, Jona shouted away the ragged children who begged beside the old stairs. They kept crowding him. He threw the expensive black satin out to them, a distraction. They shrieked at their gift, tearing at the expensive cloth like sharks, and running off with their scraps.

The mistress of the brothel nervously fluttered over to stop Jona in the stairway. Jona announced, at the top of his lungs, that he had come for Lord Elitrean's rogue son. Doors opened and closed, some clicking locked.

Jona pushed past the owner, and snarled at the whole house, again. He kicked open the first door he saw, but it wasn't Elitrean's son. The next door wasn't, either.

Women screamed and tried to cover themselves.

The owner ran up behind Jona, and begged privacy for her guests, offering a large bribe. Jona threw the money on the floor. More money appeared. Jona smacked it away.

"Tear the place down, then," she shouted, "And don't be looking for me when your wick needs burning."

The children, a flock of pigeons, snatched up as much of the spilled bribe money as they could. The owner cursed them, kicking at them, but she couldn't stop them. The children faded into empty rooms and closets.

Jona laughed.

Lord Elitrean's son waited in a room with a sword in his hand, a half-naked woman hiding behind the bed.

"Are you the man shouting for me?"

"Yeah. I'm Lord Joni," said Jona. "This was all my estate before the war."

"You're really a king's man? I thought you wore the uniform to sneak into parties," said the young lord. He sheathed his blade.

"I am a king's man, and I'm sick of all your parties, and I'm sick of you. You aren't on your own lands here," Jona sneered.

"Are you hiding behind the King's service?"

"Are you hiding in a brothel? I stripped your carriage of drapes, and exposed your house seal. If I catch you with an unmarked carriage, I'll strip it again. How you run things on your grounds is your business, but in the King's City, you will not get away with destroying your family's honor in hiding."

"My father will hear about this."

"I'm sure he already knows what you do. He'll give me a prize for trying to stop you."

The young nobleman looked back at the woman hiding behind the bed. "I'm not paying you," he said, and pushed past Jona, past the apologetic owner, and into the main street. Jona followed him, watching to make sure he got into his carriage and left.

When he was gone, Jona smiled. He turned to the owner. "So, got anyone new?"

"You get out of here!" she shouted. "Calipari won't like it you making a scene!"

Jona laughed. "My money not heavy enough for you? I want a girl, healthy and strong, and new. Who you got for me?"

"Nobody," snarled the owner. "The Sergeant won't mind I throw you out hard after what you just did in my house!"

"Go get him, then. See what he says."

She backed away looking angry enough that she just might.

Jona laughed. He went back into the brothel, and back upstairs to the room where Elitrean had been having his fun. Inside, the woman had come out of hiding. She was washing her naked chest in a basin of fresh water. She looked up at Jona without covering herself. "You next?" she said. "Must have wanted me bad to chase him off."

Jona smirked. "Something like that."

"Sixteen for the business. Anything special, you pay more."

"How much just to touch you a bit?"

"Touch me? Where?"

"Anywhere."

"Sixteen."

"Even if there isn't any business?"

"You know I'm worth it."

"Guess so," said Jona. "Stand next to the bed."

All she had on was her skirt. She stood where she was, with her hands up behind her head, waiting near the bed. Jona counted sixteen coins from his pockets, carefully placing each coin one by one on the table. He was surprised he had enough.

At the bed, Jona cupped each of her breasts. They felt heavy, like they were full of water. A little milk leaked from one of her nipples. He thought about taking her, and leaving her reeling and ill. But the milk meant she had a child hidden here, and if she got sick, her child would, too. He stopped. He shrugged at her. "Right then," he said, "sixteen well spent. Now get out of here."

"What? All that trouble, and that's it?"

"Go on," he said. "Get out of here. I want to be alone awhile. Now get going."

"I got other customers."

"Not tonight. Tell your boss to find a new room for you. I'm staying here a while."

"How long?"

"Long as I want," he said, "Now get out of here!" He slapped her lightly on her backside. Annoyed, she quickly poured the money into a bag, then pulled a robe over her shoulders. She disappeared into the hall.

Jona wiped his wet hand off on the bedsheets.

Jona didn't know why he had done what he had just done to Lord Elitrean's son, or to the woman in the room. He knew he had wanted to do it, and that no one would really stop him. So he did it. He wondered what he wanted to do next, and couldn't think of anything right away.

Jona looked around, wondering if he could find something

incriminating to justify this whole idiotic night. If he was really lucky, the owner would come in with some thugs and he could fight them and then everything would be sensible and right with the world, beating down the rough men and bouncers that brothels always drag in off the street.

Jona smiled at that thought, and snatched a heavy glass perfume bottle off a cabinet. He pulled the pillow out of its case, and turned the perfume bottle and the pillowcase into a makeshift blackjack. He slipped beside the doorway to surprise anyone who came in from looking for a fight.

He heard footsteps in the hall.

When the door opened, he raised his improvised blackjack, ready to shatter a heady stink all over whoever came through the door. He expected trouble.

A maid pushed a mop bucket into the room, dressed like a Senta.

Jona frowned. "That's it, then." He lowered his weapon.

The Senta startled and jumped away from him, tripping over herself and the mop bucket and the mop, falling over. She landed hard on her elbows.

Jona winced. "I was expecting someone else." He bent over her to help her up. "Sorry."

The Senta snarled at him. She snapped her fingers and fire singed Jona's face. It caught easily on his clothes and the sweat stain in the fabric started to singe and burn. Jona startled. He beat at his collar and rushed over to the water basin in the room. He threw filthy water on it.

"Bloody Senta," he said, dabbing at his uniform, "Look, it was an accident! You shouldn't burn a king's man. It's the same as burning the king himself!"

She stood up and adjusted her thick clothes. "The king should be burned for letting you thugs run around!"

Jona balled up his fist, but hesitated. "People don't say that to our faces," he said, instead of hitting. If he struck her, she'd probably set his clothes on fire, and the sweat stains would burn through the cloth before he could douse it all.

"People should!" said the Senta. Jona walked over, still thinking about striking her, and if he could hit her hard enough in one shot to knock her out while she was busy standing up.

She punched first. She got Jona hard, right on his nose. "Don't come near me!"

Blood. Blood all over her hand.

Jona held his breath. He clutched at his nose, and pinched it. "You shouldn't have done that." He leaned back and felt the blood seeping into his sinus cavity and into the back of his throat. He coughed.

The blood caught the edge of her long sleeves. It started to singe the cloth.

Jona smiled even through all the pain and fear, and had to try not to laugh. She'd see that. She'd see that, and he'd be done with everything. As soon as she saw that, his life was over. Even killing her wouldn't save him. Calipari would hang him for that. She wasn't some brain dead pinker, or a thug on the street. She was decent people, working hard at something.

She looked down at her sleeve, how it cooked. She beat at it.

"Don't." Jona's life flashed before his eyes. He had been lucky last time, with Calipari, that the sergeant had washed his hands before he saw how the blood had gotten on his sleeve, and anyway it all could be blamed on Aggie's broken nose.

"What is this?"

"Nothing," Jona said. "Wash your hand. Come on. Get that blood off it."

"Is this…?"

"Listen, I'm sorry I scared you. I was just bored. I thought Elitrean'd send someone tough, and I'd bust a perfume bottle on 'em for a laugh. I meant nothing by it. I swear I didn't mean to scare you, or do any real harm to anybody. Please…"

Jona should have felt more fear than this. Always, hanging over his head, running through the streets and the night, the threat of it: a bleeding wound. Now he was begging for his life.

"I don't care what you're doing here," said the Senta. "You should get something for your nose."

"It got broke a bit ago," he said. "It's not important. Please…" He pinched his nose shut, trying to stop the bleeding.

She frowned. She pulled some wet rags from her pocket and wiped at the blood on her hands and sleeves. Her hand was shaking. She offered the rags to Jona. "Soapy washcloth?" she said, "Slightly used, but still covered in soap. Might keep it from burning your shirt off."

Jona shrugged. "Why not?" He took the washcloth from her fingers.

"You…" said the woman.

"What?" he said. His eyebrows creased.

"Your blood is eating my sleeve. It's like an acid."

"I'm not," he said, forcefully. "Don't be crazy. Elishta's been sealed a thousand years."

"Right, I know. You know I'm Senta. I could find these things out."

"So go find these things out, and find out I'm not."

"Some demons' children are exceptionally long-lived."

"If you're such a Senta, why you cleaning up after whores?"

"I do what I must. Would you prefer I joined the city guard?"

"Of course not," Jona sighed. "It's just weird. Aren't you supposed to be on a corner with dice or cards or something?" He thought his voice sounded crazy with all that blood in his throat. It was hard to try and talk out of this problem when there was so much blood.

"Not every Senta finds the koans of dreamcasting in her heart." She snapped her fingers again, and a splash of fire sparked in mid-air.

"What's your name?"

"What's it to you what my name is, king's man?"

"Nothing, I guess," he said. "You like it here? You know, cleaning up brothels."

She nodded. "I like it fine."

"Well, if you need anything, you look me up, and we don't tell anybody about the blood, okay? It's not what you think it is, and a rumor can kill me over nothing when it's about my blood. My name's Sergeant Calipari," he said. "Sergeant Nicola Calipari."

"Nicola," she repeated, her expression grave. "I will."

"I have to go take care of this."

"Okay."

***

Jona left Rachel there, in the messy room alone. He rushed back to his own home to clean the blood off his uniform and out of his fingers, and make sure his nose wasn't going to open up again. If Jona's blood touched grass, the grass would die too fast to be inconspicuous.

He ran through the dark. He pushed through all the shadows in the street to run home to the light of his mother's kitchen. He ran, feeling his way around through darkness, pushing up to the basin where the old pipes still carried water from the river. He pumped water into the sink. He held one hand under the surface, then another. He washed at himself with old rags he'd have to burn.

He heard his mother's soft feet coming down the creaky stairs. He heard her bare feet padding across the room. He felt her hand on his arm.

"Jona," she said, "Are you all right?"

Jona nodded. "I'm fine, Ma."

He was lying. His stomach burned.

She rubbed his arm. She wrapped an arm around him.

"I said I'm fine," he said. "You need to stay back."

She held him. He didn't push her away. "You have to work in the morning," he said.

"Are you going to be all right?"

"I don't know," he said. "I don't know."

"Do you want to talk about it?"

"My nose opened up again. I got scared, that's all," said Jona. "I just got really scared that someone might find out about me."

"Did someone find out?"

"No," Jona said, "I just got scared."

"Don't be," she said. "How's your nose now, Jona?" She reached for his face.

He flinched away from her. "It's better. Don't touch it, ma."

"I never wanted you to be a king's man. It's dangerous. More so for you than anyone. Clean up your mess before you go to bed," she said. "I'd do it for you if I could. Good night, Jona."

"Ma, what do I do if someone finds out about me?"

She walked back to the stairs, quietly.

"What do I do if someone finds out?"

Her steps up were so slow, like each one was a sunset coming down all heavy in a valley. Her steps were so slow. Jona listened to them, and to how quiet it was between her steps.

Silence was a word, right then.

***

We hide all the time. I hide all the time.

Rachel sniffed the blood again. She definitely smelled the touch of Elishta on it. It smelled just like hers. Djoss taught Rachel her whole life to keep her blood hidden and burned. Her mother taught her that, before her brother did. When the women's dilemma arrived, she had to use rags and burn them to ash in private. If she cut a finger she had to cover it with candle wax and cloth to keep it completely sealed. People got sick around her blood.

Rachel rushed the blood-spattered sponge and rags into an abandoned strip of grass behind the brothel. She found a few blades of green grass. She sprinkled the blood on the grass. The blades withered like they were in a drought. She held her breath and tried the little experiment again with a larger plant. That plant died, too. Already, the acid had eaten through the rags, pooled in her palms in ruined ash, blown away in the wind like sand.

She had never met another like herself before in her whole life.

CHAPTER XIV

We moved here. It's better in this place. Cleaner.

"You work on the other side of the Pens, right?" Djoss was standing at the door, his arms folded. "You're by that one river—the bigger one."

Rachel sat up in her cot and stretched. "If I see you in the brothel where I'm changing those disgusting sheets all night long, I'll burn your bare behind," she said. "Don't worry about where I work."

"I'm not—look, I found a room over by there. This butcher has a whole building in the place next to his shop. He owns the block. You'll be closer."

"What about yours?"

"A few extra blocks won't kill me."

"Won't kill me either."

"It's nicer than this."

"Who needs nice? We need to stay hidden, Djoss. We need to stay out of trouble, pinch every coin, be ready to run."

Djoss sighed. He told the truth of it. "Turco needs this room," he said. "We need a nice hidden place. You and me can go be inconspicuous somewhere else."

Rachel fell back into her cot. "Baker know about that?"

"Baker won't mind, the money we'll bring in."

"Those crates wearing down?"

"Something like that," said Djoss. "Tired of working for other people. We're going to do our own thing."

"You ever smoke any of that stuff?"

"A little bit," he said. "Need to when you pick it up. Make sure it's good. If it ain't, I bust heads. I've had to bust heads a couple times already. Folks skim off the top, sell on the side. Lots of bad stuff out there."

"Djoss…"

"Better than bouncing. Safer then that. No drunks. Turco did you a favor, too, didn't he? Got you a job."

"Yeah, he did."

"So let's move," said Djoss. "Nice place. A window we can open when it's hot. No oven over our heads. Not so sweaty, so we don't need so many hammocks and cots. Come on, let's go. It'll be better."

"I'm wearing everything I own," she said. "I'm ready to go. I'm always ready to go, Djoss. Don't get too deep into anything. Don't make good friends. We can't stay here forever. We can't stay anywhere." Rachel stood up and adjusted her clothes. She was laced up tight. "They're waiting outside, aren't they?"

Djoss opened the door. Turco came in first. His red clothes were worn through in the seams. His skin was ashen. He bowed to Rachel, like a gentleman.

"Found you a new place," he said.

"Thanks, I guess."

"Could be more grateful than that," said Turco. "I try to do right, and nobody ever's grateful. Not polite."

Dog came in behind him. He walked into a corner. He touched the warm brick where the baker's ovens poured heat down into the ground, leaning into it and closing his eyes. He turned around to look at Rachel, leaning back into the warm stones.

Turco placed a hand on Djoss' shoulder. "This'll do fine. Gonna start our own thing here. No more other people's weed. Make the real money."

Rachel wanted to do more, to say more. There was nothing she could do. As horrible as Turco seemed to be, he had found her a job. In that old alley, he made room for people that didn't have anywhere else to go. He had found her brother a job, too. As much as she hated it, he was her brother's friend. He was finding her a new place instead of just throwing her out. It was hard to think of it that way, but it was true. This man, and his mute friend, were actually being as nice as they could manage.

"Turco, I'm grateful. I'm also kind of terrified that you're going to get my brother killed. Are you going to get my brother killed?"

Turco smiled. His teeth were as red as his clothes, and more ragged. "You worry too much," he said. "Plenty good stuff for everybody."

She took a deep breath. She went to Dog, and pulled him off the bricks before he burned himself. He was deep in the weed. His eyes couldn't focus. She sat him down in a different corner where he could still feel the heat, but wouldn't burn.

"He's a bit… Well, Djoss'll be watching the door. Dog's getting a little too pink for that."

Turco could have abandoned Dog, too, but he didn't. Dog was hanging on, always hanging on. She was, too, in her way.

"Who's going to be carrying the meat?" Rachel asked.

"Ragpickers, mostly," said Turco. "Little mudskippers be dividing it up, sneaking it in. Plenty coming in off the ships. Plenty for everybody, I think. Djoss'll be working here, watching for trouble, carrying meat if it's too heavy for the ragpickers."

Rachel nodded. This man was her brother's friend, and he was trying to help them. "You said this new place has a window?"

"Won't be so hot there, either, with the window," said Turco. "This is better for us. Demon weed cools you down a lot. Thins the blood." He looked over at Dog and laughed. "He's going to be mean when he comes down. Anything you need help moving?"

Rachel touched Dog's naked skull. She looked into his glassy eyes. She wanted to shout and run away from Dogsland that night. She wondered what it was like for the man she had met, in the brothel, whose nose she had punched and who had a life here, too. She'd never know anything about the man with burning blood if she ran. She smiled. "I'm ready to go," she said, sadly. "We can leave the furniture if you need it."

***

The new place was on the second story, with clean wood floors. The place had a wash tub, a decent stove, and a clothesline out the window, overlooking a narrow street.

Rachel pushed open the shutters and leaned out. The butcher kept some of his animals two buildings away, and the big killing yard of the Pens was on the other side of that and two more buildings down. Women aired their laundry out on the ropes between the bricks above the heads of playing children. The wind smelled of the slaughter houses of the district, but the stench of death also carried layers of turnips and cabbage and onions and the cloth diapers boiling clean.

"This is much better," she said. "Be sure to tell Turco thank you for me."

"I'll see about two new cots when I get back," he said.

Rachel frowned at her brother. "Where are you going?"

"Where do you think?" he said. "Got to get to work."

"Oh." She frowned. "Okay."

Rachel locked the door behind him. She touched the solid wood walls, all clean and painted with white wash. She knew bouncers and maids didn't get apartments like this, even in neighborhoods near the Pens. Money must be coming in, then.

Rachel went to her new window. She leaned out to follow his broad and strong shoulders down to the end of the street. He turned the wrong way to be going back to the old room.

There wasn't anything she could do about it.

Rachel sat in the corner, legs folded and eyes closed. She tried to call on the powers of dreamcasting again. She wanted something small from the fates. She wanted to see the fate of one night, or one face, or anything.

She opened her mind's eye slowly. She let the feeling of the dreams drift in from the top of her head like wet silk. She saw a wide gray plane, with darker shadows of visual mumbles. She heard the muffled rumblings of voices—a conversation caught in pillows. She stayed there, struggling with the koans, clearing her mind of all her sorrows and fears.

Djoss shook her awake. She had fallen asleep in a corner. It was the middle of the night. Djoss asked her what she was doing. He had brought back a bed. She had fallen asleep meditating, with her legs crossed and her hair pressed against a wall.

She shrugged. "I guess I was making my legs stiff," she said, "Help me get up."

He pulled her up into the cot. "Well, I only got the one cot for now. You can use it."

"Hey," she said, "Look at me. Can we afford all this?"

"Of course not," he said. "Why'd you think it took me so long to get it?"

"Be careful," she said. "If you're arrested and I have to run…"

He walked back to the door. "We don't have a choice, Rachel," he said. "We have nowhere else to go, and nothing else to do but this. It's this, or it's nothing."

"That's not true. We could just run," she said, "We don't have to stay here."

He smiled, sadly. "I like it here. It's been a long time since we've had a chance to settle down a little, make friends."

"You make friends. I never do. Djoss, we have to think about how we're going to run."

"We will, but we'll be fine here a while. I can feel it. This is a good place for us. I need to go. I'll bring you breakfast."

Rachel fell back on the cot. She looked up at the ceiling. She considered going down to the neighborhood fountain for water. She considered waiting for ice to melt, if she pulled upon a koan. She chose the spell. She put the first chunk of ice in her mouth to drink the water of it. The second chunk she pulled from the air went into the tub, and then another and another.

She considered the man she had found in that brothel, and what he might do if he was truly like her. He might be scared of what she knew. He might run away. He might be evil. He might try and kill her if he got scared.

It was hard to focus on anything when she got to thinking about him. All the strange things she had grown up hearing all her life—the wickedness of the demon children, the terror they brought to the world and the sickness, could not coagulate into a clear understanding of a king's man hiding behind the door for a prank with a perfume bottle in a pillowcase. They should have been plotting the rise of Elishta and the Nameless. Instead, she was pushing a mop in a brothel, and he was pushing people down in the Pens, where nobody ever plotted anything. If she could find him again, she'd want to talk to him. She wondered what his life was like.

The ice melted slowly. She placed her hand onto the surface of the water, and pulled the fire of her blood into a heat all through the water. Ice dissipated. Steam welled up from the tub.

All these tricks from the Senta koans, and all she ever used them for was lighting the cookfire or heating the bathwater and sometimes showing off to scare away a trouble. Magic could win wars, but what use was winning wars to people with no nation? Seeing the future in dreamcasting rarely meant anyone could avoid the patterns of their life. Boiling the water, lighting the cookfire: *that* was useful. The Senta sat on the street corners with tarot cards and for a coin they'd tell you if he loved you or he loved you not. They never tried for more—humility, always humility with the koans.

If she saw the man again, she'd try to find out more about him. She'd try to talk to Turco about him. She'd try to do something. The pattern of her life had to change.

She stripped off her clothes, and slipped into the water.

***

My husband found her first rented room. There weren't many bakers near the Pens. Jona had never even been inside. He had watched her walking here, once, along a street he knew all the days of his life until he could remember things and never have to remember where they happened. A lamppost was enough, for him, or the angle of a building on a corner. I had to push through his mind.

The bakery with the basement room was where it had always been, waiting for us to find it.

My husband and I walked inside and down, under the ovens, to the muddy basement. Rainwater collected in pools and runnels. The bricks were rotting. Large wooden posts lined the walls, and braced the ceiling.

We stepped among the people there sleeping in sacks, sitting in dirt, and resting along the walls where the heat wasn't so hard on their backs. They didn't even look up at us.

We had blessed apples, and dandelion wine. We poured out the wine into the rainwater puddles. Fireseeds would never clean the mud in this damp room. Not even burning the building would dig deep into the groundwater, here. We placed blessed apples in a basket in the center of the room. Wolves lived better than this, among the meadows and hills.

Upstairs, we gave notice to the baker that his house would be burned. He was to clear out the people, the upper floors, anything he wished to keep. He was to take it all to a temple for purification. The demon stain was all over his building.

"Get out of my shop," he said.

"I'm sorry," I said. "It isn't your fault. There's nothing you could have done."

"You get out!" He threw bread at my face.

We left him.

The king's men had already been informed. They waited outside with bells on their belts. The captain of the guard nodded at us.

"Give them time to clear out," I said. "This is their home, and they need time to leave it. Give them time."

The Captain looked up at the sun. "Daylight doesn't last. My boys need to get home, too. They don't start coming out, we'll ring the bells down on them. These aren't the kind to leave a place easy."

"Who is?" I replied. "It's their home."

The baker poked his head out from the door. He saw the king's men there, and us. He and his wife came down to shout at the captain. He spit at our feet. The captain struck him over the head for it. The baker fell to the ground. He clutched at his head. He wept.

I bent down. I touched his hand.

"I'm sorry," I said.

He pushed me away as hard as he could. The captain arrested him. I watched him dragged away, with his wife. The captain raised his hands. "Clear the building, boys," he said. "Everyone to temple, then to a cell they get rowdy with us."

The guard lifted their bells, ringing them. Then, the king's men swarmed the stairs. People came out, screaming. The fires were coming. The whole building had to be put down for the old demon stains in the basement. A demon's child had lived here for months, sweating into the hot bricks.

I turned away from these things, to my husband. *Do you remember the great oak on the hill above the red valley?*

I do.

Do you think it is still beautiful, in the sunset? So beautiful the pack howls late into the night because it's so beautiful that you have to shout about it, scream it out of your soul. Is it still beautiful, there?

I do.

I want to go home.

My husband said nothing. The fire raced from the basement floors, strong and hard from the stain, and all the people screaming while their home burned down. The king's men poured buckets of water on the bricks around the side to keep the fire from spreading. They formed a line of men from the wall, passing buckets around the fire. People gathered to watch. Word spread among them of demon children, I'm sure.

My husband and I remained there, silent at the fire.

***

We talk too much. I don't want to talk about anything. I just want to stay right here, and sleep.

Don't yet. Keep me company.

I don't have any exciting stories to tell you.

Anything. What did you do when you found out about me? What was that like?

What was it like for you?

I didn't want to think about it, so I didn't.

I thought about it. I didn't think of much else.

Rachel had lingered in the bath water, lost in thought. It occurred to her that she was going to be late for work if she didn't move fast. She jumped from the bath, looked around for anything to dry off with. All she saw were her clothes. She pulled them on, uncomfortably damp beneath them. Djoss should've been home by now.

She looked out before dumping the water. She didn't want anyone near. There was no one. The children had long abandoned the street.

She pulled her boots over her clawed feet, and decided she wasn't going to go back to work. If there was another demon child, he didn't know that she was one of them. If he didn't know she was a demon child, she had to be careful, and try to find him first.

She wanted to find Djoss, and tell him that there was another one like her in the city. She thought he'd be at the baker's. She left the room. It felt like she was leaving someone else's home instead of her own. It felt like she was supposed to try and hide that she had been here, in someone else's room while they were out.

Back in more familiar places, at the baker's shop, she found one of Sparrow's boys sitting outside the door.

"Hey," she said.

He sat at the door. "Can't come in. We're out."

"I'm not trying to go in. Is Djoss here?"

"Who?"

"My brother. Big guy."

The child shook his head. "Nobody's here but us."

"Turco, then, is he here?"

"Nope."

"Do you know where anyone is?"

The kid spit. He scowled at her.

She walked around a while, to the cart that only took foreign coins, and the tavern down the hill. She found no one there. She walked back to her new place. She got lost trying to find it. She wandered up and down unfamiliar streets searching for a familiar landmark. When she got home, at last, the room was empty. It didn't look like he had come home at all. Rachel closed the window. She sat down in the cot, with her back against the wall.

Her brother had been with her in tiny fishing villages, where he pulled nets on a ship, and came home for lunch. In other villages, he had held down sheep for sheering while she slept in a field nearby, hiding in the long grass where farm dogs wandered to sniff at her hair where she slept. All the days of her life it had been this way. They had worked a caravan together, on a long desert, taking turns driving the animals through the scrub grass growing between the dunes.

Then they came here on a ship. Then she didn't know where he was. It had happened so gently, like a tree growing limbs apart.

He was out. She didn't know where he was. If she were found out right now, and she had to run, she would have to think about finding him or running. She would have to decide.

She'd never leave him. She waited until nightfall. She slept in the empty room alone. She woke up, and she was still alone. If he had come in while she was sleeping and left again, not even mud on the floor marked a step.

She went out after him again, first to the tavern where he used to work. She didn't see him. She approached one of the bouncers she thought she recognized.

He looked her up and down. "No Senta tricks tonight. Got a band playing."

"No tricks," she said. "Looking for my brother. Thought he worked here. Djoss."

"He quit. You're his sister, huh?"

"Yeah."

"You don't look like him."

"Lucky for me," she said.

"Watch out for him. He's been in some bad stuff, I hear. Pink around the eyes."

All the places she knew to go, and some she didn't, late into the night, she couldn't find him anywhere else. The last place she wanted to look was the baker's room.

When she did, she saw Turco sitting outside the door in a chair. He waved at Rachel.

"Where's Djoss?" she asked.

Turco leaned back in his chair. "Thought he was with you."

"You're lying."

"Don't worry about your brother," he said. "He's fine."

"Is he really?"

Turco shrugged. "I guess he is. How's your new place?"

"Good, I think. Djoss hasn't been back. I'm worried about him. I can't find him. He's been gone for days. Turco, if you got him arrested… If you got him hung…"

"Who, me? No." Turco took a deep breath. He stood up and

stretched. He opened the door. "Come on, then."

Inside the room, the single, small hookah was planted in the center of the room. Men sat in the dirt around it. Sparrow was sitting in a corner. She glanced up at Rachel, then turned away.

"Not arrested," said Turco.

She recognize him when she saw him. He was blissed out, the edge of a hookah stem tied to his fingers. He was lying in mud, staring upwards, seeing nothing.

"Oh, no…" said Rachel. Her brother, her champion, the man who had protected her all the days of her life. "Oh, no…"

Turco untied the stem of the hookah from his hand. "I'll help you get him home." He grabbed Djoss by the arm and hefted him up. Rachel took the other arm. His legs weren't working well. He made low groaning noises.

"Is this really what you do when you're out with him late into the night? Is this what your mysterious life has been all this time?"

Turco didn't say anything about it. He helped Rachel drag her brother up the stairs, and into the store. The baker's shop was empty. Out on the streets, which were were all empty.

Djoss got his legs back under him half way to the new rented room. He smiled like it was the greatest day of his life. He looked over at Rachel and smiled at her. He was happy to see her.

When Djoss got his feet under him enough to walk on his own, Turco bowed out. He said that everything would be fine in a while. He had to get back to watch the room.

Then they were alone, Djoss still smiling.

"Hey," said Rachel. "Bad news. We have to run again."

He coughed. "What?"

"They're looking for me at the brothel. A man tried to pull my clothes off, found my scales. I spit on him. He saw my tongue. He knew everything, right away. Sentas stand out around here. They can find me easy."

"We have to go?"

"Are you in any condition to run?"

"No," he giggled. "Sorry. We have to, though. How much coin do we have?"

"Djoss, I have to tell you something."

"If we can hide a while… Maybe Turco knows a place to hide us."

"Djoss…"

"It would only be a matter of time until he found out…"

Rachel stopped, and pressed her heel into the ground because she couldn't kick him. Djoss was slow. His reactions were still blurred. He turned. He wasn't smiling anymore.

"Rachel…What is it?"

"I was lying," she snapped.

He took a breath. His face dropped cold. He turned back to the new room.

She shouted. "You can't be like that if we have to run!"

He kept walking. He got to the door before she did. He left it open behind him.

The other demon child she had discovered was the last thing on her mind. When it rose to the surface, she didn't want to talk about with Djoss. She didn't want to say anything to anyone about it.

In the morning, Djoss left again, without saying good-bye. Rachel watched him leave in silence. She didn't know what to say. She sat down on the cot. She put her head in her hands. She looked around and wondered where he was going, how long he would be there, and what would happen if she tripped and fell, and her clothes tore a little. If she were robbed and beaten and left bleeding somewhere, her blood killing grass where it spilled, then she'd have to run.

Djoss was trying to settle down here, and they should never have settled anywhere. They should have just kept running south from the boat that smuggled them in.

She started to cry. Her demon tears were her own acid blood. She wiped it away as best she could with the cot's blanket. The acidic blood melted through the ragged cloth to the wood floor, which began steaming. She wiped with her hands. She was panicking. She began crying even harder. This would be it if it ate through. She'd have to run if the tears went through the floor, and her brother missing, and people looking up through the strange holes in the floor.

"Stop crying," she said, to herself. "Stop it."

She rubbed at her eyes with her clothes. She rubbed at the blood tears that had already fallen with her shirt sleeve. She sat down on the floor, pressed the back of her leg into the acid, where she could get the most of it covered with her leg. She felt it eating up towards her skin, burning the leather and heavy cloth ragged.

"Stop crying," she said, again. The tears got through to her skin, all the way through the leather, burning her.

"Just stop." She breathed. She tried to focus her breathing and choke it all down. The koans came to her, unwanted, like a stillness. The fire came to her. It burned the ground where her tears had fallen, singing the floor. She quickly iced the fire over, before it could spread.

Once the stain was contained, it was so small: a couple of spots on the floor, no more mysterious than spilled food. When it had started, it was the greatest danger in the world. She laughed at how scared she had been. She laughed because she needed to laugh, at anything at all. She looked down at her clothes, ripped open, and she laughed at those, too. She was not a vain woman, but she thought about her clothes more than even the vainest woman in the world. She didn't have anything else to wear that wasn't precariously damaged, and Djoss was nowhere to help her. He would probably be out and angry a long time. She filled the tub with melted ice again. She tore off all her clothes, and threw them in the water. If the blood still smoked a little, the water would dilute it enough to save the rest of the clothing. Rachel knelt before the basin, scrubbing at the wilting stains with her bare hands. The clothes were ruined, of course.

She'd have to find new clothes, but in dark enough light, she might be able to keep her scales covered.

She pulled the clothes out, wet. She tugged them on. She looked down at where the leather had been gnawed through. The holes were on her arms, and the back of her leg, mostly. If she was careful and moved her arms carefully, no scale would show itself beneath the burns.

The leather was damaged, but the clothes weren't totally ruined, yet. Rachel looked around the apartment for any cloth at all to cover herself. All she saw was the cot. She stripped her boots off. It wasn't hard to tear up the cot with her talons.

She did her best to cover her leg, especially. It was in back, where she couldn't watch it. It was a place where no one would mistake the scales for some kind of blemish in her skin. She wrapped her leg in cloth where the scale was exposed. She tied it tight enough to hurt. With her wet pants on, she ran her hands over the hole. She felt nothing but cloth. It would have to do.

She pulled together all the money she had.

In the streets of Dogsland, she could find anything. She could find food. She hadn't had anything to eat in a while, and her hunger hit her like a crash. She bought food. After she ate, she felt better. She could find a new job. Djoss would come around. They'd been through too much to fall apart over this.

She traveled a long time on foot, to the north, then the east. She took a ferry across a river. She waited until sunset was gone, and the cloudy sky had no moon. She walked in a straight line towards a river. She was looking for another Senta, and a place where one might be working in a nicer crowd than the Pens.

The watchtower lights along the eastern wall blended with the night sky on the horizon, like low-lying stars.

Rachel found a Senta turning cards in the shadow of a tavern between a wool exchange and a field of mud stripped raw for a stacks of crates on pallets. Rachel had stopped here. She had seen a Senta that was blind. Her eyes were completely white with cataracts.

Rachel coughed.

The Senta pulled out her cards and touched the top of the deck.

"Hello," Rachel said.

"Hello," the Senta replied. She sounded like an old woman, but she had looked young enough in the slanting light of the tavern.

"How do you read the cards when you can't see them?"

"I can feel them," she said. She held one up, for Rachel to touch. Rachel ran her hand gently over it. The paint was thick. The strokes were clean and precise. The images were blurred from her touch. "I make them myself," she said. "They don't look like much, but I know them."

"I've never heard of that before. I, too, serve the Unity. I need new clothes. I don't know where else to go. I have coin to pay for them."

"Wealth?" said the Senta. "A waste of time."

"Do you have spare clothes?"

"I do," she said, "and I can smell yours from here. You stink. What happened?"

"An accident, I assure you."

The Senta smirked. "An accident," she said. "That is almost the truth. Show me your knowledge, Senta. Prove to me that you serve the truth. I cannot see, and I cannot believe you."

"Hold out your hand," Rachel said and reached inside of herself. She brought forth ice and placed it into the Senta's palm.

"Nothing," said the Senta. "You are barely beginning."

"As are we all," Rachel replied.

The Senta nodded. "Yes," she said, "that is true."

"You look like you're almost my size. You are dressed well. I have not been as fortunate on my path."

"Follow me."

Rachel followed the old Senta. The woman's room on the top floor of the inn was practically the whole floor. She had heavy furniture, and a bird in a cage who moved nervously from foot to foot when the two women came in.

"Your smell gives you away, demon child," she said. "You smell like damp brimstone."

"Oh?" said Rachel. She hardened her heart against the woman. "What are you going to do about it?"

"I am too old and too blind to stop you. Please, just take what you want. Please, just hurry."

"I don't want to hurt you."

"You can't help your nature," the Senta said. "Take whatever you want. I couldn't stop you. By the time I cried for help, you'd kill me, devour my flesh, and you'd still escape in time."

Rachel frowned. "I would never do that."

"Your tongue is as forked as your soul," the old woman replied. "I hear your voice, but I don't know where it comes from. It's not a human voice. The shape of your mouth is wrong."

"I don't want to steal from you, or hurt you," Rachel protested. "I just want to buy new clothes. I'm Senta, just like you."

"No, not like me," the woman said. "Please… Please, don't hurt me." She was calm. She sat down on the edge of her bed. "Take whatever you want, but please don't hurt me. I'm an old woman. I'm blind. I won't stop you."

Rachel pulled out a coin and tossed it at the woman. The coin bounced off the bedspread. It fell to the ground. Rachel picked it up from her feet. She put it on the Senta's lap. The woman snatched Rachel's wrist from the air. Her breath quickened. Her fear jumped out. "I won't report you! Just take what you want and go!"

"I'm not evil!" Rachel snarled. "You don't know anything about me!"She yanked her hand back. The old woman sat on the bed like a panting statue, breathing hard and terrified.

Rachel pulled new clothes out from drawers, and changed there. She watched the blind woman sitting inside her fear, unmoved, unmoving. Rachel didn't try to cover herself. She just changed. The old woman said nothing.

"You are a living affront to the Unity," the woman whispered, when Rachel was almost finished.

"I didn't choose my life," Rachel said. "I never had a choice about it. I just must make the best of things. I'm not evil. I don't hurt people, or dig into the ground."

"Please, just take what you want and go…"

"Treating me like a thief makes it so easy steal from you," said Rachel. She picked up the coin she had tried to give to the Senta. She left, running into the streets, back to the Pens where no one looked at anyone. She wanted to keep running, and escape the city.

CHAPTER XV

At night, I pulled the wolfskin across my back. I left my husband sleeping. I crept down the stairs on padded paw, to the main hallway. Everyone was asleep, here. The doors were closed and locked. I didn't bother with the front door. I slipped into the back room, where I know the innkeeper slept with an open window. I heard the flies buzzing in his room, and the engorged mosquitos joyfully making love in his blood. His window was open. I wasn't sure if I would fit through it. I placed my paws on the windowsill, and peered out. I saw the city there. I jumped out into the night.

My heart longed for the wild places of the world. I walked at night where the lamplights burned down, out of oil, where darkness filled the streets. The fireflies came out in great numbers, calling to each other there. I walked among them, blessed them as best I could in my wolf form. I ignored the noble estates with manicured trees and deer chained and penned for hunting. I slipped into the ruins of old buildings. I sniffed the rats and mice and owls that lived in rotting bricks.

Beyond these, the housecats and tomcats and butcher's dogs and chickens and pigs and all the creatures of the city, mindmute and indifferent to all the sorrows of the men and women of the world, sang to me of sorrow and felled trees and mud and crowds. I sang back a song of the hills. I stood upon a warehouse roof and howled my song of the hills, and the hills rolling, and the hills covered in green grass and trees, and the hills in the first rainfall of autumn. Oh, I sang.

I sang to drive them all away, somewhere else far from the world of man where they could be happy—where Erin would grant them peace.

The dogs barked at me like I was some kind of invader here, and I was. This was Dogsland. I belonged in the hills.

My husband found me soon enough. My howls were not discreet. We walked together to the reeds at the edge of southern side of the city, where snakes chased frogs in the grasses ignorant of the poor men building shacks on beams above the wetlands. A snake would not believe me if I told him he was in a city. All he was grass and rotting wood.

We walked, my husband and I, through the wild places at night.

At the end of the night my husband nudged me.

Did you see anything you recognized?

Yes. Did you?

You know what I mean.

How did you do it when you were young? What was it like?

You know.

I hate it.

We do what we must.

I hate this place.

What did Jona think of Dogsland?

He loved it here. He still does.

Still want to go home?

Not yet. No, not yet.

What do you see with our eyes?

When I went among the ruins, I smelled her. I could practically see her when I did. She walked down the street like any moment someone was going to wound her with their eyes. People never look each other in the face. She was walking, and she looked so scared.

Show me where. Take me.

So, I did.

***

Rachel walked from building to building in her new clothes. Senta clothing was usually plain. This was plain, but there was craftsmanship in the way the the red lashes splayed out below her waist and pulled tighter when she tied her belt over it all. She still had the crossing red lashes on her chest, and the fraying out where the lashes splayed into threads below her waist, but it was cut for a woman, and the pants were so baggy they were practically a dress. It would help her stay cool in the sweltering sun, and obscured her figure. Traveling women did not accentuate their hips. It had been a while since she had found clothes from a woman.

She wondered if she had wrapped it right, and if there were any scales showing. She felt for wind while she walked through the crowded streets.

She needed to get back to familiar districts to find Djoss. He wouldn't be here. This wasn't the Pens. A theatre spilled patrons into the taverns across the street. Behind the tavern, a huge, black bear fought a pack of ferocious dogs. People were cheering for the bear. They had been betting on how long it would survive. Rachel couldn't see much past the packed crowd except the ferocious bear, standing high on its hind legs and roaring at dogs.

It was a hideous thing. She wanted the dogs to tear the monster apart. She heard a dog whining in pain, and it knotted her stomach. A street performer cracked bawdy jokes from a pair of stilts, walking through the streets high above the ground like the lamplighters, looking down and shouting obscenities at the people he saw beneath him. He had a large bucket on a stick, and he pushed it down below into the crowd when a coin was offered up to him. He shouted down to Rachel. "A Senta Witch about the town! If you can see the future, you know how good

I am in bed!"

Rachel looked up at him, a mask falling over her face. She didn't want anyone to see how terrified she was. "I see a large puddle in your future," she said. "And broken stilts."

He laughed. He held down the bucket for a coin. Rachel gave him the very coin she would have given the Senta for these new clothes. She didn't want to make a scene.

For just a moment, she looked around herself, in her new clothes, in this different place, and she felt like a different person. She stood up a little straighter, felt something break inside of her, then mend: She was never more alone than in a crowd like this, people who knew they would eat tomorrow night and never have to run away. But there was someone else in the city who probably felt the same way about things with whom she might be able to talk, might form a tiny crowd of two, together. Even if he was evil, he couldn't have been much worse than Turco or Dog.

Walking on, back to the Pens, she scanned the crowd for a face. Any hint of a king's man uniform got her to turn her head quickly.

By the time she made it back to the ferry, the streetlamps drifted on and off in the dwindling oil. Strong stars fought past the night haze overhead. Rachel watched a bored city guardsman lighting matches in the dark as he waited for the ferry to come back across the river. He looked up at her, holding a match. He looked right at her.

She looked away, terrified of him, even if she wanted to talk to him alone, pour all her secrets onto him like bleeding a wound.

Jona looked right at her. He was dressed for the night, not his king's man uinform. A body had been dropped into the water already that night. Jona was trying to piece together what all these merchant men might be doing to merit death. Jona had climbed into a window, and waited for the man to come. He had choked him to death with a cord, and pulled him out through the window. Jona tied a heavy brick to the dead man's belt, and it pulled him down into the water. When he was done, Jona had gone back into the room and searched for signs of anything that made a man worth killing.

The only thing he found were tax ledgers on a rolltop desk. Jona couldn't read them in the dark. He slipped the ledgers into his shirt and left. He had to repress the urge to pull them out and study them for any signs of trouble in the night. He was in a crowd of workmen waiting for the ferry, the lamplight fading out after the long night. He bought packs of cheap matches and tried to light the whole packs like short-lived candles because he wanted more light to read once the men passed by. When they caught their ferry, Jona had the ledger out. He lit a matchbox as if it were a candle. The fire was bright and hot, but it didn't last long enough to read anything.

Jona tried just one match, enough light to find the man's name in a corner. It was a forgettable name for a forgettable man. The match bit into Jona's thumb, and he threw it into the water just as he had the man. He gave up. He shoved the ledgers back under his shirt. He sat down to think on a stray brick of a trash pile, deep in the building shadows. He had matches left, but it was hard to light them in the dark. He thought about how it was easier to kill a man than to light a cheap match, and read his name.

The ferry came for everyone. Jona was supposed to take the sewers home, but he was sick of sewers and the sewer stink and all the killing he was doing that didn't make sense. He wanted to ride the ferry over, and walk like a decent man down the street to his home. He'd be at work by full sunrise, an honest king's man, walking the streets, watching for trouble. He looked through the crowd out of habit, toying with his last cheap box of matches. He stopped in his tracks. His gut twisted. He stepped away from the ferry. He slipped back into the shadows.

He saw her, looking at him like she knew him.

When the ferry cast off, he used the crowd for cover to escape.

He ran to the sewer line to pass over the water on a workmen's little ferry boat, to the Pens, and then to his home.

Jona didn't want to kill anyone anymore. He especially didn't want to kill her.

***

What did you do when you saw me?
Nothing. I went home. I had a fight with Djoss. You?
I went home, too. I didn't do anything.
What were you fighting about?
I'd rather not talk about it.

Djoss came home, at last, and saw Rachel sprawled out on the cloth from the destroyed cot.

"What happened?"

Rachel sat up, yawning. "I broke it," she said. "I got a new job. I'm working down closer to you. Go get two cots. Actually, get beds. Get large, soft, feather beds." She threw him some coins from her pockets.

"Your clothes look different," said Djoss. "They wear out again?"

"I washed them," said Rachel. "Where have you been?"

"What?"

Rachel sighed. "You've been gone forever."

Djoss frowned. He sat down on the cold stove and folded his hands. "I was working."

"Oh," she said. "I have to work tonight, too."

"You broke the cot?"

She stood up. She stretched again. "Come on. You've got money, right? You're making real money? Let's get some beds, with mattresses."

Together they took to the street. The wind off the ocean was strong and beautiful, and it carried away any words they might have shared. And if anyone saw the rugged bouncer and the Senta standing next to each other, waiting for a gap in the carriages to cross the street, they would've known they were related by their silence. Only relatives can be so quietly together like that.

They bought two beds with barely a word. Djoss had plenty of money. They didn't even need to use Rachel's coins. Djoss carried both mattresses on his back, walking slowly behind the carter from the store. He and Djoss dragged the new furniture upstairs. Lying down on a bed, with a mattress of stuffed hay and feather, was at once comforting and frightening. Djoss didn't seem to notice. He fell asleep the moment he laid down. Rachel remembered holding a mattress, and jumping out a window. She looked over at Djoss, and wondered if he really knew what he was doing. It was like watching a stranger in Djoss' skin. His face blanked and his body slackened, and everything about him that was full and alive sank down into the mattress, and the Djoss she knew was gone. It was like how he looked when she found him in the basement at a hookah.

He rolled over away from her, and his shirt rode up his back. Someone had dug fingernails into him. She got up from her new bed. She pushed the shirt up higher and studied the marks on his back: fingernails.

Rachel frowned.

She had seen Djoss one time, when he was working, and he had Sparrow's three boys beside, walking towards the basement. Too late in the night to be carrying meat like that, it stood out. Djoss had one whole sow slung over his strong back, and the kids had a pole that two of them carried with a pig on it. The third, the youngest, carried a piglet slung over his shoulder just like Djoss' sow. The animals' bellies had been cut already, and sewn back together with white twine.

The next morning, he had come home with fresh pork sausage, a teapot and four fine, white cups.

"Djoss, don't," she said.

"Why not?"

"Better to have the coin, instead. Better to just take coin and keep it. We don't need things as much as coin."

"We deserve to have a better life, for once. I'm making good money here. We can leave it if we have to. We can sell it back if we have time."

Rachel decided not to say anything. The memory of the twine along the pig's bellies made her think of running again. It made her think about Djoss blissed out beside a hookah.

She wondered if he had taken to Sparrow as Turco and Dog had. This thought was worse than the twine. He could afford furniture and teacups. That's fine. If he could afford a woman who wanted food for three boys, he was hiding how much he was making because he knew Rachel would believe it was dangerous.

She had watched him eating, how he chewed his food and held it and ate it. She imagined her brother with Sparrow, how he would cut into her like that, devour Sparrow's body, and how Turco and Dog would be there. She couldn't eat.

"Djoss, I think it's time to leave," she said.

He grunted. "You're just not used to settling down. This is a good place. Plenty of room for us to hide out."

"No, Djoss."

"I like it here."

"Do we at least have a plan? Big city with lots of guards. We need a plan."

"Plan is don't get caught. Run to water. That's always the plan."

"I'm really scared about something and I don't know what," she said.

"You find out, you tell me," he said. He was done eating. He stood up. The chair made a terrible sound across the wooden floor. Djoss didn't seem to notice.

Rachel opened her mouth at his back. Then, she closed it. If he hadn't been so busy making friends, making money, she'd have told him that she had encountered a man who had blood like hers, and maybe they should find him and talk to this man, or just run away from him. If it was just him and her, like it had always been and always would be, then she would tell Djoss everything. Right now, she thought it would be hard for him, when they ran. It was going to be so hard for him.

***

I'd rather not talk about it.

If Djoss was burning coins with friends, she needed to work hard.

In the morning, she got a new job at a new brothel, far away from her room. Turco didn't know anything, and didn't need to know. It was worth the walk to keep all her pay. Rachel mopped floors and changed sheets.

Sometimes drunks there asked the Senta for a prophecy, and if she couldn't actually see anything, she'd make something up. She needed the money. She never told anyone bad news. She didn't want to lose her job over a future they probably already saw for themselves. Usually the things that kill us are things we do every single day. Even Erin teaches that. Men in brothels who do not realize that would never believe their futures, anyway.

Rachel stripped off filthy, dusty, sweaty sheets and threw them in a big bag. Then, she spread a less filthy, damp sheet over the mattress. She ran a mop across the floor, and dumped any chamber pots out in the basement where a sewer grate opened to this stinking river of sewer that flooded in the summer rains.

The roof leaked constantly. When hard rain fell, Rachel also had to keep the many buckets across the top floor from spilling onto the floor, emptying them into a barrel near a window. She dumped the full barrel out the window, and put the barrel back where it was. She wiped the wetness off the floor with a dirty towel.

Women and men came and went all night. They didn't look at her. The only thing lower than a cheap sailor's whore was the whore's maid. And with all the whores to gawk at, and all the men to attract, the night maids slipped in and out like breezes with candles, and days went by when no one even talked to her.

When the night wore down, Rachel scrubbed sheets in the tiny yard cut into the sidewalk. By the time the sun edged against the horizon, she piled the damp sheets into the closets on each floor.

Rachel picked up her night's pay each morning. She counted it on the spot, right in front of the man that paid her. He didn't pay attention to her once the money was in her hands. He just busied himself with the rolls of accounting behind his scrawny desk, counting the coins his girls had earned.

They weren't even human to her. Rachel watched the birds flittering around the hallways, and the bears chasing after them. She counted the money like golden fruit pulled from a farm.

Weeks passed. Djoss only came home to push food into a cupboard. He dripped into his bed and slept with his arm draped over his eyes to keep the light out. They were both too tired to fight.

***

A heavy storm rolled in for three days. Rain, rain, rain. The streets emptied. The girls smoked corncob pipes from the balconies. The ships couldn't come to port in such wild waters. No sailors. Few marks. No one worked.

Rachel finished early, and the owner of the brothel told her not to come back until the rains stopped.

She walked home in the rain a while, but she didn't want to go home. She walked towards Djoss' work at the bakery room. He was hunched outside a butcher shop, looking up and down the street.

Rachel slipped into a narrow alley before he could see her. She peered around a corner at him. How could she destroy this barely-spoken arguing if she didn't even know what he was fighting to keep from her?

CHAPTER XVI

We searched for Salvatore. We slipped the wolfskins over our backs and prowled the sewer lines. I led. My husband followed. We sniffed the air for his scent.

I thought I had him once, near the Nameless' pointless temple. I caught his scent near the door where the coin is paid. There were other ways inside, but this was his. I thought I had his smell. Jona was a demon's child, not a Walker and not a wolf. He couldn't tell me anything about what Salvatore smelled like.

We followed the smell that might have been Salvatore. It was sour, and cold, like rotten fruit left to freeze in a snowy field.

I lost the scent of him at the water's edge, where the workmen kept their boats. The rowboat ferried us across fine, but once there, there was no sign of Salvatore's scent. The street had too many pedestrians, and too many horses. We couldn't smell anything there. We scared people, too, as big as we were. When anyone dared to come near, we snapped at them and ran off. Back into the sewers, and back onto his trail. No sign. Every night, no sign.

He had been here, somewhere.

I knew so much from Jona's mind, but never enough. Salvatore's patterns broke with his heart.

He was here. He had to be here.

***

Jona snuck the tax ledgers he'd stolen in to the station house, and slipped them into a pile of pending reports on Calipari's desk. The Night Sergeant was in, but he was fast asleep, a bottle resting on the desk beside him. The night crew were about, bringing trouble off the street, but nobody was doing it right then. The scriveners had probably scattered when they saw the Sergeant had fallen asleep, drunk. Jona wrote a note to put with the ledgers. He used his left hand to hide his identity from Calipari's sharp eyes.

Night King is real. She's in here, somewhere. Tell no one until you're sure.

He had studied the ledgers too. The man was working for the noblemen, providing wine and meat for the balls of nobility coming with the arrival of the dry season. With him gone, there was one less merchant to supply the noble balls. That's all he was in his tax ledger. The Night King had wanted him killed for something, and it was hard to imagine that it was something to do with nobleman dancing long into the night.

***

Jona was at a pub near the Pens, where he had slipped Geek's buddy Djoss a spare coin to get him inside even though the line was out the door because this troupe of dancers was in town. They could pull their legs behind their head and do cartwheels. Jona was there with Geek, Jaime, and Jaime's wife. Jaime and his wife immediately started dancing—he wouldn't touch a drop if she was looking. Geek saw the red door in the back and went gambling, no mind if it was illegal because they let him win a little for the privilege of staying open. Jona was left standing there all by himself in this big, crowded pub.

Jona went up to the bar and raised his hand at one of the barmaids. The only thing for him to do at a time like this was to get drunk as quickly as possible. He tossed his money on the counter and threw back his mug like it was going to fly away if he didn't drink it fast enough. He raised his hand again. When he turned around with his drink, a woman stood directly in front of his face.

Rachel.

"Excuse me," said Jona, "help you?" He fingered through his pockets for coins. He wondered if he had enough to bribe her. He was in a crowd. He didn't have a way to kill her in a crowd. He didn't have a knife, or any poison or anything. He was tired of killing people. He put the cup down on the bar beside him. He was tired.

"I remember you," she said. "Don't I remember you?"

"Maybe," said Jona. He smiled. So, that was it.

"I busted your nose?" she said. "I want to talk to you somewhere. Somewhere away from here."

She should have been screaming for the guard, shouting at everyone that this man in a uniform was an impostor. He looked like a man, but he was not a man at all. He was a demon's child. He was trying to damn them all. Jona raised his glass to take a sip, and quickly brought it down. His hand was shaking too much. He couldn't hold the mug. He sneered.

"I didn't hear you," he said.

"We need to talk," she said. "Please, I don't want to do anything awful to you. I just want to talk, where we can be alone."

"Why?"

"I punched you," she said. "Don't you remember?" She mimicked punching him in the nose. She was trying to be friendly. "I'm not afraid of you, if you think... Look, we need to talk, okay? That's all."

"Shouldn't confess to punching a king's man," he said. "King don't like it when people punch us."

"Your blood!" she shouted. Her voice didn't carry well over the music and the crowd. Someone bumped her from behind. She fell against Jona a little. He pushed her back.

He pounded the top of the bar. "What about it?" He couldn't get through the crowd if he had to run.

"Nothing, okay? I don't want to hurt you, or tell anyone. Please, can we just talk?" She touched his hand, gently. "I just want to talk to you. Please?"

She pointed at the kitchen door. He shrugged and followed her. He was thinking about killing her. She was pretty. She led him by his collar through the crowd. He tried to think of what his mother would want him to do, but couldn't think of anything. It was hard to imagine her telling her son to kill a woman.

It was bound to happen. It was in the air, always in the air.

What was there to talk about? There was nothing to talk about. He was what he was, and if anyone else knew, he'd be dead. If he had killed her when she struck him, everything would be different. If he had run back to the brothel where she struck him, after the bleeding had stopped, and hunted her, then he would still be alive in the morning.

He hardened behind a shell. His eyes closed, then opened. He looked around for any chance to get away with it.

She had him by the hand, back into the kitchen where a fat man wiped the glasses furiously, then out the back, where it wasn't crowded, but there were still people.

"Where can we go?" she said. He looked at her. She was just as scared as he was. She let go of his hand and bit her lip. "We need to go somewhere private."

Jona shook his head. "You really want to go somewhere private?"

"Please…" she said. She took a deep breath. "Anywhere. I'm new here. I don't know where we can go."

He looked up and down the street. "I know where to take you."

A canal was near.

Jona led her down to the waters' edge to an empty place, where the homeless cleared out at the sight of Jona's uniform—a perfect place to choke the girl in privacy and drop her in the water. He'd have to be careful and fast. Sentas had tricks up their sleeves, he knew.

"Private spot," said Jona.

"Okay," she said. "I wanted to tell you that…" She looked around. "Please, don't hurt me. You don't have any reason to hurt me."

"I don't want to hurt you," said Jona. "I really don't."

"Okay," she said, again. She looked at the water.

Then, she leaned in close to Jona, close enough he could smell her skin, and she smelled like bleach and brimstone. Horrible. The ale hit him, maybe. Something hit him; something washed over him. Jona realized that he wanted to taste her neck. She spoke softly. "You were telling me over and over to wash my hands."

"What do you want?" he whispered. "Want me to pay you? I don't have a lot of money, but I'll pay if I have to."

"I'm not going to blackmail you," she said. "I don't want to do anything to you. I just… I just want to talk."

"So talk."

"I don't really know what to say."

"If you tell anybody, I'll be burned alive. My mother arrested…"

"No," she said. "No, no no… I know, I don't want that."

Jona's fist clenched. She might just be wearing the clothes for the protection of them. "Are you really Senta?"

"Yes."

Jona looked away from her, towards the murky canal water. "I don't believe in that," he said. "Don't believe in Erin or Imam or the Unity."

"Everyone believes in something."

He didn't want to kill her. "Where's Elishta in all that, huh? Where am I? Nowhere. Evil. What am I supposed to do, worship demons?" He looked her in the face. She was terrified. "I can't change what I am."

"I'd have already turned you in, you know. If I was going to do that. If I wanted money, I'd have asked for it by now, back in the bar where it's…" she looked over at the canal. "You know… Safer."

"Right."

"This isn't exactly what I meant when I said somewhere private."

"It's the best we can do."

"I just want to know how it happened, for you? That's all. I'm just curious about you."

"Right." He'd never said it all out loud in his entire life. "All my secrets, then? My father and my father's father, and maybe even my father's father's father were all like me, but they were a little worse. I was born with demon wings, and my mother cut them off me, sanded the stumps down to the bone. I have big scars there. Tell people I fell on a gate. I never sleep. Not even a little. What else do you want to know? There's nothing else to know about it. That's all there is. Satisfied?"

"My name's Rachel. Rachel Nolander. I want to do something to you, and it might hurt a little, but it'll be all right, I promise."

They stood there, looking at each other. Jona wanted to laugh. He wanted to walk away as if this never happened, pretend it was all a joke.

"I don't know what to say," she said.

Jona snorted. "So, I'll see you around. You tell anybody what I said, it's the end of my life. Maybe the end of yours. You think about that."

"No." Rachel grabbed Jona's hand. She lifted his palm up to look at it. "Just give me a second." She ran a finger over his palm.

Jona shivered. Her finger was so warm, that a chill ran up his spine.

Rachel circled her naked finger over Jona's palm, calling small bursts of fire into his skin, underneath it.

"That hurts," he said.

She closed her eyes. She didn't let go of his palm.

"That hurts!" he said, louder. He tried to curl his palm, but she wouldn't let go.

"Stop," she said. "I'm done."

"What did you do?"

She still clutched his hand. "Listen, I know more about your heritage than you do. My mother taught me. When the oceans were born, they weren't salty at all, and ran pure as liquid crystal. The rain came, and the rain fell over the naked ground, and the minerals on the rocks leached into the water. And the water grew dank with saline and brine. We can measure the precise moment the heavenly Unity touched the water, because the salt in our tears is only so lightly salty, and the rivers keep pouring the minerals and filth into the oceans. We can look for the place where the water is as salty as our tears, and the length of the journey will be the length of time human beings have been alive on these shores."

Jona coughed. He was sweating. He had trouble breathing. He rubbed his hand. He had a burn mark under his skin.

"Elishta, far below our feet, has no life, only demons, and their wickedness seeks to destroy our life for theirs. They sent emissaries to enrapture the mortal world into the darkness below the waters, below the ground, where the burning of souls is the only light. When a demon-touched child is born, they are... supposed to be evil destroyers of life."

She let go of his hand.

"And, everything I just said, what they teach about you, well... It's all wrong. I think it's all wrong. I know, because I'm not like that. I'm not a destroyer of life. I'm just me. I'm all I ever was."

Jona leaned back against the wall, rubbing his hand. He looked down at it. He didn't say anything. He didn't have anything to say. She unlashed her sleeve. She pulled it down a little to expose her shoulder. She leaned over to Jona. "What do you see?" she said.

Jona squinted in the dim lamplight. She had white skin, like a corpse, on her face and hands. Her shoulder was black as pitch. It shined in the moonlight. He reached out a finger and touched it. Too hard to be moles, to supple to be armor.

"My father, too," she said. "My mother was a Senta he had beaten into submission. One day, my brother poisoned him, and killed the evil inside of him. I wasn't evil like he was. My mother was killed when people found my demonic father's body. My brother isn't like us. He was born before I was, when my father wasn't what he became. My brother hid me, and ran to get my mother, but he was too late. Him and me ever since, and no one else. These scales are all over my body. My feet are demon claws."

Jona touched the skin in front of him. He ran his fingers on the scales.

Rachel let him touch her scaled forearm. He pushed the rest of her sleeve up higher, exposing more of her arm, and above the elbow it was only scales, like the smooth armor of a warm snake. He ran his hands over the scales, gently.

Rachel pulled the sleeve down sharply. She bound it shut. "So," she said, "are you evil?"

"What?"

"We're supposed to be evil, right? Are you evil?"

"I don't think so. My name's Jona, I'm the Lord of Joni but that doesn't mean anything anymore. I'm just Jona. I'm trying to rebuild my family name. I make officer, and I raise my mostly-human kids to be a little stronger than me, a little better. I'm not as bad as my father was, not as bad as my grandfather."

"I don't have anything. I don't even have a shadow."

Rachel held her arm out against the wall. The lamplight shadows ended at the sleeve. Her hand had no shadow.

"Crazy." Jona held out his own arm next to hers, his shadow parallel to her arm until the hand. Hers was absent. Then, he touched her hand. It felt real.

Rachel checked the lashes of her sleeve. She pulled it tighter, and checked the seams.

"I guess Senta's a good disguise for you," he said.

She raised an eyebrow. "No disguise," she said. "Didn't you see me with the koans? Maybe someday the Senta will figure out how the demon children fit into everything."

Jona searched around the night for anything to help him know what he should say or do. She was waiting for him to speak. Was there anything else to say? Jona didn't know. He looked at her, and remembered that he was going to kill her if he had to. It felt like a memory from a thousand years ago. It felt like a different life, and it was. It was the life where there wasn't anyone like him that he could talk to about it. Salvatore was something else, a creature or a monster or a force of selfish energy. He wasn't like her. Meeting her was different.

"What now?" asked Jona.

"I don't know," she said, "I've never met another."

"I met one other, once."

"Was he evil?"

"He was evil, but he was no worse than the people he worked for. Haven't seen him in a while. He doesn't know about me, what I really am, but I know about him." Jona scratched his neck and grinned, sheepishly. "You know, I don't sleep with prostitutes. I just go now and then when I'm putting on the show of it for the boys. If I did, they'd just get sick, and I'd have a reputation that might catch up with me."

"Yeah," she said. "Oh, I didn't show you my tongue."

She opened her mouth. It came out, like a lizard's tongue. It had a fork on the end of it. She pulled it back in quickly. "Sorry, it's kind of gross."

"No worse than my wings," he said. "You talk fine."

"I have to. It took practice. I fold it up a lot, inside my mouth. If I get drunk, it starts to slip a little, so I don't get drunk. I've got all these scales to keep covered all the time, and my tongue, and I don't think I have anything else wrong with me. I think that's all I got." She bit her lip.

"Are you hungry? We should go somewhere else."

He looked down at the canal. He had an image in his mind of a body falling into the water, tied to a heavy stone. He lost his appetite.

"I'm not hungry," she said.

"Neither am I," he replied. "Doesn't matter, does it?"

They walked a bit, to a cafe at the edge of the Pens that stayed open all night serving the sailors who rolled out of the taverns looking for something to eat before they stumbled back to their boats. Rachel and Jona didn't eat anything. They drank bitter tea as stale as sea biscuits.

***

Hunting, always hunting. Jona's mind dropped away from Salvatore, but we did not. I found a trail as black as pitch among the sewers, and old enough it only came through because the stain lingered while other things did not. It led deep into the city, to a building cracked down the center, and half fallen away.

I took to the stairwell, there, straight to Salvatore's room. My husband scoured the rooms for anyone alive inside. There was no one. It was deep night here. I climbed the stairs. I knew the stairs. I had seen them in Jona's mind. I knew the door, too. I opened the door, and saw the room.

The hammock was still there. Dust covered everything. The floorboards had rotted, as had the ceiling. Fingers of moonlight pushed through. I smelled him here. I smelled him everywhere.

I pulled the wolfskin from my back and I stood up tall. I tested the hammock. It still seemed strong. I sat on it, and leaned back. I imagined a life lived like this, in this small room.

My husband said nothing when he came in, searching the floorboards and the walls for anything that remained that might tell us where Salvatore had gone.

He pulled the skin from his own back.

The Night King knows where he is.

She will not welcome us.

She knows exactly where he is. He's too hard to find if he was just by himself. He's not this smart. He can't be without much memory to guide him. He has friends even if he doesn't remember them.

Is anyone here?

No.

It will rain tonight. It is a good night to burn this building down.

***

Jona and Rachel were walking on her way back from work. She noticed how the people looked at her differently now that she walked with a king's man. She didn't know what to think about that, but she liked him.

She took his hand. She smiled.

He looked down at her hand as if he didn't quite understand why it was in his. She squeezed, and let go. He nodded at her. "Oh," he said.

"Sorry." She let go.

"Sorry, nothing." He took her hand. He held onto it.

He didn't want to let go.

CHAPTER XVII

We hunt the living not the dead. Salvatore eludes us. Rachel may return to Dogsland, if her brother returns.

I see with my eyes, my senses, deep enough into Jona's memories. I can see more than he ever did. His memories lead where they lead, and there is never too much information for hunters to know their prey.

Is it real? Will it help us if it isn't real?

No memory is real.

If it helps us hunt her, then it is real enough.

***

The next evening, Rachel opened the window to a dreary sky drenched in gray clouds and rolling thunder. She sipped her tea and watched the storm coming.

"It'll pass," said Djoss. "A dry spell is coming."

"Since when do you know anything about the weather here? We've only been here a few months."

"People are saying it."

"You think they'll want us to work tonight?"

"No," he said.

"Have we got enough for rent?"

"We do," he said.

"Do we have enough for me to have some fun?"

"Like what?" he asked.

"Oh, I don't know," she said. "I want to go dancing! Come dancing with me, Djoss!"

Djoss shrugged. "All right," he said, "Where?"

"Anywhere. Just don't leave me alone. I miss you."

He sighed. "I miss you, too," he said. "I have some things I have to do first."

"What?" she said.

He squinted his eyes, thinking. "You know what? I guess I can skip it until tomorrow. You wouldn't like it, anyway."

"No, I'll come with you," she said. "What is it?"

"Nothing," he said. "Just… We'll go do something fun. It will be empty except for us. It'll be our own, personal, flooded city. One of these days we need to invest in some parasols."

The first thing they did was slip into the night between the worst of the storms. The second thing they did was slip into a bar, drenched from head to toe from the rain. The bar wasn't playing any music. They stepped outside. They clomped across a bridge of planks to the other side of the road. The bending boards sank the edges of their boots into the water that had emerged from the sewers. This late in the season, the sewer water mostly ran clear. Anything that hadn't washed out into the bay by now was never going to leave. The heat was coming back. The dry time was coming, when it wouldn't rain for weeks at a time, and then only a little.

The next tavern they found only had one musician, a single drummer. Djoss and his sister danced awkwardly—her in all her Senta attire, and him terrified of stepping on her feet with his huge boots.

The drummer smoked a pipe while he drummed. When his pipe ran low, he gave the two dancers a loud, fast finish.

Djoss, Rachel, and the bartender clapped for him. No one else was there. Djoss got them both a drink and a little stew. She asked him where he'd been all these nights. He asked her the same thing. Neither of them wanted to admit to anything.

Djoss tossed some more money at the drummer, and they danced some more. They didn't have to talk if they were dancing.

When the drummer ran out of weed again, they sat back down and drank some more. They talked about the different ales they had had from all the different places they had been, and at last, after false starts and too much effort, they gave up. They stepped back out into the street.

Looking ahead, Rachel saw the widow's middle child leaning against a wall and glaring at them. He faded into the night behind the storms of another weeping cloud.

Djoss and Rachel went home, eventually. She borrowed one of his huge shirts. He had three of them, now. None of them ragged thin. She sat on her cot in the dark, looking down at her legs. She rarely looked at her own body. When she did, it didn't seem real to her. Sometimes she could forget that she wasn't a normal person, and she walked and moved among the people as if she was safe. She ran her hands over the jagged scales. She was so dirty, and so smooth.

Djoss scrubbed their clothes in the bathtub with a washboard he had picked up with all his new money. Rachel had stopped yelling at him about buying new things. They had furniture, cutlery, and herbs in pots in the window. He hung her clothes to dry in the apartment because of the rain outside.

In the apartment above them, two people were making slow love.

Rachel took a deep breath. "Djoss, I want to tell you something important."

"What is it?"

"I think we need to run, and soon."

"Why?"

"I found someone else like me, I think. I did. We should run."

"If no one knows about you, we should stay. This has been

good for us. We've never had it so good. Beds, clean clothes, and everything. You just stay away from her. You see her, you turn the other way. She doesn't need to know about us if she gets caught."

"It's a man, Djoss. We're both getting used to this place," she said. "It scares me. How's Turco doing? How is your thing with him?"

"Basement's flooded out. Nobody's going down there until it dries. He's looking for a new place."

She knew he was lying. She had been in the basement in the worst of the rains and it had never flooded. "Do we still have enough money?"

"We've been keeping our hands busy," said Djoss.

"Doing what?"

He didn't say anything.

"Djoss, doing what?"

"Try to get some sleep. Plenty of work in the dry season, and no monsoon rains us out."

She looked down the shirt she was wearing. Some of the sweat stains on it were a strange rust-color, like blood, diluted.

***

When the rain faded, Djoss and Rachel went back to work as quiet as ever. The night passed easily enough. Sailors had money and whores had easy lies and no shame. Rachel cleaned up after them without a word.

In her mind, she saw a whole city spread out before her full of taverns and brothels and men looking for women and women looking for money and her brother punching people and smuggling from one building to another to pay the rent for the woman he kept on the side and her kids who were growing up to be criminals and the daylight world was just noise, while she slept, of shopkeepers and people that don't talk to each other and everything in the city was lonely and wrong and sickening and nothing was good in her world. The only person she was talking to then was Jona, in cafes and quiet corners of the city where they could speak alone and only for themselves.

When she told that to Jona, he hugged her. He said, *It isn't all bad all the time. It's just like that when you stay in the Pens too long. I'll take you to a ball. You'll see something new, something wonderful. Do you have a gown?*

Of course not.

Well, I'll find you one.

I don't want to go to a ball. I want to go to a place where I don't have to hide who I am. I'd have to do more than hide at a ball. Jona, I don't know what I want.

Well, when you know, tell me. I'll help you. We're friends. We should help each other.

Maybe. I'll think about it. What do you want?

I want to know what dreams are like.

Oh.

That next day, the shift ended, and Djoss was missing, and Rachel couldn't stand it anymore. She went straight to the baker's basement. She walked in, and ignored the baker, and went to the stairs in back.

The basement wasn't flooded out. She had been there in the rains. She knew Djoss had been lying to her.

She knocked on the door. Sparrow opened it. Rachel had expected Sparrow to be there, with her stooped shoulders and her mean face. This was no surprise.

Rachel pushed her way inside. The widow said nothing. She sat down in the mud leaning back against a post.

"What do you want?" said Sparrow.

"Djoss keeps you here, doesn't he?"

"He does. Turco's spreading out. Didn't need this anymore. People don't like how muddy it is. Djoss said we could stay here."

"He'll never stay with you. Not for long."

"I thought you said you were his sister."

"I am. I'm not jealous. Djoss and I... It's only a matter of time before we have to leave this town. I hate it, but that's the way it is. And when we go, no one follows us. We're just gone. Poof. Like smoke."

"For now, my boys get to sleep indoors. You take him with you, you take care of him when he's stumbling in here too pink to walk straight."

Rachel leaned against a wall. "When does Djoss get here?"

Sparrow shrugged.

"How dangerous is this stuff they're doing, him and Turco and Dog?"

"What do you care what he does long as the coin's solid?"

"We have enough bad business on our own without looking for more. What's he smuggling?"

"Bad business?" the widow echoed. "I knew those tricks of yours weren't good for anything. Turco says they ain't stealing. Might be lying, but it's none of my business. You done? I don't want you around when the boys come back."

She could have meant her sons, or the men that kept her here. Rachel looked around. The squalid room had not improved from the recent rains. A few more wooden posts had been put up to prop the bowing floor above. It didn't seem like enough.

Rachel had a room above ground with a window, a table and a bed. It made Rachel want to strangle her brother for what he was doing to this woman, how he was using her, but she knew that he'd stay with Rachel if she had to run. She wasn't losing him. For now, he wanted to pretend like he was a different man, and have a secret life away from her.

Sparrow went to a corner of the room. She had a jug there that could have been rain water. It could have been anything. She took a deep swallow from it. She didn't offer anything to Rachel. She didn't even look up.

In the street, Rachel saw Djoss' back pushing through the crowd. She ran after him. She ran beside him. He slowed down. There was blood all over his hands. "Pig's blood," he said. She didn't believe him, but she didn't know how to tell the difference. They walked back to the apartment. He went to his bed with dirty hands. She went to her cot with her muddy boots still on.

She thought about Jona, walking the streets. She thought about having her own secret life. She thought about how handsome he was in his uniform, even if he was a little mean sometimes.

***

Two nights later they both got their night off on the same day. Djoss rented a small skiff. They took to the bay, running along the sides of the galleons and the cutter ships, and the low freighters. Djoss could sail a little, and Rachel could manipulate the winds when she wanted. They picked up speed, and bounced from wave to wave.

Rachel laughed and laughed.

And everything was fine between them again for a while. Djoss was going back to see the widow now and then. Rachel knew but didn't talk about it. She was out, too, meeting Jona in a café, sitting in the sun and talking to him about her life. She had never had anyone to talk to like that.

What was your face before you were born?

What is life like for you?

How do you live?

When she closed her eyes, she tried to picture him with wings. Would they have grown large like a gargoyle's, or small and deformed? She tried to imagine his scars, and how'd they feel if she ran her hands over them.

***

Rachel waved at Djoss in the street. He nodded at her. He was carrying something. Rachel picked up step beside him.

"Hey," she said.

"I know," he slurred. He had a sheen over his eyes, like a crystal veil, and his shirt collar was pink from his sweat. He was having trouble focusing.

"What do you know?" said Rachel. She folded her arms. She knew what.

"Don't use the stuff," he said.

"Just make the money on it. Don't use it."

"Turco pays me enough to pay for a decent apartment for a change."

"Right."

"I'm not really into this stuff."

"I believe you."

"You don't."

"No, I believe you," said Rachel. "I have to, Djoss. You're all I have in the world." She looked up and down the street. She knew where he was going next. "You know what else you should know? It isn't a nice thing to do to that woman, or her boys. I wish you wouldn't. I'm going home. Come with me, instead."

He smiled, sadly. "Yeah," he said. "I will. But Sparrow helped us when no one would. Her and Turco and Dog, they're my friends. Rachel, when's the last time we had friends?"

"I'm your friend," she said.

"You know what I mean."

"I don't, Djoss," she said. She was lying. She knew exactly what he meant. She was going to meet Jona for tea under a willow tree. The rains were fading away, and people could live outside again most days without a parasol. Djoss said he'd be home later, and he was lying, too.

Rachel didn't let him off easy this time. All this fighting with her brother, and Jona could wait one day. She wanted to make Djoss give this lie up, before it hurt even more. She followed him back to the baker's room.

She watched him go in alone. The three boys came out and sat on a stoop. They pulled out their dice and tossed them in turns, but there didn't seem to be a game to it. No one was winning. Rachel walked up to them. She smiled. They didn't smile up at her.

The eldest pulled a spike from his ratty boot. He picked at his teeth with it. The rust matched the color of his teeth.

Inside, the baker was nowhere. Downstairs, the door was quietly ajar. Rachel heard the sounds of two people grunting softly, male and female. She thought about knocking. She pulled the door completely closed. She covered her ears. She didn't want to confront them until they were dressed again.

The eldest boy came into the stairwell after Rachel, still picking at his teeth.

She pressed a finger over her mouth. *Hush.* The boy raised the spike in his hand and pointed at Rachel. "You leave us alone," he snarled. He jumped at her from the top of the stairs.

Rachel grabbed for him in the air. "Djoss!" she shouted. The boy tried to stab her, howling. She couldn't hold him back for long like this, he was so wiry and angry and fast.

Djoss came out, naked with his pants in his hand. He looked down confused at the boy fighting Rachel, stabbing at her body with the spike, cutting at her clothes, and tearing into the places in her body that should have been soft with hands and teeth.

The widow shouted from the room, "Please…!"

Djoss got his free hand on the boy's leg and threw him against the wall hard. Rachel snapped her fingers, and the boy's clothes caught fire. He howled like a little wolf. He smacked at the fire, then ignored it. He lunged at Rachel with the spike again.

Djoss had his pants halfway on. He couldn't stop it in time. The spike caught between two of Rachel's exposed scales catching the spike like armor under her clothes. The boy tried again. He would never break through with a rusty spike. Rachel tried to block with her arms to protect her clothes.

"What's that!?" the boy shouted. Finally, the fight went out of him. His knees weakened and he leaned back into the stove. He coughed. He hadn't drawn any blood, but he had tried. He had bit and clawed and shoved.

The widow said, "Djoss, please don't."

"Don't what?" he said.

"Don't hurt him."

Rachel was exposed. Her scales showed through the cuts in her clothes. Djoss grabbed the blanket that the widow had been clutching over herself and handed it to her. Rachel couldn't think. She had to cover the holes in her shirt where the boy had slashed at her. She had to hide herself.

The widow said nothing. The other two boys came in from the street.

Djoss broke the silence in the room. "If you tell anyone about my sister, I'll kill you with my bare hands. If you tell Turco or Dog, I'll kill them, too. You know I could."

He found his shirt, pulled on his boots while standing up, one foot at a time, and nodded at Rachel.

Sparrow was crying. She reached out to her children. She grabbed at them. She looked up, terrified.

"Time for you to leave town," said Djoss. "Time for you to take your boys and get out of the Pens. I see them again, it won't be good."

Sparrow pulled on her clothes quickly, her hands trembling. She took her boys hands.

"Go on. Get out of town. Get out of town forever."

Sparrow led them up the stairs.

Djoss' face was a mask, like a brick.

***

Back to their apartment near the butcher's, Djoss pulled out a sewing kit and fixed Rachel's shirt. She waited in her cot, with the blanket wrapped over her body.

"How long were you following me?" he said. He was a better sewer than she was. He had done it longer. He could pull leather taut and was strong enough to push needles through it.

"You don't want to know," she said. "I'm sorry. Did you mean what you said to them?"

"Of course not."

"Because if you did…"

"No."

"Her boy just tried to kill me, and it's your fault"

"I know," he said. "I'm sorry, Rachel. It's not what I wanted. It's not what I wanted for any of us."

"What do you want, Djoss?"

They sat quietly a while. He sewed. She watched him.

"I don't want to run. She'll leave. She'll take her boys," Djoss said.

"I hope you're right."

He put down his work. He folded his hands on his lap. "Do you want to run?"

"No," she said. "I like it here, too. I don't think Sparrow will hurt us. Djoss, I'm so tired of running."

"What do you think it'll be like if we stay here?"

"Like this," she said. "Like this until we have to run. It never, ever stops. Nothing changes. Nothing gets better. We just keep on running until we die."

Djoss picked up his sewing again. "Good," he said. He handed her clothes as he finished repairing them.

By evening twilight, they both had work to do. She checked it for new holes in his mending. She put all her Senta clothes on. "Check me," she said.

He checked over her whole body for a hint of a scale, or a flash of skin. He found none. Outside, they stopped at a street vendor for something to eat. They came home at the end of the day, slept, and did it again and again.

And that was their life. That will be their life everywhere they go.

***

Jona's mother piled ladles of stew into a bowl for him. She set the bowl before him and sat at the table, eating nothing.

"So," she said, "how's work?"

"Eh," he said, "it's work. You?"

"I finished the dress for that Carroha girl. You know the one, with those fat hips. I never had hips like that. When she walks, it's like a ship's floating sideways. She's rich, though. Money makes any girl pretty."

"No, it really doesn't," said Jona. "I hate those girls."

"You need to marry one of those girls. You cut a fine cloth in a uniform. Get a promotion, maybe a commission, and you find yourself a rich girl, and one that isn't too pretty because then she won't mind you."

"You were pretty once."

"Your father was rich once. Any big plans tonight?"

"No."

"The balls are starting soon. Lady Sabachthani's the only one throwing any good ones. You should go to them. If you go out, pick up some tea. You drank a ton of tea yesterday. Honestly, I've never seen someone drink so much tea. How's the stew?"

"It's fine, Ma."

Jona hunched over his stew. He tried to ignore his mother staring at him. She just kept staring at him, every night staring at him. Jona never saw her eat anyting, but she always cooked for him and watched him chew and swallow.

CHAPTER XVIII

Salvatore was being kept from us. We were sure of it. Someone had told him we were here. They pulled him away. His trail was cold and getting colder every night.

The Night King knows.

We can't trust her. I did not want to contact her. The money he made for her would not be enough to justify protecting him from us. We were the only two people in all of Dogsland that were not afraid of her, and did not bow to the authority of kings.

We should have her arrested. We need some kind of leverage to get the truth out of her.

You're thinking like him. We already know the truth. It is the only leverage we need.

When I dream, I do not know where I begin and he ends.

Give it time. All memories fade.

My husband was trying to comfort me, but this only made it worse. I thought about how Salvatore had eluded us. I was losing memories every moment, even as I was digging deeper inside of them, writing everything down as best I could. We had to face the Night King, and demand the truth. To do this, we needed to arrange a meeting, where we wouldn't be killed just for demanding a meeting. We chose our own main temple, near the king's palace.

We sent word to her in her father's house. We wanted to send a clear message to her that we knew who she was, and that we had the power to reveal what we knew. We told her where we would be.

The temple of Erin in the city was open to the sky. If it rained during a service, it rained. The grass turned into mud too quickly, here, with all the crowds and all the rain. The temple here kept gravel stones across the yard instead of a lawn because of all the rains and the crowd of feet that would ruin everything into mud. The stones made walking noisier. We heard her long before we saw her, her dainty shoes as narrow as a hummgbird's nostril compared to her heavy ankles. She was in widow's black, but she wasn't a widow. Her face was veiled.

We wore the wolfskin in the shade of a tree. We did not want to take them off. This place was a comfort to us in the city. There was dandelion wine and apple trees and on any other day children would be playing here.

I considered letting my husband speak for us, but I knew he wouldn't speak kindly to anyone from her father's house.

Let her speak first, I thought. Let her squirm and wonder if we were the Walkers or if we were just wolves.

She sat on a root that had grown out of the ground like a curving bench. She placed her hands in her lap, demure.

I yawned. I had very sharp teeth, and she could see them all. Well?" she said.

I flicked my ears at an imaginary fly.

"You sent for me, and rudely I might add. I don't know who you think I am…"

My tongue slipped loose. The wolfskin peeled away from my mouth. "I know who you are, Ela. I wanted you to know that the Temple of Erin knows exactly who you are."

She peeled off her veil. Ela Sabachthani looked older in real life. Jona remembered her with more alabaster powder on her skin, and a vitality that her face no longer held. "Do you feel better, intimidating me and calling me silly names? I am not the king of the night."

"Your magic will not save you when you die," I said.

"Your concern for my soul is noted," she snapped. "Now, what else did you ask me here to talk about?"

"Salvatore," I said.

"You can't have him," she said.

"He is an abomination of Elishta."

"He is a person," she said. "A very sad, lonely, little man, who can't remember his own name if we don't remind him."

"A demon child!" I snarled. I stood up on my wolf paws. I was level with Ela's face. "Polluter of flesh, seducer of innocents, betrayer and destroyer of life!"

She stood up, unabashed. "He's mine," she said.

My husband pulled the wolfskin fully from his back. He was tall, and strong. He bowed to her.

"Lady Sabachthani, sit down," he said. "My wife carries Jona's mind. She feels strongly about Salvatore, and what he did before Jona died."

Ela folded her arms. She looked to the gates of the temple. "Why should I stay? You're only going to insult me with cheap threats and slander my friends."

"He's already dead," I said. "His mind is dead. This city is already your father's, and the night is already yours. We are not concerned for these things. We only want the demon child, Salvatore. All those men Jona killed, all just men, helping other nobles throw parties that you would not permit to be better than yours. You had men killed for party favors. Do you think the king would listen to us? Do you think we couldn't make him listen?"

Lady Ela Sabachthani frowned. "Jona was going to get in trouble if I didn't keep him busy. I had to find something for him to do until I was ready for him. Stand up, like your man. I don't like talking to beasts."

I remained a wolf.

"Jona didn't know everything about me," she said. "And it took him a long time to figure it out. You carry his mind with you. Tell me something. Tell me what he felt, deep in his heart. Was he a sad, lonely, little man?"

I said nothing.

"Because that's what I thought he was. Why Salvatore? What about the other one? Have you found that awful maid?"

"She has gone north, beyond the red valley."

"Why don't you just chase her? Leave Salvatore alone. He's mine, and I take good care with him."

"She's less dangerous," said my husband. "She tries to protect people from what's inside of her. Salvatore cannot. Him first. Then her."

"I want you to go after her first. By the time you find her, I'll be done with Salvatore, and he'll be on his own. What can I give you to get you to do that? A new temple? A place for your ministry among my advisors when I ascend to the throne?"

"What do you have to give that we would want except for Salvatore?" I said. I stood up. I am not Jona. I can stand against her. I can threaten her with truth. "What do you want with demon children? What spell is this?"

She put her veil back on. "No spell this time. And, I give you what is mine to give. What do you think I will give you? Jona would know the answer to that."

I said nothing.

"Tell me he would have married me anyway, just for the money."

I shook my head.

"Never?"

"His heart was never yours."

She turned away. "My sad, lonely, little man. It was so hard to keep him busy, all those aimless nights." She walked towards the gate.

I called to her back. "Why do you do what you do to them?"

She said nothing.

My husband frowned. He looked at me. *That didn't go as I expected.*

We need to leave, now.

We need to keep all the skulls away from her. We cannot permit any in the city.

Jona knew what she meant. Lady Ela Sabachthani, king of the night, had only one thing to give us: our lives.

***

My husband and I left for her estate on the island right away, trying to reach her land before she could get there, send word about her gift to us. We traveled as man and woman, and cautiously. We took ferries over canals, and carts over the mud-patches that would leave our footprints to be followed by anyone she might send after us. On the last ferry to her estate on the island, we stood between the horses of two fine carriages.

I touched the neck of a white horse. The horse warned me of a strange smell on the ferry. I smelled it, too. I thanked the creature with a stroke of my palm. My husband and I were being watched.

The ferry landed. Two sleepy king's men sat on chairs and waved at everyone to pass. My husband and I stepped onto the smooth cobblestones. Our shadow was not a demon child. He was only wicked. Wicked is a common thing.

My husband and I looked at each other and nodded. We pulled the wolfskins over our backs and bolted for the Sabachthani estate as fast as horses. We did not bother with the guards. We jumped over the wall and ran.

We followed the shadows of trees to the willow grove where the two hulking forms of steel and meat stood like carriage-sized mantises. They raised their arms at us, menacingly. My husband peeled the wolfskin from his back. "Back, demon," he said. He raised his hand. We are holy servants of Erin. He threw holy water at them. It burned on their metal shell. They froze up, trembling at us. We could hurt them. They had never known anything that could do that.

My husband stood up next to one of the juggernauts. It stared down at him, like a tree gazing into a man's face. The monstrous creation shivered like a broken clock. It was so old. Meat rots, no matter how much magic is cast upon it. Dead meat rots.

Steel was fused with muscle and bone to make the beastly things. One of them had a broken, bent-up leg. The other was missing part of its long, mantis-talon. The exposed bones were black beneath the meat that held it. Maggots had tried to grow inside of the wounds, but they died long before they could be born.

Be careful. Don't touch them.

My husband didn't listen to me. He touched just the steel face of a monster. He pressed salt through the eye holes, with holy water. This made steam and puss burst and bubble. The steel face loosened. My husband pulled the steel away from the sticky flesh. It had the skull of a man underneath, except all warped and bent into the steel that contained it. This skull had two horns like an ibyx.

I peeled the wolfskin from my back. I had more salt and holy water, for the other construction and the other skull. The magic burned away like acid with the rotting meat. These wounds we made were mortal wounds. The construction of meat and steal would never move again.

My husband carefully wrapped the horned skull in leaves and leather rags. He slipped it into the bag on his back. The final skull stared back at us, mute.

"Salvatore," I said. "Is your name Salvatore?"

We gingerly peeled back the mask of metal for the skull. It was almost human, but warped in the jaw and one of the eyes. We collected its skull and poured a ring of salt around the rotting demon flesh. Fireseeds took to the back of the monstrous heaps. Ignited, they burned strong and long.

Sabachthani's alarms had been called in the house. Horses hooves' galloped. My husband and I had to leave right away. Over the wall, and away into an alley, my husband yanked open a sewer grate we knew. Down, then, and running hard through the dark waterways, we didn't bother with rowboats. We jumped hard into the water, swam across to the other side of rivers and canals, ran on damp as bathers. We moved so fast, up from the sewer, to the walls, to the woods, and away where no hand of the night could touch our pelts.

At night, we slept in peace on a stone that carried heat long into the night. In the morning, I felt Jona's mind inside the frayed sea wall at the edge of my consciousness. He was a formless thing, there, inside my head. I walled him in with the scent of the woods. This was my memory, of all the days of my lives.

Salvatore, said my husband. *I wonder if I don't know where he might be.*

Where?

He wasn't in the city. She would have known we were looking for him.

Where would he be?

Have I ever shown you the mountain, where I killed the demon's child before you were born?

This will be your face before I was born?

Does Jona's memory make you a Senta? Have you looked too long upon Rachel's life that you are dreamcasting? It is a place to look, and to rest if he is not. It is a guess, but I think it is a good guess because it was a good place to hide once. We have new skulls to study.

They're only children. We should not call upon Erin for that. I know their life already, warped like that and so young. We already know who did it to them, too.

To the hills, to the highest of the hills, we howled to the wolf packs. We called them with baleful hunting songs. They howled love songs to death over the hills, singing us on.

We climbed the mountain quickly. Sabachthani would have sent word to him that we had left the city. She would have called her pet back home.

The cave was abandoned when we arrived. The bird cages had long ago collapsed into heaps of rain-washed wood and rust. Deep in the back of it, we found a hammock in the dark. It smelled of Salvatore.

My husband laughed. *I didn't think we'd find him here.*

We haven't found him, yet.

The smells of him were old. He had slept here. We read the tracks of him, walking in with soft boots. He had traps he was using to capture his meat. He cleaned and cooked it himself in a corner. Birds, mostly, with some rabbits, and anything he could find in the hills to eat—acorns ground up against a rock, wild onions, and rosemary. He was here, and now he was gone.

I leaned into his hammock. I swung a little, there. *The new skulls,* I said.

My husband pulled them out. He placed them on rocks. *No,* he said. *There's no need. They know nothing.*

Are you sure?

Look at them again, next to Jona's.

I did. They were deformed, but more than that, they were smaller.

Children, I said. *We must go back. They deserved a quick death. They did not deserve what Lord Sabachthani did to those young children.*

Sleep a while here. Rest your mind. Dream your own dreams. You have walked long in other lives. I will search my own demon child's memories from my youth. I will sleep here and remember his life and the people in it, and I will search for Lord Sabachthani.

So, that's what I did.

We will return to the city, in the depth of night, but not yet.

Salvatore had lived long and long before we knew him. Like the city that hid him from us, Erin will come for him and tear all the buildings down around him. Sunflowers will grow tall and golden there. The wolves will run the dogs away and rule the rocky ground where the bricks lay broken.

I slept in the hammock, and dreamed of the mountain where I

was born, far to the east. I dreamed of my own mother's tongue licking my palm.

I dreamed only of myself.

About the Author

J. M. McDermott's critically-acclaimed first novel, *Last Dragon*, was on Amazon.com's Year's Best Science Fiction and Fantasy of 2008 list, and was shortlisted for an IAFA William Crawford Award, among other accolades. He lives and works north of Atlanta, inside a maze of bookshelves and empty coffee cups.